WICKED LITTLE THINGS

WICKED LITTLE THINGS

Justin Arnold

Tiny Ghost Press

ISBN:
E-book 978-1-7399834-6-8
Paperback 978-1-7399834-7-5
Hardcover 978-1-7399834-8-2

Cover artwork by: Lio Pressland
Illustrations designed by: Freepik

To find out more about our books visit www.tinyghostpress.com and sign up for out newsletter.

For Cayla and for Rachel. You know everything.

THE HOLLOW: SEPTEMBER FIFTEENTH

Grant Allen hadn't thought about dying. He'd thought only of getting the picture and leaving. Enter, click, run. It should have been easy. The woods of Jasper Hollow are usually silent and empty.

Tonight, however, is different. Boots clomp through mud, whoops and yelps echo among the trees. A pack of guys—three maybe—get closer and closer. Grant knew he'd been spotted the second he entered these woods, decked out like a freak in this stupid dress and heels. They'll waste no time in pulverizing him.

And now he hides behind a tree, barely breathing, refusing to move even an eyebrow as the whoops cut closer. And closer.

He kicks off the heels and pulls at the red sash around the vintage white sundress. He'll choke the bastards with it if he has to. He crouches in the brush and waits. Listens.

As silently as he can, he pulls his phone from the dress pocket and holds it up, snapping a quick selfie, the camera's flash one brief reprieve from the dark. He stares back at himself, a jock in a freaking dress, crouching in the woods and trying not to die.

He sends the picture to Dane, saved as Lil Cousin in his phone, with a text:

Okay, I did it. Happy Birthday. Forgive me?

He stares at the screen. Three dots appear, just for a second, and then— nothing.

Grant wants to call his cousin and chew him out. Tell him to get over himself and to leave Grant alone, especially with all that freaky stuff he's been able to do lately. The least he could do is slap a Like on the picture. It was five months ago! What is he supposed to do, sashay down Main Street, ruin his whole life to make Dane feel better? He clicks through and makes the call. If nothing else, maybe these guys won't jump him if someone can hear.

Dane doesn't answer.

Okay then, I guess we aren't family anymore.

Grant shoves down the white-hot anger threatening to erupt through his hands and crush the phone. He slips it back into his pocket.

He'll have it out with Dane right after he survives these assholes.

"Shit!"

Grant jumps to his feet and yelps as something brushes against his leg.

A gaunt brown rabbit hops across his foot and dips under the brush. Grant breathes out with relief, then purses his lips, realizing how loud he just was.

He listens. He waits. But all is quiet again in the woods. Grant sighs, turns to plot his next move and—

"Hi, dollface," a burnout with hair as blond as Grant's stares back with red, pot-glazed eyes.

A fist slams into Grant's back and he's flung forward. The burnout catches him as the other two rush at him from behind. They grab his arms and drag him from the brush and across the open, moonlit floor of the woods.

"Get off me!" Grant roars, his deep voice grinding like gravel in his throat.

One of the burnouts loses their grip and Grant slams his fist into the guy's jaw, sending him to the ground, a string of spit spraying the dirt. He whirls to take on the other two, but they're faster, grabbing Grant's shoulders and kneeing him in the crotch. Grant doubles over and falls down. The two guys kick him. And kick him. And kick him.

One of them lifts a foot and aims for Grant's head. Grant squeezes his eyes shut and tries to duck out of the way.

But the impact never comes. Instead, he hears the screams. The sound of ripping flesh. Three heavy knocks against the trees.

Then silence.

Grant's first idiotic thought is that they've exploded. Finally, he peels his eyes open and blinks, his breath rushing in uneven waves through his chest as he stares at the sight.

Ten feet from him, all that remains of his tormentors are fleshy, pulped parts on the ground. Red-black blood drips down tree trunks.

They did *explode*.

Grant blinks again. There's a man on the other side of the clearing, half in shadow, half in moonlight.

Stretched and skeletal, his body is clad in a corroded plaid suit that must have once been the color of mustard. A mask of furs, strung together with black stitches, covers his face so that he looks like a rabbit. Two long, furry ears stick out of the mask, like those of a demonic easter bunny. One is cocked—listening.

He steps closer, heavy on his right foot. His breathing is loud but ragged, suffocated by the mouthless rabbit face.

Grant can't get himself to move as the "man" closes in, thudding in a pair of dirty leather shoes, a long toenail pushing out from a hole in the front.

He stops now that he towers over Grant, wheezing through the mask. Two gray, cloudy eyes peer from crudely cut holes.

Finally, Grant breaks from his stunned silence and screams.

The rabbit-masked man stoops and presses a finger to Grant's lips.

Cringing, sucking in the cheesy smell of sweat and spit from that dirty, earth-covered finger, Grant finds his words at last. "I-I-I shouldn't have worn this stupid dress."

The hint of a smile pulls upward beneath the mask. Waxy hands slide over Grant's face and down his shoulders, to the bust of the sundress, then lower, swooping across the skirt and down Grant's leg to his ankle, where his mother's heels have cut his skin.

"F-f-f-f," the rabbit-masked man stutters.

"No."

"F-f-fresh. *Fresh*."

Grant tries to pull his legs up and run but his feet won't move. He fumbles for his phone. Maybe he won't get away, but someone will know. Someone will hear something.

The rabbit-masked man lunges for his arm as he dials 9-1-1, and Grant writhes and bucks his torso against the man hovering over him as he pounds the green Dial button.

Someone answers on the first ring, and the rabbit-masked man stops fighting. Grant locks gazes with him, and he stares back with those strange, clouded eyes.

"Help! I'm in the woods, my name is Grant Allen, I'm seventeen—"

Grant stops, shudders. He hasn't reached the police. On the other end, the voice of a child is singing a playful melody.

"Rabbit Skins. Rabbit Skins... Here to cleanse you of your sins. Drags you down and eats your bones. Keeps you for his very own."

Grant screams as his right ankle twists under the rabbit-masked man's grip. The phone falls to the ground and bounces, childlike laughter pouring out of it till the line cuts off.

Rabbit Skins straightens to his full height and drags Grant, who hadn't thought about dying, deeper into the woods, until his screams fade beneath the silence of the trees.

1

FUNERALS MAKE FOR THE BEST REUNIONS

ighting things on fire is simply not what good gay sons do. But make no mistake—I would *love* to flick my fingers and bust a flame on something. That's what happens if I freak out, get mad, or put myself around people who peeve me off.

Weird things happen. Deadly things...

And right now, well, I'm doing all of the freaking out, getting mad, *and* being around peevish people. But I promised my mom not to cause a scene at a funeral.

Yes, I'm at a funeral. Grant's funeral. There's a blood-red tie on my lap—the one my Aunt Bella wanted me to wear. She wanted everyone to wear something red since it was his favorite color. But if I put it on, then it's real. Then I'm really at my cousin's funeral.

My cousin who was murdered on my sixteenth birthday—then found a week and a half later at the edge of the Jasper Hollow Woods, so mangled and unrecognizable that we can't even look at him before he's buried.

Why? Oh! I saved the best part for last: the killer cut off most of his face.

My fingers burn hot, begging me to let just a *little* fire out. While I think Mom would understand my need to, she'd also probably put me up for adoption, or just leave me in a box on the corner with a note saying Free to a Good Home. So I rake my fingers through my curls and pull at them instead.

Across from my safe spot on a green lounge in the foyer of the parlor, a crotchety looking funeral director barks, "Sign the book," at a pair of newcomers. They immediately go to the guest book and scribble their names. I wonder if they notice that I myself wrote *Captain Hook* and *Peter Pan* for Mom and me. I've been keeping myself distracted that way. Trying to tell if anyone notices and if they can keep a straight face. I tilt my head slightly and read in on them.

It's a thing I've been able to do for as long as I can remember: pick up things about people without them knowing. Like glancing in a notebook that someone's left on a table. I can extract just a little bit of information, just enough to know what they're thinking. If they're hiding something. Like Twitter in my mind, but way more personal. I hear their thoughts as I would my own.

I stare at the back of the man's head. *"This place smells like my grandmother's house."*

Okay, so no one is present enough to notice that beloved characters of literature are here. That's fair.

I really should go see my family. Well, those of us left, anyways. I've been planted on this lounge for ten minutes, putting off the uncomfortable inevitable. But that's yet another bit of proof. If I see my aunt and my remaining cousin at a funeral, then Grant is, in fact, dead.

My heart thuds and the fire burns through my arms, desperately wanting release. I shake my hands as though that will extinguish it, then venture farther into the funeral home. I sense the casket at the end of the long viewing room and make a point not to look at it. Closed or not, I'm not ready to see.

The room is packed with people my age. All of Grant's bros, fan club, and wannabes, I'm sure. Maybe I'm being unkind, but my cousin's popularity was undeniable.

It's half the reason I couldn't stand him by the end.

Hannah's not hard to spot among them. She's a dead ember in a world of confetti, not even a drop of red on her. My morbid cousin has truly embraced her dark side, with her hair, as blonde as Grant's, dyed the color of ink. Her black dress falls around her in straight lines without a hint of figure.

"Hey." I step next to her.

"Hey."

"So—"

"Everyone's so happy they don't have to see a dead body. Look at them."

I scan over the surrounding teens, the older mourners in the corner. Everyone does seem mostly at ease, I guess, talking as though they're at a picnic in the park. "Yeah."

"Mom got to see his body when she identified him," Hannah continues. "I wanted to look but they wouldn't let me. It's unfair, he was *my* twin."

She's staring at the casket, and I risk a tiny glance. A big, polished white box with gold-colored handles. A massive corsage of roses and baby's breath crowns it. *He's in there. Or, parts of him, anyways.*

"Yeah. It's unfair."

"Sorry." Hannah lets out a gust of breath, shaking her head. "That was messed up. I just—I don't know. Have to see it to believe it? Like, you know for a fact where he is and what he looks like now, you know? It's not left up to the imagination that way. I find the finality...soothing?"

She gives me a sheepish look, her pale cheeks flushing pink. I get the feeling she wants me to say something, anything, to normalize the fact that she's a Grim-Reaper-worshipping weirdo.

I force a smile and say, "Whatever, freak."

She half snorts and stares at her hands, and I notice she's wearing red nail polish. Her lips twist and pucker out in thought. That's the mark that we're related. Grant and Hannah got their dad's hair, eyes, and tall physique. I'm stuck with the Craven branding: mud-colored hair, big-ass mud-colored eyes, and the stature of an urchin working the assembly lines of Victorian London. But the twisting lips? One hundred percent Craven stock. Like we're inquisitive ducks.

Before the silence can become uncomfortable, I say, "So, how you doin'?"

Her dead blue eyes slide to me, and she breaks a forced grin. "I'm just peachy."

I cringe. "Right. Yeah. Sorry."

Across the room, Aunt Bella sits in the front row of white folding chairs. The dark circles around her eyes tell me she hasn't slept in a week and probably hasn't really eaten either. Mom sits next to her, hand on her arm. She whispers something to her and nudges a silver flask into her hand. Aunt Bella takes a swig of whatever it is (wine probably, knowing my mother) and I force myself not to read in on them.

Hannah grabs my arm with no warning, and I jump. "I'm really happy you're here, Dane. I'm not always prickly. I'm a damned ball of sunshine, you know that."

"Yeah, I know. Strange situation."

"We've always been like siblings. You, Grant, and I. I still think of you as a brother."

I wink. "You too."

A genuine laugh, a small one, breaks out of Hannah and I feel my shoulders relax. She looks toward the doors. "I need a break."

"God, me too."

We head into the foyer, and I reclaim the green lounge for us. It feels more rigid here, where the funeral director stalks back and forth, glaring at a cluster of loitering teens.

"Any more news on...well, on who...um—"

"Who the killer is?"

"Yeah."

Hannah shrugs, a bit forcefully. "Of course not. Murder sells. This shithole is going to milk it as long as they can. Tourism or some other shit. But I'm just conspiracy theorizing. My guess? Occult. Which, fantastic, way to make it look bad."

My stomach tightens, and the right corner of my lip twitches. Hannah claims she's a witch of sorts. What she doesn't know is that she's sitting next to someone capable of way more than crystal healing and tarot-card readings.

Grant knew. He found out six months ago—in April. The last night we spoke. If Hannah knew, she'd probably not speak to me either.

The door swings open and a blast of cold September air sends a few orange and scarlet leaves across the floor. The funeral director rushes to catch the door as it bangs against the wall.

"Easy!" he shouts.

The cluster of teens scamper when they see whoever it is. By the time they pass, three figures stand in the doorway. The bright, late-morning sunlight behind them casts halos around their heads, leaving their faces in shadow.

The one in the center steps forward, the other two following. Three girls, around my age, each arguably prettier than the last. Actually, they're *beautiful*. Or maybe it's just because they're in a pack. I can't decide.

Each wears a red jacket. I know that everyone is wearing some sort of red, but this is different. Seriously. Each is wearing a jacket, and they're all similar. Not exact, but similar *enough* that it seems like a uniform, and the job is being *those* girls.

"Sign the book!" orders the funeral director, closing the door behind them.

Hannah stands and bolts into the viewing room as the girls finish with the book.

I follow her and when she finally stops, I ask, "What's wrong?"

"They have no business being here," says Hannah through clenched teeth.

"Who are they?"

Hannah grunts. "They're called the Reds. Your garden-variety bitch club whose sole purpose is to make people miserable. They didn't even hang out with

Grant. The blonde one turned him down, and she never turns jocks down. Which, good for her, but that says something."

"Deep breath," I say. I'm worried she's going to shank them with her crossbone earrings. "This is *your* court."

The girls, *the Reds*, pass by. I tilt my head and focus, trying to read in on the middle girl first. She sweeps a windblown hair from her light brown cheek and tucks it behind her ear. I want to find out how she–how all three of them–look so movie-star-perfect, as though a swarm of pixies greet them every morning with their own magical salon. But her book won't open. I try the other two but am cut off when their eyes slide to me in perfect unison. I dart between their gazes, feeling myself shrink. I wish I had on my trusty hoodie so I could shrink into it and disappear.

The middle girl, who's obviously the leader, stops and winks a honey-colored eye at me.

"Love the tie."

"Thank you."

"Back it up, Madelaine," Hannah warns. "We're in mourning here."

Madelaine snaps her eyes to Hannah. "Sorry, Igor. I didn't see you there."

The blonde claps excitedly while the third shoots us a look like she just smelled the world's most rotten egg as Madelaine leads their way to the other end of the room.

Hannah snorts. "Psh. Igor. Get real. Obviously, I'm Elvira."

When they're safely out of earshot, I ask, "What even was that?"

"I told you, they're bitches, but Madelaine Wednesday is the worst one," says Hannah.

We watch as Madelaine takes a seat toward the back and pulls her large—probably designer—purse onto her lap. The head of a white cat peeks out.

"And she brought Ambrose the freaking cat. Somehow, she got papers to document him as a service animal. He goes to *school* with her. Can you imagine being that attached to a freaking cat?"

"Who are the other two?"

"The blonde is Chloe. She claps a lot. Then there's Elena." She nods to the girl with tan skin and dark hair. With her unimpressed expression, she seems like she'd win the zombie apocalypse with only a glare. "I'm pretty sure she eats children. Especially little boys with hair like cotton candy."

I put my hand on my head. "It is *not* like cotton candy!"

"Without product, yes, it is."

"Screw you, Igor."

"Elvira."

Aunt Bella comes at me, sweeping me into a giant hug and cutting off my retort.

"Daney-Waney-Yuletide," she coos.

Damn it. Whoever let my mother give me that middle name needs their ass kicked. *Yuletide.* As though I'm Santa's favorite elf, destined to save Christmas in vivid Claymation. "Hi, Aunt Bella."

She releases me from the bear-trap hug and smiles, looking me up and down. "You look so healthy. I'm glad you're taking care of yourself again."

I tense and slide my eyes to Mom. How much did she tell her?

A weird feeling snakes through my gut as I look around and take in the whole family. No grandparents or anything anymore. Just me, Mom, Aunt Bella, Hannah, and Grant—well, parts of Grant. Together again. Funerals make for the best reunions, I guess.

The funeral director approaches us, wearing a tight expression that reminds me of an angry turtle. "You need to take your seats," he spits out. "We're starting."

Aunt Bella raises her eyebrows at him. "Oh, go sign the book."

Mom tugs Aunt Bella's arm and heads toward the chairs, nudging the flask into her hand. "He's just doing his job."

Hannah and I give each other an awkward look of *moms* before following them to sit down.

This is it, I want to scream out loud as the service begins. This is Grant's funeral. It really is real.

The reverend—or pastor—shaman?—I don't know what he is, says a lot of words about god and heaven. Plans and paths. Tooth fairies and wizards in emerald cities. Okay, I have no clue what he's talking about. My family was never religious, so I can't tell you why he's even here. I just stare at the floor and try not to look at the casket. Instead, I work to keep my pounding heart from exploding.

"Now..." The reverend-priest-man's voice comes back into focus. "The deceased's cousin will say a few words."

Shit.

Mom nudges my leg. "Dane."

Mom was going to say a few words, but I offered. Maybe it was out of guilt or because I honestly wanted to. Let's go with both. But now that I'm here, and the casket is there, nailed shut with Grant inside, I can't. Not in front of all these people. I'm supposed to be lying low, *especially* where he's concerned. Not swearing on a holy bible that he was a beautiful person who could do no wrong.

"Dane..."

Dane can't come to the podium right now. He's too busy digging a hole to crawl into.

"Honey." Mom jabs me in the arm.

"Yes!" My voice cracks.

A stifled snort echoes behind me and I push myself to my feet.

When I reach the podium, I force myself to face the pack of people here to say goodbye to a pile of body parts. My hands rest on the soft paper of the open bible, where my written eulogy ought to be. I haven't been able to plan anything. I couldn't bring myself to.

My arms are already hot and tingling again.

I squeeze my eyes shut and words start bursting from my chest like water from a broken pipe. My lips purse as they ricochet around my mouth, because I know what's coming but I can't stop it. I don't *want* to say what I'm about to. Why in queso's name am I trying to say—

"Yo-yo-yo, D-Frizzle in the hizzle!" *Stop the words!* "We interrupt your education for this breaking news report!"

Oh. My. God.

I pull my eyes open and stare out. Faces gape, some smile in disbelief. A wave of sweat pours down my forehead. I can't believe I just said that. It was my byline back when I read the school news announcements in sixth period. Back when I didn't care if people thought I was a weirdo.

Out in the crowd, the Reds stare back. Madelaine has her arms crossed, head cocked, as though she already knows exactly who I am and all of my dirty secrets. I wish I could crawl through a crack between the floorboards.

"Let me start again." I take a deep breath and exhale through O-shaped lips. "I loved Grant. I know that much. He was my cousin. I...I really don't know *how* to feel beyond that. Sometimes I think this is all a horrible mistake and he's still out there. And other times"—my eyes fall back into contact with Madelaine's—"he's dead to me."

I look at the ceiling and push my hands hard against the open bible to steady myself. I hadn't meant to say that. I'd wanted to say that he's gone. Not—

"He's dead to me!" I say it again. *Stop the words!*

I feel my chest exploding, all of the anger and resentment boiling up before I can stop it. My entire body feels hot. "Okay, look. If you're in this room then you already know it. Grant was an asshole."

A pocket of people laugh, and to my surprise, Aunt Bella is one of them, probably thanks to the flask. But my mother shoots me her death glare. The one that says, "It's cheaper to take you out of this world than to keep you in it."

But more words are coming, and I can't stop. "He hurt *a lot* of people.

If not by bullying them in the bathroom, then by trying to get his junk in anything moving." The laughs turn to gasps. "Well. Now he's gone. He's never going to put his junk anywhere because he doesn't have junk—" *Stop. Talking.* "And I'll never get to tell him how much he hurt me. I'll never tell him he was wrong, and I'll never kick his ass the way it deserved to be kicked. And what really, *really*, sucks is that I'll never get to say sorry. Because you know what? I'm an asshole too."

Madelaine looks down at her lap, and I notice that the one Hannah called Elena gives a polite nod. Like she's *satisfied.*

"Dane." Mom stands.

Thin plumes of smoke rise from under each of my hands. I pull them away to see my handprints, black and charred, where passages of scripture used to be. A cry pours from my throat.

"Son?" the reverend puts a hand on my back.

"Don't touch me!" I slam the bible shut.

I fling backward, trying to get away from anything flammable. My foot catches on the reverend's ankle and I fall back against Grant's casket. I reach out to catch myself against it and—

A room of cold steel. Gloved hands putting a faceless corpse in the casket. It's missing an arm. A leg. Most of its blond hair.

"I think I'm gonna grab Hallow Bean for lunch," someone says. "Wanna come?"

"No thanks," another responds. "I've lost my appetite."

I yank my hands off the casket and cradle them beneath my armpits as another sob escapes me. That's something else I'm able to do. See the history around objects. But I definitely didn't mean to do it this time, and I feel like I'm going to vomit.

"Need to sit down?" the reverend comes toward me.

"I don't know what's happening to me," I say. "I'm so sorry."

I flee the viewing room, knocking the podium over as I go. Everyone is talking, muttering about the freak kid.

"Dane!" Mom shouts after me.

"Let him go," Aunt Bella says. "It's fine."

2

TELL NO TALES

I feel light-headed and dizzy between reading in on the casket and burning the bible. Really, Dane? *The bible?* Not to mention the fact that I just threw all that dirty laundry at a room of mourners. Hell, I don't care about the randos. They don't really know Grant or my family.

I feel bad that Aunt Bella and Hannah had to hear it.

The fire in my arms turns into hot tears that push from my eyes as I come down the ramp of the funeral home and stomp into the graveyard. I want to be as far away from people as possible.

A gnarled and knobby tree stands in the middle of all the crumbling old tombstones. Grant and I used to call this the Tell No Tales Tree, back when we were kids. Not much else to do in Jasper Hollow. This was where we played and shared secrets that we wouldn't even let Hannah in on. It was our "boys only" radius. Up until this past April.

It's your fault, my thoughts scream. *You didn't answer the phone.*

I let myself cry as I reach into the breast pocket of my suit jacket and check my phone. Nothing. No condolences or encouraging messages. Which isn't surprising, since I have no friends. I click into my recent calls.

Grant phoned me on September 15 at 11:35 p.m. The minute I turned sixteen. The day he went missing.

You didn't answer the phone.

I click his name and open our texts. A column of green notes that I never responded to comes to a halt with the picture he sent just moments before the call.

Here he is, my golden-boy cousin. Blond, athletic, blue-eyed, wearing a white sundress in the woods.

He went to the woods because you made him, and you didn't answer the phone.

I'd said that I'd forgive what he did if he embarrassed himself. I named the one thing that would make an arrogant, homophobic, cis male feel as hopeless and tortured as I did.

And now he's dead. And I didn't answer the phone.

The phone falls to the ground as the next wave of tears push out, and I can't fight the fire anymore. Splaying my fingers, I watch as flames ignite across my fingertips like ten unholy birthday candles. This, unlike reading minds and objects, is somewhat new. This first started in April—that last night before things between us fell apart.

If you're wondering if he outed me, yes, he did. But that's not the whole problem.

The breeze picks up and the flames extinguish. I cringe at the smell of the air and twist my face up. This town smells like blood.

I know that's insane. And I'll admit that I've never mentioned it to anyone, so it could just be me. But Jasper Hollow smells like *blood.* Sometimes more and sometimes less, but it's always there, covering the town with iron and rot. Like the entire Kentucky state came here to bleed out or something. I've been living in Lexington for so long, I almost forgot about it. But it seems stronger now.

Almost like it's been fucking waiting.

Stuffing my hands in my pockets, I lean my forehead against the trunk of the Tell No Tales Tree and look over at a tombstone. In this grave was the man, we said when we were kids, who would rise from the dead and kill whoever snitched on us. I squat before it and trace the name. Charles Frederick. 1880–1901. The rest has eroded with time.

Two faint, red thumbprints remain on his tombstone. We always sealed our secrets with blood. Coming out to him was no exception.

Grant broke the seal by outing me, and now he's dead. I'm old enough to know that ghosts don't just rise up from the ground and start killing people. But the timing is too eerie not to think about it.

Someone must have known about our pact. Right? And I need to find out who.

After all, it could be my fault. Couldn't it?

I take a deep breath and shake my head as nausea picks up in my stomach. Too much thinking. I need to get inside before anyone comes looking for me. Pushing myself up, I turn to head back to the funeral home, but halt.

People have begun trickling out into the parking lot. I've missed the end of the service and it's time to go to the gravesite. Among the thin throng, the Reds stand at the top of the ramp, that white cat rubbing against Madelaine's leg. Elena stares at me with narrowed eyes, like a sculptor sizing up a hunk of clay. Chloe smiles back like I'm her next best friend.

And Madelaine is tilting her head, focusing her eyes very hard on my forehead.

I can't explain how I know. But I suddenly feel bad for ever reading anyone's thoughts. Because it feels awful. Like after you find a spider crawling on you. You know it's gone and there aren't any more but can still *feel* a hundred insects on your arms.

Madelaine Wednesday is able to read my mind. She's doing it right now.

"Dane. Yuletide."

I wince. "Merry Christmas."

To be fair, I should've seen this coming. Mom was silent when I came back inside, and she maintained that icy quiet during the procession to the new cemetery and halfway through dinner at the church.

But when she cocked her head toward the stairwell, I knew it was time. Now, she stands with her fists on her hips—her signature stance for when I've gone too far. "I said you could be a little shit *tomorrow*. Is it tomorrow?"

"No," I mutter. "I freaked out. I'm really sorry."

"Don't tell me, tell your Aunt Bella." Mom points behind me, where Aunt Bella has followed us in.

"I'm sorry, Aunt Bella."

"Honey, it's fine," Aunt Bella says in a resigned tone that tells me deep down it's really not all that fine. She puts a gentle hand on my shoulder, and I don't flinch. "It's fine, Robyn."

"It's not fine!" Mom's voice climbs into a soprano's octave. "Calling him an asshole at his own funeral is not fine!"

"They always talked like that." Aunt Bella puts her arm around my shoulder. This makes me feel worse, letting her smooth it over for me. "*We* talk like that. Cravens have always been that kind of family."

"Well, *I* thought it rocked."

We all look back to see that Hannah has made her way into the stairwell. She nibbles on her red-polished thumbnail. "I just wish I'd had my phone out so it could go viral."

Aunt Bella sighs. "He would have liked that."

"Oh, swell." Mom sits on one of the stairs and presses her forehead into her palm. "Dane can be a meme. That's what I always hoped you'd be when you grew up, *D-Frizzle*."

I tense and sway my arms rigidly back and forth. I always do this when I'm pent up with embarrassment. I call it my Muppet move. "I'm *sorry!*"

But there were strange girls in red jackets trying to read my mind, and I lit a bible on fire, not to mention that a killer might have my phone number.

Mom's eyes dart to me and I shrink away. Why do I get the feeling she just heard that?

"It's not okay, Dane," she says.

"I'm okay," says Aunt Bella. "Hannah is, too. You are the one who isn't."

Mom looks to Aunt Bella. "You're fragile and upset."

Aunt Bella points at Mom. "Okay, *big sis*, I'm not twelve anymore. Don't tell me how I feel."

Hannah and I exchange a quick glance. *Here we go.*

Mom sighs and pushes herself back to her feet. "You're right. I'm sorry, Bells. It's not my place to do that. How about we all take a deep breath and have a fresh start?"

Aunt Bella nods. "Sounds good. Hi, Robyn, I've missed you."

"I've missed you, too," Mom says. "Hannah, hello. I can't believe how pretty you're getting."

Hannah snorts. "You're lying. Hi, Aunt Robyn. Hi, Dane."

"Hi, Elvira," I say. Hannah smiles at this. "Hi, Aunt Bella."

"Hi, Dane."

Mom sighs. "All right. Let's go act like we want to be here a little longer, and then we can get out of this place."

"I couldn't put it any better myself," Aunt Bella says. I think she's about to cry but she inhales sharply through her nose and pivots toward the dining hall. "I'm exhausted."

Hannah gives me a sheepish look and follows her mother. This isn't the first time Aunt Bella has had to hold it together. Hannah and I were little when Uncle Richard died of an aneurysm. Not to mention my maternal grandparents who died before I was even born. Mom says the Cravens dropped like flies, and the Allens were tethered to us by marriage.

Speaking of Mom, she steps to block my path as I head to leave the stairwell. She narrows her eyes at me. "How are your hands?"

I've got them shoved inside my pants pockets. The tingling's been better since I let the fire out, but I still feel like I'm going to set this entire church ablaze.

Mom hasn't said exactly what the fire is or if this is normal to us. But she hasn't said it isn't, either.

"Fine," I say.

"I just don't want anyone to see anything they shouldn't. People can be—"

"Yeah," I step around her. "My hands are fine."

I push into the dining hall before she can say anything else. Mom's always been like that. Everything is private, nothing is worth discussing. No approval or disapproval of the fire. Nothing about my sexuality. As long as I'm alive and not causing a scene, she doesn't care.

I think that's a form of love—or at least tolerance—but I wouldn't know any different.

I shake my head to clear the existential crisis brewing in my cranium and find Hannah at a table, poking a meatless chicken leg. She doesn't say anything when I scoot my chair next to her and plop down, so I make the first gesture.

"You want a drink or anything?"

"Not unless you've got schnapps." She doesn't look at me.

"Fresh out." The silence resumes and I listen to the click of her fingernail against the chicken bone, louder than the low rumble of the eating mourners. "Hannah, I really am sorry. I don't know what made me say all of that stuff—"

"I said it rocked." She finally looks at me, and a smile plasters across her face. "I'm not upset about your eulogy, Dane."

Pursing my lips, I blush. "Of course. Yeah. Sorry. I don't know how to—"

"Navigate the feelings of grief, loss, anger, and resentment?" Hannah squints and her smile becomes more genuine. "Me either. That's why I deleted emotions from my hard drive. Look, maybe tonight we can just hang out and pretend things are normal for a while? I don't think I can take another quiet night at the house. Mom's been going to the den so I don't hear her crying, and I don't think I can pace anymore—"

"Yes!" I sit up straight. "Everything is absolutely normal! We'll get milkshakes and sing in the car, and we can scream into the void that is Jasper Hollow."

"God, I love screaming into voids."

I relax, relieved to pretend for a bit and not think about murders and roaming killers. But it's cut short when the Reds enter the dining hall. They're impossible to miss, their red jackets bright like fresh blood under the fluorescents.

"Shit," I mutter. "Your friends are here."

Hannah glances back over her shoulder and grunts. "They are *not* my friends. Don't worry. If Madelaine sics her cat on you, I'll punt it."

"You don't need to—"

"I'll punt it with a smile."

The Reds snap their attention to me, as though they were looking for me. I shrink beneath their glares and pretend to be interested in something Hannah is saying, but that's a bust since her mouth isn't even open. I sense them heading for our table.

"The hell do they want?" I whisper.

"Maybe they want to adopt you and make you a pretty girl," says Hannah.

"Shut up."

That's not entirely ridiculous. When I was outed, girls came running to claim their mythical gay best friend. It seems like a crap deal to me.

"Hey," one of them stage whispers. "Come here!"

I whirl my head and see Chloe wave as they take an empty table.

"You've been summoned." Hannah scrunches her nose.

I don't know these girls. I've been here for barely one day and likely won't be staying long, so why do I even care?

"Less gawking, more walking," Madelaine calls out.

I want to tell her where to shove her cat, but I get up and stumble to their table. Let's face it. When it comes right down to it, I am but a jellyfish destined for the net of SpongeBob.

"What." I punch the word to make it a challenge.

"You with Igor?" asks Elena.

"It's Elvira, bitch." Hannah steps behind me.

Madelaine pulls her purse onto her lap and reaches in to caress the white cat.

"You're having a hard time, so we'll let that slide," she says.

Hannah raises a finger (whether to cuss Madelaine out or place a Sicilian curse on her, it's really anyone's guess), but I cut her off. "I'm her cousin."

"I know that," Madelaine says. "You were Grant's cousin, too."

Were. My heart sinks.

"I'm Madelaine Wednesday. This is Chloe White, and Elena Gallegos." She gestures to each of the girls in turn before locking eyes with me. "And you're the Craven kid."

"Mhm," I say. "Well, ladies, I'd love to stay and chat, but now's not a good time and—"

"Sit," Madelaine commands.

What is wrong with this girl? "No, I'm good, but—"

"I said *sit*."

I slide into an empty chair, the one next to Chloe. Hannah gawks at me as though I've throat-punched her. But there's some sort of pull working inside me. I don't feel like I have to sit; I want to. Like the marrow in my bones is magnetic, and these girls are the refrigerator.

"Good boy." Madelaine's tone sweetens.

Hannah grabs a chair from another table and slams it next to Madelaine. She plops down with a huff.

Elena curls her nose. "Who asked you to join?"

"Oh, I did," says Hannah. "Silently, of course. I politely invited myself, and so I cordially accepted."

Elena opens her mouth to respond, but Madelaine waves her hand in front of her to cut her off without moving her eyes from me. "Here's the thing. We know your secret. But it's not really a secret anymore, now is it?"

My arms tingle. How could she possibly know about this? "McScuse me?"

"That's cute," she laughs. "You know, that you're gay?"

Okay. I see what's up now. They've found a boy with a limp wrist. With me as their new BFF, the Reds would be diverse enough to pose for the covers of college brochures and fool students with our front of inclusion.

"Apt observation."

"Wait!" Chloe bounces in her seat. She whispers, "Do you think any of the guys here are cute?"

"N-no," I lie, but I feel my face turn red. There're easily five of Grant's classmates here that I would give a second look.

Chloe *tsks* and reaches a hand out to me. "Take my hand. I want to show you something."

"Not now, Chloe!" barks Elena.

Chloe whimpers in response.

Madelaine laughs, her eyes still on me. "No worries. You're welcome here."

"Golly gee, thank you."

Hannah rolls her eyes. "How is this any of y'all's business?"

Elena side-eyes her. "If you're going to sit in, the least you can do is be quiet."

"My apologies, I didn't realize I was crashing an investigation."

I nudge her leg under the table. "It's fine, Hannah."

"Actually, we're going to a little party right now." Madelaine cocks her head at me with doe eyes. "Want to come?"

Hannah grabs the edge of the table, and it shakes under her grip. "Do you realize this is my brother's *funeral*?!"

"Yes," Madelaine drops her smile. "That's why we need Dane."

As if that makes any sense, I tilt my head back and forth, at least pretending to consider. "Thank you, but I don't think my mom would be okay with that."

Madelaine smiles. "Elena?"

Elena reaches into her jacket. She pulls out a phone and taps the screen. My cracking voice fills my ears.

"Yo-yo-yo, D-Frizzle in the hizzle! We interrupt your education for this breaking news report!"

I almost fall out of my chair as the Reds break into hysterical laughter. Hannah sits up and raises her eyebrows at Elena.

"Can you send that to me?"

"No," I say. "She can't! She doesn't have service!"

Elena can hardly breathe. "I have full bars."

"No, you don't!"

Madelaine clasps her hands together. "I'm going to ask again. Would you like to come to the party? Or should we let everyone back home know that D-Frizzle was, indeed, in the hizzle?"

Kill me.

3

LIBRARY, VANILLA, CINNAMON

"Get your elbow off my boob." Chloe pushes my arm away.

"Sorry," I say, my face hot.

I'm stuck between her and Hannah in the back seat of Madelaine's pink car. Of course it's pink. What else would do for Barbie's Murder Mobile? I fiddle with the tie in my hands and try not to freak out too much. Dying in a car fire is *not* how I promised Hannah we'd spend the evening. But the last time a group of my so-called peers invited me to a party...

I peer at Hannah. "Why couldn't you drive us?"

Madelaine looks at me in the rearview mirror. "Yeah, because you wouldn't just speed off in the other direction."

"Look," I say. "I'm not really much fun at parties. I can't even dance!"

Hannah nods. "Even other white guys are embarrassed for him."

"Thank you, Hannah." I force a smile. "See? I'd only ruin your stainless reputation. So, if you want to pull over, I'll just make my way home."

"Nope," says Madelaine.

"Oh, come on!"

"Does anyone have a pacifier?" Elena asks from the front passenger seat, scrolling on her phone. "For the baby in the back?"

Ahead, the lights of a four-way stop turn yellow and Madelaine speeds up. They blink red, and she goes even faster, speeding through the intersection.

On cue, a dark car pulls out behind us, and red and blue lights flash.

Madelaine grunts and slows down. She pulls the car over to the curb and makes a hard break.

"Well, now it's gone to hell," I say. "We're so grounded. Better head home right after."

"Shut up," Madelaine flips the map light on and rolls her window down. "It's just Doyle."

A sheriff makes his way to the car. He lumbers around the driver's side and shines his flashlight in on Madelaine.

"How many times we gonna do this, Wednesday?" he asks. His voice is heavy with Kentucky drawl.

"I'm on the clock, Sheriff," says Madelaine. "Call my boss and ask her."

I lift an eyebrow at Hannah, who shrugs and shakes her head.

Sheriff Doyle rests his elbow on the door. He looks slowly around the car with gray eyes under a furrowed and suntanned forehead. When he gets to me, he stares. "You Robyn's boy?" I nod. He looks back at Madelaine. "Give him back. I told you girls to stop stealing boys."

This time, my face snaps to Hannah, but she's beat me to it, with the signature family expression of "What the hell."

"Don't worry, Sheriff." I can practically hear Madelaine's smile. "He strayed into the car. I couldn't leave him."

With a grunt, Sheriff Doyle looks to the street, then back at all of us. "What is it? A Code Silver? Code Scarlet?"

"Code None Ya."

"You girls realize there's a killer on the loose?" asks Sheriff Doyle. I feel Hannah tense next to me. "There's three others still reported missing. You know that?"

I glance at Hannah. There are three others besides Grant?

"Why do you think I'm on the clock?" asks Madelaine.

Sheriff Doyle squints at Madelaine, then sighs. "Stop runnin' lights. I'll ticket you next time, and I'll make up for all the other times while I'm at it."

"Yes, sir."

"And get the cat outta your lap! You're driving."

Madelaine picks up the cat and tosses it to Elena, who yelps in surprise.

He looks back at me. "Sorry for your loss." Then, his mouth lifts into a half grin. "And tell your mom that Todd Doyle said hi."

He winks, pushes himself off the door, and heads back to his car.

Madelaine rolls up her window and sighs. "It's as easy as luring boys from GameStop."

Yeah, I'm definitely about to die.

"Help—"

Chloe slaps a hand over my mouth.

"For the record," Madelaine says as she pulls down a dead-end street marked Poplar Lane and turns into a dark driveway, "Doyle and I were joking. I don't steal boys."

I mutter something, but no one understands me. I can't say anything outright because Chloe still has her hand on my mouth. I've tried everything. I licked her palm. Thrust my head back and forth. I even pointed over her shoulder enticingly to get her to look the other way. Sadly, she's stronger than I thought, and Hannah seems too entertained to help my plight.

"Let him go," Madelaine says. "What did you say?"

I pant as Chloe drops her hand. "I said, 'Could've fooled me.'"

Chloe inspects her palm. "Your lips are really soft. What ChapStick do you use?"

Hannah leans over me and looks out the windshield. "Are we where I think we are?"

I push her head away to get a good look. The headlights illuminate a gate, closed with the iron heads of two black cats at its center. Their lifeless gold eyes peer right back at me. Must be the murder compound.

"You bet your death-loving life, Igor," says Elena.

Madelaine inches the car forward and the gates creak open. Must be motion activated. Right?

"Um, and where is that?" I gape at Hannah.

"Collingwood Hall," says Hannah. "The founder's old house. But it's a museum now, not a good party spot."

Chloe leans across me to look at Hannah. "I didn't think you'd mind breaking a few laws."

Hannah darts her eyes to Chloe. "I don't. Just ask the shiv in my pocket."

We pull up a winding drive toward an estate. The windows are dark, and I can barely make out the massive outline of the house against the moonlight. Headlights slice across white pillars, and Madelaine halts the car at the steps to the veranda.

"Get out." Madelaine peers at me through the rearview mirror.

"What are the magic words?" I raise my eyebrows.

"Out!"

Hannah swings her door open with a grunt and I slide across the seat to join her. A gag seizes my throat the second I step out of the car. This is the most pungent the blood smell has been since my arrival—as though this is where the smell is brewed. Definitely a murder compound. Or a slaughterhouse.

I look up at the looming antebellum-style structure. My eyes dart to an upper window, where I think I see a flash of something cross the pane.

Madelaine comes around the car, arms crossed. The white cat follows her. "Know about this place?"

"No," I say.

"They don't let us pass elementary school without knowing," Hannah says. "Lester Collingwood settled the area that is now Jasper Hollow. He named it after his bloodhound."

"Jasper is named after a dog?"

"But the house wasn't lived in very long," Hannah continues, and her eyebrows rise. "After the shit that went down."

A shiver threatens the back of my neck. "What happened?"

"Tabitha." Madelaine makes her way to the veranda. Elena and Chloe flank me and leave me no choice but to follow, and Hannah bounds to catch up. "She made it all possible."

The front door swings open, but I don't think I saw Madelaine ever touch the knob. She crosses the threshold and turns around, hanging off the doorway with both hands. "Oh, and by the way, Igor, you heard none of what I'm about to tell you."

"I make it a point not to listen to anything you say," challenges Hannah.

Madelaine, to my surprise, laughs and disappears inside the blackened house.

So, this is where they bring the stolen boys. I gulp. *Probably gouge out our eyes and keep them in jars. Make pink milkshakes with our brains.*

"Ew!" shouts Elena.

"Stop reading in," I say, swatting the nonexistent bugs off my arms.

Hannah shoots me a curious look, but how can I possibly explain that? We step into the dark house. An amber glow fades up to my right, revealing a parlor where Madelaine stands waiting, holding the cat like a baby and petting its tummy.

I exhale. I'd been holding my breath, anticipating the blood smell to knock me down. But it doesn't smell like blood in here. It smells like an old library, mixed with vanilla and cinnamon. I sniff in, relieved to catch a break.

"It's a safe space for us," Madelaine explains, and the nonexistent bugs come back. "For people like me. People like you."

"Gay boys?"

Madelaine smirks. "I'm honored. But no. Hannah, what can you tell us about Tabitha Collingwood, please?"

Hannah puts her fists on her hips. "Well, I didn't know there'd be an oral essay assigned. But from what I remember, she was eccentric. Always wearing black and going out to the smokehouse. She threw wild parties and liked to walk around the graveyard. My kind of bitch, honestly."

"Well, there's something they don't tell you in school." Madelaine cocks her head to an oil painting above the fireplace. "She killed her husband."

I slide my eyes to the painting. A tall and hard-faced woman stares back with eyes that I'm pretty sure would follow my every step. She wears a black hoopskirt and a red hat with feathers. I notice that her right index finger is subtly pointed downward, as though to hint at something below the ground.

"They said he was murdered by an antiabolitionist, and they found no evidence to suggest it was her."

"I'm telling you, she killed him. Had one of those wild parties in the smokehouse. A bunch of people dancing around naked."

I side-eye Hannah. "I don't like this party."

Madelaine ignores me. "Lured Lester Collingwood out there and—*splat*. Cut him up with the help of her coven. A human sacrifice so that we could connect with our patron and have power."

"Nope!" I make to flee, but Chloe blocks my path, shooing me back a foot.

Madelaine laughs and drops the cat, who lands with a thud and a hiss. She makes her way to the next room. "Relax, that was the first and last human sacrifice. Come on."

I grab Hannah's arm and start to follow, but Elena steps in front of us. "Not you, Igor."

"I'm not going anywhere without her," I say.

"Need I remind you of my shiv?" Hannah folds her arms.

Elena glances at Hannah's pocket. "It's an old Dum-Dum stick."

"How did you—"

Elena snaps her fingers, and Hannah looks to the floor, frozen, her eyes half-closed. She's totally zoned out. I wave my hand in front of her face. Shake her shoulder. She remains unreachable. I look at Elena, trembling. "What did you do?"

"She can't know about all of this," she says, unenthused, as though that explains everything.

"Hurry," Madelaine calls. "That run-in with Doyle's made us late."

Chloe scurries into the next room. With a hard nudge from Elena, I hesitantly follow, cramming my hands deeper into my pockets. As we walk I look back at Hannah, who stands frozen like a shopping-mall mannequin.

When I reach the archway leading into the room, I halt.

It's the dining room. A long oak table stands at its center, red velvet ropes around it. A mirror hangs on the opposite wall. Madelaine stands before it, checking her reflection. She smooths her hair, blows herself a kiss, then tilts the mirror.

A square of the floor drops away, revealing a set of steps.

"No!" I turn, but Elena and Chloe block the exit. Again. "I am not going down into the murder factory, thank you very much."

"Yes, you are." Elena pushes me toward the stairs, as though she's a pirate and I'm next up on the plank.

"Elena, you stay with Igor." Madelaine crosses to follow me. "Make sure she doesn't come out of that waking coma until we're done."

"Fine with me." Elena shrugs. "I feel like Ada's in a weird mood down there."

"She's *always* in a weird mood." Madelaine rolls her eyes. Then she stares me down until I take the first step.

The floorboard groans beneath me, and I force myself to keep going. I really don't like this. At all. But I also kind of feel okay? Like I'm supposed to be here? It's the magnets inside, like at the church. I feel pulled to whatever waits below.

The farther I go, the more the steps feel soft beneath the soles of my shoes. Madelaine pulls out her phone and flips its flashlight on, illuminating the rest of my way. Rose-colored shaggy carpet that must've been here since the '80s covers the remaining steps. They turn at the bottom, leading to an open door where the light pools across the floor.

I hesitate when I cross through, finding myself in a basement with stone walls and a concrete floor. It's decorated with white bulbs on strings that cross back and forth across the beamed ceiling. There's a large sofa with fluffy, fuzzy pillows of various colors, and a Muppet-skin rug to match.

This isn't a murder factory, it's Tinker Bell's Nightmare Sorority.

Madelaine drags me over to the fuzzy couch and forces me to plop down. A Hello Kitty stuffy falls into my lap. Madelaine crosses to an equally fuzzy chair and takes her seat as the white cat snuggles next to her.

"Good Ambrose," she coos and scratches its head.

"Efron?" Chloe skips down the stairs.

Fur brushes my leg and I shout, pulling my knees to my chest. A fat orange cat bolts to Chloe and leaps into her arms.

"You named your cat after Zac Efron?" I slap my chest to calm the adrenaline.

"Why not?" Chloe crosses the room. "They're both adorable."

I take in the other side of the room, which is blocked off by pink sheets. It gives the appearance of a fake wall, with magazine cutouts and gold stars stapled onto them.

"Ahem," an earthy voice says from behind the sheets.

I jump.

"Oh, crap." Chloe drops Efron and scampers to a teal record player. She fumbles through a stack of vinyls, dropping a slew of them. Finally, she picks one and puts it on the turntable. "Presenting the incomparable, the wonderful, the mystical"—she looks back at Madelaine—"the *irritable*—"

"Ahem!" the voice repeats.

"I'm getting there!" Chloe drops the needle on the record. "The fabulous Miss Ada!"

Chloe claps as she skips to the sofa and jumps down next to me. I hug myself and lean away.

The record scratches to life, crackling out the unmistakable sound of the Rolling Stones. Tinkling piano gives way to trumpets and horns. The sheets part and in dances a woman who can only be described as, well—she's like a *rainbow!*

A tall, lanky woman, with a huge mane of orange hair, sashays about in flip-flops and a flowing robe of red tie-dye. She looks like a dancing lava lamp.

Despite her wild movements, her face is completely stoic, eyebrows raised in a no-nonsense expression. She spins, tossing her hair and flaunting a yellow feather boa across her shoulders.

Wait a minute. I squint. That's not a feather boa—*it's a motherfucking copperhead snake.*

The incomparable, irritable, evangelical, whatever, Ada throws her arms to the sky and freezes. She flicks one wrist and the music screeches to a halt. She's eyeing me like a madwoman. "Who—*what* is that?"

"Hm?" is all I can manage.

"It's Robyn's kid," says Madelaine with narrowed eyes. "You told us to get him. Remember?"

"I did tell you to get Robyn's kid," says Ada. She keeps looking me over like she's not sure if I'm the right sweater to put on that morning. "But I meant for you to get *her*. Not *him*."

"There is no *her*," Madelaine mimics Ada's voice. "There's only *him*."

"Impossible," says Ada. She squints. "Do you think this is some kind of joke, male?"

"No, ma'am," I say.

"Then why are you laughing?"

It's true. I have started laughing. Whoops. "I'm sorry, it's just...what was that?"

"I beg your pardon?"

"You literally just danced in here like a drag queen. I didn't know whether to scream or tip you."

The copperhead hisses at me and I force the laughter back down. I plead to the snake with a look that I can only hope says, "Please don't bite me."

"Not now, Louisa." Ada pets the snake's head, and it purrs. She looks back at me. "You can't be the Craven kid. You're so—so masculine."

My face flushes. "I am?"

"Madelaine, this can't be right!" Ada looks away from me and I feel a bit relieved. "It's a boy. Sixteen years ago, Isabella Craven Allen reported that Robyn gave birth to a *daughter*. What did you do with her?"

"Maybe I ate her in the womb." I shrug.

Ada casts her eyes to the ceiling. "My god, it *is* Robyn's kid. Everyone out! Out!"

Madelaine and Chloe both stand and head to the stairs. I go to follow them, but when I lift my foot to take the first step, something wraps around my ankle. I look down and cry out: it's the copperhead. I double-take at Ada, who has seated herself in Madelaine's spot, her robe spread out like an ancient queen.

"Not you," she says. "Sit down. Let's have a little chat."

Maybe it's the magnets in my marrow, maybe it's morbid curiosity. But when Louisa uncurls herself from my foot, I return to the sofa. Louisa slithers to her owner and crawls over her feet.

"Tell me," she begins. "What sort of things do you do? And for how long?"

I don't respond at first. Part of me wants to begin with everything. Reading minds, the first time I touched an object and saw its past. But another, stronger part of me doesn't want to give her anything.

"Well, since birth, I suppose," I say. "At first, I just kind of laid there. Cried a lot. But soon, I graduated to crawling, and eventually, my legs figured out how to walk—"

"Don't be a smart-ass." Ada leans forward. "I see you, and I see that wall."

"The one behind me?"

"You think if you keep making jokes, no one will see those insecurities. Well, let me tell you, Craven Kid, that might work on everyone else, but that's not going to work with me."

I tense my jaw, feeling the deep scowl cross over my face. *Fuck you.*

"Watch your mouth," Ada raises an eyebrow at me. "Even in your mind. How much has your mother told you?"

"About what?"

Ada sighs. "Classic Robyn. Just run and let the problems solve themselves."

I open my mouth to ask what she means, but she cuts me off.

"Let's try this another way. Have you ever, let's say, done strange things? Read minds? Accidentally made things happen?"

Under my sleeves, my arms are hot. Lighting this sofa on fire sounds fantastic right about now. I look at the floor instead of responding.

"To put it simply, you're a witch."

I bolt to my feet.

"An untrained one," Ada continues, "but a witch, all the same."

"You're on drugs," I protest, remembering Mom's warning not to let anyone see what they shouldn't.

"Oh, can we please skip this part where you deny it? I'm tired of it already. You were born beneath a blood-ringed moon—"

"And I'm sure it was in the seventh house, and Jupiter was aligned with Mars, but that means nothing. I don't fly on brooms or cast spells."

"We're not basic witches," Ada shrugs. "It might take some time to process, but every Red comes to her senses after a day or so. Even if the *her* is a *him*—if that's your preferred pronoun. Miss Elena has been 'educating' me, as she says."

"Well, this has been lovely," I give Ada a polite half bow. "It really has. Thank you for that amazing performance, and for introducing me to your lethal little friend there, but I need to go. Good night."

I make for the stairs.

"Not so fast!"

I take the first step. "Good. Night."

"There's a killer on the loose."

I halt. My stomach bunches up. I stare ahead at the wall.

"You know that, of course," continues Ada. "We can find them before they get anyone else. As long as we're all together."

Slowly, I crane my neck to look at her. She sits demurely, hands on her lap as if to say, "Now that I have your attention."

"I don't care about anyone else," I say. "I only care about my cousin. We literally *just* buried him."

Ada lifts her eyes to mine. A half smirk appears. "There's not much I can do about that. But we can stop whoever did it. Join a coven, catch the killer. Not a bad trade, eh?"

"I'm getting out of here." I stumble up the stairs. "I want to go home!"

Ada laughs. "Oh, sweetheart," she calls after me, "you *are* home."

4

FAMILIAR TO ME

There's a picture of us at fourteen or so, tacked to Grant's bedroom mirror. He's got me trapped in a headlock and we're flashing what Mom always called our 'shit-eating grins.' I remember when this was taken because it was Easter. April. We only have two years left, and we don't even know it.

I slide my fingers across the photo and close my eyes—try to dig past its glossy surface and into its atoms so it can show itself to me like a tiny ghost reel. But nothing comes. Ada's words play on a loop in my mind, breaking my focus.

Witch. An untrained one. Killer on the loose. Witch. An untrained one. Killer on the—Witch. Witch. Witch. Witch.

Join a coven. Catch the killer.

My hand drops and I open my eyes. I stare at Grant. "Who killed you? Was it our pact?"

His shit-eating grin stares back. I push my thumb to his face and focus on myself for a minute. I look genuinely happy. Accepted, I guess? Grant was the one guy my own age who didn't make me uncomfortable. I never felt like I had to be super boyish or straight-acting. He'd known me since birth. The sight of my happy face pisses me off. Heat rushes from my cheeks down to my shoulders. My hands tingle and when I pull my thumb away, I gasp.

A hole has burned through the picture, removing Grant's face forever.

"Shit!" I tear the picture off the wall, and a few more flakes crumble away, Grant's body disintegrating before my eyes. "No! Stop!"

I slam it face down on his dresser and hold my hands up in surrender, but it's too late. Photo Grant is gone. *Witch.* A chuckle escapes my throat, startling me.

I run my thumbs over my fingertips, savoring the phantom heat as it dissipates back down to that dark place inside me. Having the power to make fire has to be a bad thing. But why does letting it out feel so good? Why, deep down, do I feel this microscopic bit of glee at having burned off Grant's photographic face?

I think of the Wicked Witch of the West, shooting fireballs at scarecrows, of Glinda drifting in a bubble.

Are you a good witch? Or a bad witch?

What kind am I?

We're not your basic witches. Join a coven. Catch the killer.

Shaking the thoughts from my head, I try his wrestling trophies next. The cracked spine of his copy of *It.* The red comforter pulled across his bed. Nothing reveals any history to me. It's like his energy has already left the room, leaving behind only the stink of his body spray and dust.

Morning light floods through the window. Everyone will be awake soon, and I don't feel ready to talk about last night. Especially with Mom. What am I even supposed to say? "Hey Mom, some lady with a copperhead told me we have powers that can catch a serial killer. Is that legit or nah?"

It was awkward enough around Hannah, who clearly had no idea how much time had passed in her daze. She acted like it never happened at all and commanded we drive around and sing after the Reds returned us to the church parking lot. I had no choice but to belt out all of *Beetlejuice the Musical* and act like I didn't just discover my whole life is a lie.

Crossing to the window, I lean against the pane and look over the backyard. Aunt Bella's house stands just outside of town, at the edge of the Hollow Woods, which I was never allowed to go into when we visited.

Catch the killer. Witch.

The magnetic feeling inside me returns. Fog rolls from the trees, wispy gray clouds stretching out like the arms of a welcoming stranger. *"Come on,"* the trees seem to whisper. *"Let me show you something."*

No matter how much my bones beg, I shouldn't go in. But what if I can see the answers there, hidden in the atoms of leaves? What if I can find out who killed Grant, without Ada and the Reds, and put a stop to all of this here and now?

I drag myself from the room and descend the stairs two steps at a time. Footsteps echo from Aunt Bella's room, and I bolt out the kitchen door.

Moments later, I'm nearing the first tree at the yard's edge and forcing myself to breathe through the rotten scent of the fog. I close my eyes and put my hand to the tree.

Nothing.

With a glance at the house to ensure no one is looking, I duck through the brush and into the woods.

The canopy of leaves blocks out most of the morning light. A panorama of moss and mud, thick with tangled brush that's probably home to big-ass pink moths, lizards, and other Kentucky backwoods shit I don't like. I have to weave around foliage in the way.

I nearly stumble on a root arching from the ground, and I jump. I swear, it looks more like a human rib.

Here, the air feels different—stiffer and clouded with the intangible feeling of doom. Like entering a room after an argument without knowing it, you can feel that something bad just happened.

The shrill chirping of morning birds echoes from above, and a wild turkey gobbles in the distance. Are they welcoming the morning, or desperately grateful for its arrival?

My palm lands on another tree. Still nothing. Do trees even save their histories? I try a leaf. Nada. A twig. No, sir. I beat my fist against the tree and whirl around, lean my back against it. I try to soothe my frustration with deep breaths through my nose.

I'm just being weird, but it sounds like the birds are chanting, "Witch. Witch. Witch."

Something tiny jabs my shoulder. *"Click-click-click—"*

I cry out and stumble from the tree, swatting at the air and whatever just touched me. I spin around and—

A raccoon stares back at me. I grab at my heart and double over to calm myself. I look back at the raccoon, and its round black eyes lock onto mine.

Calm down, I think. *Just a fucking adorable raccoon.*

The raccoon makes its clicking sound again, and I swear it actually just said, *"Watch your tongue, young man. And thank you."*

Okay. I can take reading minds and some flickering lights. I can deal with a copperhead hissing at me, and you know what? I'm working through the whole flamethrowers-in-my-fingers thing. But a talking raccoon? Not even the raccoon in Disney's *Pocahontas* could talk.

I rub my eyes, half expecting to wake up and start the day all over again. But the raccoon is still there, and now he's grinning at me.

"Are-are you talking to me?" I point at my chest like an idiot.

The raccoon nods and clicks, *"Of course, young master."*

It scurries a few feet down the side of the tree, and I stumble a few more steps back.

"Your soul called to me, and I answered."

My face heats up. "I... I've gone crazy."

"I hope not," clicks the raccoon. *"For then you would be a fox, and I can't abide foxes. But at any rate, young master, we ought to be getting you out of these woods. Dreadful things happen to humans here and I don't think the ghosts of the woods appreciate humans of your kind."*

"Humans of my kind?"

"Witches, sir." The raccoon blinks.

A chill sweeps up my arms. This has gone far enough, thank you. I push my hands into the large front pocket of my hoodie. Okay, I'll humor him if it gets him away, or at least kills time until whatever drug the Reds must have slipped me wears off. Because this isn't happening.

"What's your name?" I ask.

"Click-click-click—"

"In English!"

"Aloysius, sir." I swear to god, the raccoon just bowed like a dandy.

"Aloe-wishes," I phonetically punch the name. A chuckle escapes. "What a helluva—"

"I see that the name tickles you, sir. I knew it would, and that's why I named myself. Just as I knew you would adore this whimsical British accent. You've always loved your whimsy."

"And, *Aloysius*," I say, "why are you talking to me?"

"Oh, I must," clicks the raccoon. *"I am your familiar. An extension of you. Your most faithful companion though you've only just now learned it."*

"I don't think—"

"If you reflect deep down, you might find that you've always dearly loved raccoons. I seem to recall a stuffy you once favored?"

I widen my eyes. How does he know about Wowcoo the raccoon stuffy? Aloysius grins at me again and starts to laugh, a disorienting mix of high-pitched chuckles and clicks. Ada's words ring through my head yet again, and I get the urge to cover my ears.

Witch. An untrained one.

How much has your mother told you?

Oh, that does it. I bend down, scoop him up in my arms, and make a beeline out of the woods.

"Oh!" cries Aloysius. *"Put me down!"*

"No!" I quicken my pace and wrap my arms tighter around the struggling raccoon. "I need proof that I'm not insane."

His striped tail swats at my arm but I don't ease up. Finally, I make it through the yard and up the deck stairs. I toss him under one arm and push open the door.

Aunt Bella sits at the kitchen table, lifting a mug of coffee to her lips while she scans the funeral guest book.

"Good morning, Peter," she says without looking up. Then she swivels in her chair and looks through the archway that leads into the living room. "It says here that Peter Pan and Captain Hook came to the service!"

I wait patiently, Aloysius still trying to squeeze out of my hold.

"I told him not to be a little shit!" calls Mom from the living room.

"I do believe in fairies," snorts Hannah. She stands at the stove in a yellow apron with her back turned, making pancakes.

It always unnerves me a little, to see the devil's bride going into Pioneer Woman mode, but we all have our hobbies, I guess.

She flips a pancake onto a plate, turns, sees me holding a raccoon, and nearly drops it. "What the fuck?!"

Under my arm, Aloysius covers his ears. *"Such language!"*

Aunt Bella finally looks up and startles, a splash of coffee staining the guest book. "Robyn! Get in here!"

Mom comes wide-eyed into the kitchen. When she sees me, she pales. I hold up Aloysius by the scruff of the neck.

"It's talking to me!" I shout. "Care to explain that?"

Mom stares at the raccoon and paints on a tight-lipped smile. "Raccoons don't talk. I think you're just confused and tired."

"Robyn." Aunt Bella sighs. "Don't gaslight your child."

Mom looks at Aunt Bella, her glare a threat. "We're leaving soon, what does it matter?"

"It's time."

Mom huffs out through her nose and looks at me. Her face reddens. "Living room."

I swing Aloysius back under my arm and follow her from the kitchen. Hannah is quick to join us, stuffing half a pancake in her mouth.

Mom plops into an armchair and rubs her temples. "Sit down."

I sit on the couch and Aloysius gives up his struggle and settles in my lap. *"Don't ask questions you don't want answers to,"* he clicks.

"We never should have come here," Mom says under her breath. She looks up at Aunt Bella, who has made her way in and is leaning against the arch.

"I'm sorry, Bells, but we really shouldn't have. I knew it was almost time, and still—never should have come."

Aunt Bella shrugs. "They were supposed to be looking for a girl."

"It was only a matter of time before they knew that was a lie," Mom says.

"I tried."

"I know."

Hannah looks down at the other half of her pancake. "I should have made popcorn for this."

"Oh, she has popcorn!" clicks Aloysius. *"Young master, tell her I would appreciate—"*

"Shh."

Aunt Bella gently takes the pancake from Hannah's hand. "Give me that. I don't want you dropping it on my rug in a moment."

"Why would I—"

"We're witches!" Mom almost shouts, her voice cracking. Her eyes widen even more, as though she can't decide whether she's relieved or afraid to have finally said it.

I can't help but grin at Mom. "You don't reckon!"

Mom leans forward, resting her elbows on her knees. "I should've told you years ago, but I was afraid to. But that's what this is. I'm a witch, and you're a witch. And my mother was a witch, and her mother. You're the next generation of Craven family heretics."

"Yeah, I figured that out when the hippie lady with the snake told me." I narrow my eyes.

"The lady with..." Mom takes a deep breath and begins again. "Who?"

"She called herself Ada," I say. "That is of course, after the girls in the red jackets kept making me say things at the funeral and proceeded to kidnap me."

"I knew something was off!" says Hannah. "We were in that house maybe two minutes before you were running and about to piss yourself."

Mom pushes to her feet and paces. "They've already found you? Shit. Shit! Shit! Why did we believe them when they said they were going for ice cream?"

Aloysius shifts on my lap. *"It's been so long since I've found a cone in the rubbish. Young master, could you—"*

"Zip it!" I bop a finger on his snoot.

Hannah comes to the couch and sits next to me, eyeing the raccoon with confusion and a bit of disgust. "So let me get this straight," she begins slowly. "There are actual witches in this room, a talking raccoon, and this isn't a dream, and I'm not high?"

Mom nods. "Yes."

"You better not be," Aunt Bella adds at the same time.

Hannah stares at the wall. "That's awesome."

I roll my eyes. "I'm glad *you're* hyped."

"So, what can I do?" she asks. "Can I turn people into frogs? Can I cast a spell that makes it storm? What?"

Aunt Bella stiffens and exchanges a look with Mom. "Oh, honey. I'm sorry. The power only comes once in a generation, if that. We're pretty much normal," she looks to Hannah's earrings, black skulls with knives stuck in their craniums. "Well, normal-ish."

"That's bullshit!" Hannah points to the ceiling. The old Sicilian curse again.

"So why didn't you tell me?" I take the conversation back. "Why didn't you just give me 'the talk' like with puberty? You knew I could do things."

"Honey, I didn't give you that talk, you googled it."

"*Because* you didn't tell me, and I thought I was dying!" I do my Muppet move and try not to yell. "I can't exactly google *this*. Did you even know I'd be a witch?"

Mom sighs. "Yes, I knew. I knew while you were being conceived—"

"I don't need *that* story—"

"I hoped it was a mistake. But then when you were three you kept sneaking into the kitchen of our old apartment to talk to some old woman. You said she smelled like cookies. I tried so hard to expel her, but my powers have faded a lot since leaving the Hollow. I wasn't strong enough to do it anymore."

I remember my babysitter, Miss June. I liked hugging the fat of her legs. She did always have cookies baking. Did I ever actually eat one? I realize now that I don't remember her eyes.

"Then you were getting in fights in kindergarten for things that kids never even said to you, and I knew you were reading minds. I couldn't explain it away to myself after that. And then..." Mom glances at Aunt Bella and Hannah, then silences. I know what she was going to say. She was going to mention what happened in April.

"I sense a story there," Aloysius clicks, more quietly than usual. *"I'm here if you ever want to talk about it."*

"What I wanted was for you to have a normal life. Without death, and spells, and all this crap. But I should have known better. So. Craven blood is very special," Mom concludes. "And now you know."

"Well let's hope I don't get sick." I force a smile. "I'd never find a matching blood donor."

"Honey—"

"Okay, I get it. Witch. Cool."

Hannah breaks her silence. "So, if you can talk to ghosts... If you're so magical, then where the hell is Grant? Who's his killer? Why can't you just see it or something?"

"I've been wondering the same thing," I say.

"It's not that simple." Aunt Bella reaches a hand out, but Hannah folds her arms and stands, storming to the corner. "It's not magic wands and broomsticks, and a witch isn't an oracle."

Hannah guffaws at this.

"We need to leave," Mom says. "We have to get you out of here before the coven comes for you. I don't want you near it."

"They already know about me," I say. "I don't understand. If they were looking for a girl, then how'd they even tell I was a witch at all?"

Mom narrows her eyes. "Did you try to read in on them?"

Shit.

Mom smirks. "You need to be more selective with that. And also, keep your mind walled up. They probably read every four-letter word you thought."

"And the raccoon?" I point to Aloysius, still on my lap.

"He's your best friend now."

I stand, and Aloysius slides off me with a grunt. "I need to get away." I pull my hood over my head and stuff my hands into the front pocket. "Hannah, don't you need to get away?"

"Yes, I do. I'll get my keys," Hannah says and darts into the kitchen.

"No," says Mom. "You can't—"

"If you want me to take this lying down, then I need air!"

Mom gestures to Aloysius and he scampers after me. "Let the raccoon protect you."

I swing open the front door. "I don't need a protector! I'm not going to be a—"

"Young master, I must protest—"

"Stop calling me that!" I whirl around. "Everyone just leave me alone!"

"You need to listen!" Mom raises her hands and the fireplace lights on its own. She turns around and gasps at the flames that are burning and spitting there, threatening to escape the hearth. I flinch, thinking of all the times I've lost control like this. The bible, charred and black. Photo Grant's ashes upstairs. The green door...

Aunt Bella falls weakly into the armchair. "I didn't know you could do that."

"I didn't do it," Mom whispers. She looks back at me. "We need to leave town."

"*We* aren't doing anything. I don't even know who the hell you are anymore." I stumble out the front door.

"Wait!"

"Just leave me alone!"

Hannah follows, rattling her keys, and we run to the car. Aloysius scampers after me down the porch steps and hops up onto the floorboard as I tear open the door and slide into the passenger seat. I try to push him out of the car, but Mom is running toward us, so I slam the door shut instead.

"He's coming with us?" Hannah snarls.

"Just drive!"

Hannah turns the key in the ignition and throws the car in reverse, nearly flipping us over as her wheels screech out of the driveway. I look back to see Mom at the foot of the porch steps, her face buried in her hands.

5

HALLOW BEAN

"Slow down!" With my feet against the dashboard, I grip the door handle and beg the door not to swing open.

"Can it!" Hannah punches the radio, and death metal screams from her speakers.

Aloysius tries to crawl onto the seat with me but jabs my ass with his sharp paws instead. I wince.

"My apologies!" he clicks. *"I don't wish to die!"*

Hannah spins the car onto Main Street and, thankfully, slows down at a red light. I breathe out. "Why must you always try to kill me?"

"I'm due for a near-death experience." She grips the wheel and revs the engine as we wait. "Don't get too cozy. As soon as we blow this town it's *vroom-vroom*, baby, all the way."

I scan the street for something, anything, to get her to pull over. There isn't much here. A few antique shops, a billiard room called TJ's, and an abandoned video rental place. My eyes fall a block down on a slab of rescued barn wood with a coffee bean etched into it. That will do nicely! "I need a coffee break."

"I'd rather have the erotic embrace of near death."

I gesture to Aloysius. "Hannah. The *raccoon* is talking to me. I haven't had any coffee today and I *need* it. I'm an addict. Give me a hit, man!"

Hannah turns to me, her eyes narrowed. "You know what? That's an excellent idea. And while we sit, you can show me this *magic* that you do."

She yanks at the wheel and pulls the car to the curb, slamming the break.

"She's going to make me sick," Aloysius clicks.

Hannah points at him. "You can start with why that thing keeps screeching at you!"

"Screeching? Well, I never!"

I pull Aloysius onto my lap and pet the top of his head. "He's my familiar. My soul called and he answered. That's what he says, anyways. And he's not screeching, he's literally talking to me. I can understand every single click."

"That's weird shit, Dane!" Hannah pushes her back against the window.

"You're telling me!" I spit out. "You heard what our moms said."

Hannah rubs her temples. "Okay."

I push my door open and get out. Aloysius hops from the car and trots ahead, keeping his head in the air like a pompous noble. A shopkeeper sweeping the sidewalk eyes us with suspicion.

"You go enjoy yourself, young master," he clicks. *"I smell a rubbish bin around the corner, and I'm peckish."*

My face burns, feeling the stare of the shopkeeper, and I whisper, "Fine."

Hannah and I make our way down Main Street. It's already littered with autumn leaves that graze my bare legs in the breeze. I don't remember the last time fall came this fast. Usually, it shows up just in time to get eaten by winter. But that's Kentucky. Weather isn't real, and your clothes don't matter. If I wasn't so hot blooded, these gym shorts would be leaving me frozen right now.

We near the entrance to the coffee shop and I note that the Open sign has a cartoon ghost painted on it. Above that is a sign marking the shop as Hallow Bean. My heart drops. This is the place the mortician went for lunch that day. The day they prepared what was left of Grant's body.

I inhale to steady my instant nausea.

The door swings back and a guy around my age stumbles from the shop, a large coffee in his hand. He trips over himself a bit to keep from knocking into me, and stares at me with unblinking, dark-circled eyes accentuated by his long, thin face.

"Logan," says Hannah. "Do we look like an exhibit to you?"

The guy gawks at her and runs shaky, black-polished fingers through his unkempt hair. "Sorry. I mean—hi, Hannah. Uh, I gotta go."

He brushes past me, heading to a beat-up Chrysler. I slide my eyes to Hannah. "Ex-boyfriend?"

"Uh, no," Hannah says pointedly. "Just a Hollowian I know from school. Guess the townsfolk aren't ready to see me out and about."

Folding her arms, she leans against the window of the shop, and her reflection conjures the illusion of twins. My heart sinks, but I don't know what to say to her.

"Anyways, let's not," Hannah waves me away, but I notice her voice crack. "You have big-boy secrets to spill, remember?"

I push open the door and brace myself for the smell of blood mixed with coffee, but when I pass inside, I'm welcomed with the aroma of roasted coffee beans and fresh brew in office-style pots. I sigh. Maybe Hannah *did* kill us on the road, and I've entered my own personal circle of heaven.

Hannah steps in next to me. "Why do you look like you just had the best orgasm ever?"

"I thought it would smell like blood in here."

"Kinky." Hannah narrows her eyes. "Care to explain that little nugget of what-the-hell?"

"It's nothing. I need my fix."

Hannah's brow furrows and she pats her pocket. "Oh crap. I left my cash in the console. Back in five."

"You promise you're not just abandoning me here forever?" I ask. "Considering?"

Pulling the door back open, Hannah gives me a dismissive wave as she exits. "Haven't decided yet."

I hustle past shelves of whole beans in canisters and a rack of T-shirts that say Hallow on the Inside and I Ain't Afraid of No Roast with a *Ghostbusters*-inspired logo. At the polished wood counter, I eyeball the rows of flavor syrup bottles to ensure they have my beloved cinnamon roll. But there are no baristas around—not even out busing tables. I could call out, but instead I take a second to get myself together.

Hannah knows about my powers now, and there's no pretending that things are normal anymore. How long until I need to tell everyone why Grant was in the woods to begin with? How long until everyone knows every dark little thing about me? The beds of my fingernails burn just thinking about it.

Laying my palms on the counter, I rest my forehead against the back of my hands. I need to make my head stop swimming. I need to process. I need—

"You know there's probably a slew of bacteria on that counter, right?"

The voice is confident, sweet if a bit gravelly. I open my eyes and tilt my head up. A barista in a swiveled brown ball cap looks down at me. His face is pale, but he has that glow that tells me he must have only just come in from the sun. He smiles at me with an amused and toothy grin, which reminds me of a dog waiting for a frisbee to be thrown. But god, his eyes are so blue.

"Aren't you supposed to clean it?" I squint one eye.

"Touché!" he says. "Welcome to Hallow Bean. My name is EJ and my pronouns are he/him/his. What can I get for you?"

I push myself from the counter and shove my hands into my hoodie pocket. "Hot Americano with three shots, hold the water."

The barista, EJ, stops punching the register buttons and eyes me. "That's just three shots of—"

"All right, you've talked me into it!" I roll my neck. "Fill it to the top with half-and-half and add three pumps of cinnamon-roll syrup. Please."

He chuckles. *He gave me a chuckle!* My stomach erupts with butterflies, and I combat them back into submission. He probably just thinks I'm weird or something. In my pocket, I link my fingers together and pull as tightly as I can, as though that'll reduce the anxiety.

Behind me, the chimes of the shop ring and Hannah enters. "Oh hi, EJ."

EJ gets a pleasant greeting from the queen of darkness? Okay, who is this boy?

He smirks. "Hey."

"Did you order?" Hannah asks me, but she turns to EJ before I can respond. "Can I get a dirty chai?"

With a nod, EJ clicks at the register, and I catch myself staring super hard at his thick black eyebrows. Why are they so pleasing to look at? "Is this together or separate?"

"Eh, together," Hannah says.

"No, separate!" I interject. EJ locks eyes with me. Word vomit comes up my throat and I try to choke it back, but instead I say, "She's not my girlfriend."

Sweat drips through my curls instantly. I want to face-slam this counter so hard right now.

"I'd hope not," says EJ. "But then again, this *is* Kentucky." He must sense my confusion because he adds, "I was, um, there...yesterday."

My eyes widen. No. He could not have been there. Because if he was, then it means he saw—

"Should I write D-Frizzle on the order?"

Hannah cackles. "Please!"

"I'll uh...get us a table." I beeline to the farthest table on the opposite side of the coffee shop. My cheeks burn so hot they must be scarlet, and I imagine incinerating EJ's ball cap to a pile of dust. Of course, he wants to poke fun at the high-strung gay kid running around town. I hate that I'm still attracted to him.

Dear EJ's parents, did you have to make his eyes so pretty?

"What is it, boo boo?" Hannah sits at the table, and I untwist my lips from their position on the side of my mouth. "He was joking. EJ's nice to everyone, so I don't hate him like I do everyone else in existence."

"You don't get it," I say, lowering my voice. "I wasn't trying to say that stuff. I'm pretty sure the Reds were making me do it."

"Yeah about that," says Hannah, leaning across the table. "What's this about how you're a special little witch boy?"

I look over at EJ, who's busy making our drinks. I notice the faint promise of a bicep under his Hallow Bean T-shirt as he plunges the steam wand into a stainless-steel pitcher. The dial turns and steam shoots up around his face. He moves the pitcher up and down.

Up and down. Up...and down.

"Dane," Hannah whispers. "Dane!"

"Mm?" I look over at her.

"Save it for the shower," she spits back. "Now what's this about the you-know-what?"

I shake my head and let out a sigh. "You pretty much heard everything that I know."

"So, what do you do, then?"

"I can read minds," I mutter. "Sometimes I read objects."

"You what?"

"I. Read. Objects."

Hannah squints. "I read tarot. Doesn't make me Sabrina."

I purse my lips and keep quiet as EJ finishes our drinks and comes over to the table with two large mugs. "Dirty chai, and a Drizzled Dane."

My cheeks burn. "A what now?"

"I don't know," EJ shrugs. "It sounded catchy and is a lot easier to say than all of the ingredients."

Hannah lifts her mug and arches an eyebrow. "He drizzled you, Dane."

A cough escapes EJ and he shakes his head. I kick Hannah under the table, but my sneaker lands against steel toe and I cry out.

"That's what you get," she says.

"Anyways," EJ looks at me with those eyes. "I'm sorry for bringing up the, well, you know. I didn't mean to embarrass you."

"Oh, it's okay." Half of my vocal cords don't work as I stare up at him, and my tone is light and squeaky.

"Let me know if I'm hot enough for you." His ears turn scarlet immediately, and my eyebrows shoot up like a rocket. "Uh— the drink! I meant the drink. Both of your drinks. The wand isn't great."

"This is sad," Hannah says. "This is *so* sad."

EJ walks backward, nearly stumbling over a table as he makes his way into the kitchen.

Hannah takes a sip of her chai. "Mm. He made it dirty enough."

"I will end you," I say and take a sip of my Drizzled Dane. Oh, sweet god on high. This is good.

"See? He's a weirdo, too. Not everyone wants to humiliate you." Hannah sets down her mug. "So, what about this object reading? Why's it so special?"

"Give me your car keys." I put my mug on the table and hold my palm out. "Or your bag, your driver's license. It doesn't matter what."

I can't believe I'm about to willingly demonstrate this. What if I can't do it, like this morning?

Hannah fumbles in her pocket and tosses a wadded-up gum wrapper across the table. I pinch it between my fingers and hold it up.

"I've never read in on anything this tiny," I say. "But I'll try. You have to be quiet, though."

Hannah pulls her fingers across her lips and pretends to turn a key. I shut my eyes and squeeze the balled-up wrapper, memorizing its every crease and jagged edge.

Blonde Hannah.

I lean into it further, rolling the tiny paper ball over and over against my thumb and index finger.

Right before the black dye. Friday night. Late spring. The windshield glazes in the evening's humidity. Streetlights glow against the glass.

A weird, intangible feeling creeps into my fingers. I lean closer into the vision.

"All right, weirdo," Hannah reaches out for the wrapper. "Give it back."

"Hold on," I say. "I'm actually getting something."

Emotions creep from the wrapper as the scene plays out in my mind. I've never picked up on emotions or thoughts before in objects.

"Long fingers rub the back of my hand," I say, narrating what I see and feel. "My belly is full of Twizzlers, and the remnants of licorice stick to the back of my teeth. The boy next to me hasn't kissed me yet."

"That is every girl's Saturday in this town," says Hannah. "Nice try."

"Spearmint gum tingles my tongue, ready for when he is. Should I bite his lip when he kisses me? I should bite his lip. Why doesn't he want to kiss me? I'm not pretty enough. You're ugly, you know."

"Okay." Hannah shifts in her seat.

I should stop and put the wrapper down. I know that I should, before I get too deep in thoughts that aren't mine. But I can't get myself to let go. It's like it has to play out before I can stop.

"What are you doing here? You hate people, especially guys. Gotta do something. God, I hate my hair. I look like Grant in drag. That's why this guy asked me out. Wants to be cool. He'll be the douche who nailed Grant Allen's sister. He doesn't really want me. He's not going to score anything, he'll just tell everyone he did—"

"Okay!" Hannah knocks the wrapper from my fingers and stands up. "We get it. I have angst. Thank you, Dr. Phil."

Yanked out of the vision, I gasp for air and steady my hands on the tabletop. My fingers, for once, feel ice cold. "I'm sorry," I whisper, daring a peek at Hannah. "Once I started, I couldn't stop." Hannah looks down into her mug for a second, forcing a laugh. "Eh, it's fine. I'll just put you in cement later so you can't tell anyone."

"Who would I tell?"

"I gotta piss," Hannah scoots her chair back and leaves the table. She stops about halfway. "Dane?"

"Yes?"

"Don't touch my shit anymore."

She disappears under the signs for the bathrooms. Her phone lies left behind on the table. Probably some sort of test to see if I'll leave it alone. No problem.

I rub my temples, my head swimming with her memories, her feelings. It's nauseating. I don't think I've stayed to watch an object's history for that long. Never seen anything so intimate. It feels wrong.

I drink, focusing on the mug. The bell chimes and another customer ventures into the shop, but I don't look up. I stare down into my drink, feeling like crap. Whoever it is takes four steps inside and stops. Must be buying whole beans.

The inside of my mug goes black as the shop plunges into shadow. The walls buzz and let out a sigh as the power completely blows. I look up, toward the customer, and the blood drops out of my face.

Grant stares back at me.

6

BROKEN PLANES

ousin Grant. The dead one. Or *some version* of him. He's staring back at me. He appears to be about ten years old, his face round, his hair growing in thick blond locks long before they heard of gel. But his clothes are ones I've never seen on him before, ones I could never imagine Grant wearing.

A bright-yellow plaid suit.

"H-hi," I stammer, my voice a half whisper.

Grant lifts his hands, revealing that in each palm are the remnants of a blue model airplane, propellers and a tail sticking out from the wreckage. A chill sweeps up my spine.

"I broke it," he says. "I'm sorry, Dane."

It was *my* plane, once. I'd forgotten all about it. The time I brought it over and we played with it at the woods' edge. He threw it so hard that it smashed against a tree. It was an accident, but I was mad at him for the rest of the day. Our first fight.

"It's okay," I say, gripping the handle of my mug. "I forgive you."

Little Grant squeezes his hands, closing them around the broken pieces. He winces. He releases his fingers and drops the pieces to the floor, sniffling. He takes three steps toward me, and the red glow of the coffee pots cuts across his face. Tears of blood red and silver streak his cheeks, but his face is void of any sort of expression. "You didn't answer the phone."

My heart skips a beat before dropping into my stomach. "I-I'm sorry—"

"You let him take me away." Little Grant sighs. He puts a hand to the right side of his face, digs his nails into the flesh of his forehead.

"Hannah?" I can barely call out.

"He took me away," Little Grant singsongs. He drags his fingers down his forehead, pulling the flesh with it. "Took me a-*way*."

"Hannah!" My voice is a strangled half cry.

EJ stumbles out of the back room, waving his phone, the flashlight on. "I'm sorry, I'm trying to figure out what's—"

He stops behind the counter, his gaze moving between me and child Grant. He slowly lowers the phone.

"But if you're very good," Little Grant continues, half of his face now pulled off, scraps of skin and muscle falling onto his suit, "I'll take *you* away, too."

"Keep still." EJ lays his phone face down on the counter. I dart my eyes between him and Little Grant. He slowly reaches for the counter behind him. "Don't move."

Little Grant moves his other hand to the remaining side of his face and scrapes the flesh off. He shudders and buries the skinless brown-and-green skull in his hands. He lets out an unbroken baby laugh. Then he starts to hum—quietly at first, but soon he hums louder, and I recognize it as some sort of melody, like a nursery rhyme. With each note, he rises in height, his form growing tall, slender, and crooked. Dirt pours from holes that rip through his suit as he ascends, the suit aging and corroding the taller he gets. Worms and maggots push their way out, falling to the linoleum

"I'll drag you down and eat your bones!" Little Grant is now a full-grown man. He pulls his dirty hands from his skull to reveal a crude patchwork of furs. A mask. His head is covered in the mask of a rabbit. His voice is deep and monstrous as he keeps repeating, "Come on home! Come on home! Come on home!"

The bells chime as the café door swings open. A gust of October wind blasts inside and the masked man spins around, then halts. The Reds strut into the coffee shop in a perfect V, like three bolts of scarlet lightning in their jackets.

Madelaine stops when she sees the man, thrusts her arms out to keep Elena and Chloe from coming any closer.

"It's worse than we thought," she says to no one in particular. She turns her hands over, and the girls take her palms in theirs.

They grip their fingers closed, shut their eyes, and begin to hum. A long, singular note, like a dial tone, vibrates deep in their throats.

The man whirls around and looks as though he's going to run.

EJ jumps over the counter with a kitchen knife thrust in the air, like a

Musketeer poised to attack, but the man who was Little Grant vanishes. Behind the Reds, the door swings open on its own. The girls jump, letting go of each other's hands. Chloe pulls her jacket closer around her and Elena shudders.

Madelaine twists up her mouth, her face clouding over in frustration. She points to the ceiling and the power comes back on.

"Why did you do that?" she struts toward us, her eyes on EJ. "We almost had him."

"What was that?" I whisper.

Chloe massages the top of her head. "God, that gave me such a headache."

Elena sucks in deep through her nose and drops into a chair in the opposite corner of the room. "I think I might be sick."

I slowly push myself to my feet and manage a few steps with quaking legs. "What. Was. That?"

"A ghost," says Madelaine. "I think."

I can't help but laugh through my trembling. "You think?"

"I don't know."

Chloe leans against the counter, burying her face in her hands. "I didn't like that at all."

Madelaine crosses her arms and sizes EJ up. "Please leave the witch shit to us." She lifts her thumb and middle finger, poised to snap them together. "Or do we have to go through this again?"

EJ cocks an eyebrow and twirls his knife like a cowboy's pistol. "Go on, Wednesday. I dare you."

Madelaine raises her fingers even higher as a warning and EJ shrinks back the tiniest bit. But they both maintain an icy stare down. I glance between Elena and Chloe, who are side-eyeing each other as though debating if they'll step in. Finally, Madelaine lowers her fingers and paints on a tightlipped smile. EJ's shoulders relax.

"Fine. Go to the back."

"Excuse you—"

"Please," Madelaine forces out through gritted teeth.

EJ shoots an unsure glance at me, and goes with resignation to the back room, like a puppy shamed. I hate seeing him go, but maybe now is not the time to worry about that.

Hannah tumbles out from under the bathroom signs, looking bewildered. "What the hell?! I thought I'd died on the toilet for a nanosecond!"

"You almost did, Igor." Elena laughs, then winces and clutches the top of her head.

Hannah curls her nose in disgust as she eyes Elena, but I notice a hand goes to the top of her head. As though to protect her mind from those snapping fingers. "What are you doing here?"

"We went to your house first," says Chloe, raising an eyebrow in conspiracy, "but you weren't there. So I thought, 'Where would I go if I were a basic witch,' and let's be real"—her smile breaks through and she points at herself with pride—"I can be one! And here you are!"

Madelaine drops her fingers and shrugs. "Looks like we got here just in time. But your moms said to come home now."

I reach for my mug and nearly spill it, my hands are still shaking so hard. "Yeah, no. I needed a break, and I *definitely* need one now."

"Why?" Hannah looks at me. "Did I miss something?"

Just your brother. Ten-year-old him, anyways. But it wasn't him, not really. I don't respond to her. Instead, I sip my drink, try to focus my feelings, and ditch the part of me that feels upset it wasn't really him—that he wasn't finally haunting me.

"Where's your familiar?" asks Madelaine. "Your mom said you got one."

"He's...around," I say.

"Well, find him and get your ass home." Madelaine makes for the door. "We'll be there with Ada around six, and if you aren't there waiting, we'll find you."

Hannah looks like she's about to stab them, and I don't know that I'll try to stop her. "Why are you coming to my house?"

"Jesus, don't you all get it?" Madelaine spins around, wringing her hands. "We need Dane to complete our circle."

She, Elena, and Chloe look at me, those damn eyes sliding in unison. When Madelaine speaks again, her voice is low, void of her usual airs. She sounds afraid. "Before anyone else is next."

7

HAPPY OTHER BIRTHDAY

"And then he just pulled his face off," I say. "And it wasn't him anymore. It was someone else."

Hannah turns the key and shuts the car engine off. "Who was it? Could it have been—"

"I don't know."

We sit in my aunt's driveway. My stomach is still a bit askew from spending so much time in the car with Hannah, who drives like a Tasmanian devil escaping the petting zoo. We spent most of the day driving aimlessly, recklessly, while I told her everything she missed. Then told her again because she didn't believe me. Then again, while sitting on park swings.

Each time, I kept getting the feeling she's upset she missed Grant. Even if it wasn't him.

My heart falls, landing in my stomach like a ball on a kettledrum. Madelaine said, "Before anyone else is next." This man, this thing, could be Grant's killer. And he isn't even alive.

A ghost has left its grave. Immediately, the phrase *Your fault* slithers through my inner ear. I look to the front door, but can't will myself to go inside yet. I'm still processing everything, and I don't think seeing Mom—or whatever it is that Ada and the Reds are planning, for that matter—is going to help.

I just want to go to my room, at my own house, in my own city, resign myself to endless unfunny TikToks, and forget any of this ever happened.

In the back seat, Aloysius crinkles a plastic wrapper.

"I'll never understand mortals who don't finish a banana Moon Pie," he

clicks. *"But nevertheless, I thank them."*

"He says he likes Moon Pies," I translate when Hannah gives me a look. I reach into the back seat and lift him as though he's a cat, bring him to my lap, and pet his head. He vibrates under my hand. It's weird how the magnets click together inside me. The longer I hold him, the more he feels like a beloved family pet instead of a varmint who crawled out of the woods this morning.

"That feels nice," he clicks softly. *"A bit to the left, if you please."*

"That's so weird." Hannah shakes her head. "Every time he clicks it's— please make him stop."

"His name is Aloysius."

"Gesundheit," says Hannah.

"Listen," I say, "about Grant—"

"I don't want to talk about my brother anymore." Hannah gets out, slamming the door to end the conversation.

I sigh and unbuckle my seat belt.

"What were you going to say, young master?" asks Aloysius, wiping crumbs from his paws.

"Nothing," I say. "Was just going to reiterate it wasn't him."

"To her or yourself?"

"Both, smarty. By the way, just call me Dane."

Aloysius gasps and wrings his hands, his eyes wide and glassy. *"Oh!"* he whimpers. *"It wouldn't be proper!"*

"Well, you have to, because I don't want to be called 'young master.' It's weird, and dare I say, a bit pervy?"

Aloysius blinks and nods. *"Very well, young m—Dane. Oh!"*

I push the passenger door open and carry him out of the car. I make my way behind Hannah and when we reach the porch, I stop and sniff.

"I smell pumpkin spice." I push past Hannah.

I set Aloysius down and swing the front door open. He scampers inside. The smell of Hollow blood outside is quickly scared away by the flood of autumn's official scent, and for a split second I think I've died and gone to a Starbucks-sponsored circle of hell.

But what confuses me are all the leaves. Reds, oranges, and browns all scattered across the floor, some tacked to walls between neon blue and green pentagrams drawn in sidewalk chalk. Twigs wrapped in black ribbons hang from the ceiling.

Hannah steps behind me. "She's at it again. Mom's been into therapeutic decorating since Dad died, but this is ridiculous."

Mom drifts in from the kitchen, practically levitating in a flowing sleeveless white gown with a red sash. Her hair flows freely, glowing like she's had a fresh dye job.

"Ah, there he is." She smiles and drapes herself over the armchair like a goddess ready to be fed some grapes. Her voice is breathy, almost cooing.

"What did I tell you about your Elizabeth Taylor impression?" I try her.

"Oh, chill out," Mom breathes. "Here, I have a vial of something if you want to relax. But no driving if you drink."

"Are you high?"

Mom waves her hands like she's calling the winds and grins. "No, I'm liberated."

Behind us Aunt Bella squeals and sashays down the stairs in an oversized white dress shirt. Her hair is pulled back in a red ribbon. She isn't wearing pants or shoes.

"They're definitely high," says Hannah.

Mom sits up. "Bells, what are you wearing?"

"Well, I was going to wear the same dress I wore for *your* awakening"—Aunt Bella squeezes her waist—"which I can still fit into, just so you know. But I couldn't find it. The only thing I have in white is Richard's old shirt. But it fits like a dress."

I squeeze my eyes shut and shake my head. "Why are you dressed like this? What is with the leaves and the twigs, and the, um"—I look at the pentagrams—"cave drawings? And why does it smell like a pumpkin ejaculated?"

"I'm baking a cake," Aunt Bella announces proudly.

Hannah elbows me. "I wonder what green goodies are *in* it."

Mom stands and sweeps over to me. I take two steps back. "When you left," she begins, "I was a bit upset."

"Same," I shoot back.

"So I brewed your Aunt Bella and myself a little somethin' to drink. You know, butterfly wings and a dried toad's foot to get hoppy. Some nice lavender." I think about the flask Mom passed Aunt Bella at the funeral. No wonder she was able to keep it together. "I'm sorry for keeping our family history from you. You were brave enough to tell me what you can do, and I acted like it was unique to you. I wanted you to have the *chance* to be normal. And then I realized..."

"Realized what?" I say through gritted teeth.

"You need a coven, honey."

I stuff my hands in my hoodie and shake my head as hard as I can. "No, thank you! I'm good!"

"Every witch needs a coven." Mom puts her hands on my shoulders. "And you need friends, too."

"I don't like them!" I shoot back.

Aloysius scampers back into the living room and jabs his paw at my shin.

"Could you please ask for a water bowl on my behalf? We raccoons are sanitary beings who always wash our paws before we eat."

"Later," I whisper.

Loud music pipes in from the front yard. I know this song because it's one of the oldies I like to put on. Hannah and I cross to the window and peek through the curtains to see Ada, dancing on the grass with that monstrous copperhead wrapped around her shoulders. She's traded her robe for another one—this time all white except for the sleeves, which are red. She looks like a demented choirmaster.

On the curb, the Reds hang from the open car doors. The girl on the radio sings about having a brand-new pair of roller skates and someone having a brand-new key.

Aunt Bella yanks open the front door and runs onto the porch.

"Quit that!" she shouts. "The neighbors will see!"

Madelaine leans into the car and cuts the music off. Ada stops dancing and looks across the street, to the empty field.

"Yes," she says. "We wouldn't want any horses to notice." She drifts to the bottom of the porch steps and grins up at my aunt, casting a glance at her dress-shirt ensemble. "But, Isabella, I thought you didn't care what others think of you."

"I care when there's a band of freaks on the lawn," says Aunt Bella.

"I prefer the term *witch*."

"The witchcraft isn't the problem." Aunt Bella turns around and comes back to the door. "Do come in."

Hannah sinks into the couch. "Don't let them snap their fingers at me."

Aunt Bella steps inside as Ada ascends the porch steps, the Reds rushing behind her. Each one carries a familiar, all of them cats, and each wears a white dress under her jacket.

When Ada crosses the threshold, Louisa the snake hisses at Aloysius, who clicks his teeth fiercely.

"A raccoon for a familiar." Ada sizes up first Aloysius, then me with a dry expression. "Can this get any cuter?"

Madelaine puts Ambrose down, who bats his paw at my raccoon.

"Disgusting house pet." Aloysius rushes to me and hops up into my lap. *"Couldn't tip a rubbish bin if they tried, and then who'd feed them?"*

Madelaine scoops the white cat back up and crushes it to her chest. "Be nice, Ambrose. We talked about this."

Hannah starts to choke, wrapping her hands around her throat.

I sit up. "Are you okay?!"

She stops hacking and takes a strangled breath. "There's...prep smell...in my abode."

Elena crosses the threshold, carrying a tabby. "Shut up, Igor, you're upsetting Caesar."

"You shut up, you melted Bratz doll!"

"All of you shut up, the grown-ups are speaking!" Ada glares at the Reds, then turns to my mother. "Robyn, darling. I didn't know you were still alive."

"And still younger than you." My mother fakes a smile that I've seen her flash two thousand times in the grocery store. They pretend to kiss each other's cheek with a *muah* on each side. "Is that a new fragrance you're wearing? Formaldehyde?"

Ada's eyes drop into slits and her lips pinch together. "It's sage and patchouli."

"Oh." Mom drops into an armchair. "I must be smelling your embalmed sense of fashion."

Chloe drops Efron to clap. "The library is open!"

Ada pets Louisa. "Now, now. Let's not be petty witches."

I take in everyone's familiar. "Mom, where's yours?"

She raises an eyebrow at me, and I gesture to the cats and the snake, while petting Aloysius on my lap.

"Oh," she says, "well—"

"Delilah left her," Ada cuts her off. "Took off as soon as Robyn here had the inkling of fleeing. Such a shame, she was a faithful blue jay."

"I haven't really missed her," Mom says through gritted teeth.

The room falls silent for a few moments, and I'm not really sure what's supposed to happen now. Mom stands and makes her way to the kitchen. "We made a sort of birthday lunch," she says, glancing at me. She must pick up on my confusion because she adds, "Your witch birthday, I mean. I thought it would be nice."

"How charming," says Ada. "Pizza rolls?"

"I also have kale chips," my mother calls over her shoulder, disappearing into the kitchen.

Ada shrugs. "She does know me, body and soul."

Elena wrinkles her nose. "Ew."

"Get your mind out of the gutter and into the grave," says Ada. "Let's eat junk food."

She follows Aunt Bella to the kitchen, leaving me with Hannah,

Aloysius, and the Reds staring straight at me.

"I can't wait to get you in your jacket," Chloe giggles.

Elena tilts her head and studies me. "I've been dying to do something with that hair."

Madelaine smiles. "You're gonna look so cute when we've finished."

"Hannah," I say, setting Aloysius on the floor. "Junk food?"

"I hope I choke on it," she says and follows me.

We all go into the kitchen, where the table is draped in a wine-colored cloth. Large plastic plates decorated with purple spiders and candy corns sprawl across it, holding miniature cupcakes, bowls of pretzels and potato chips, kale chips, brownies, a veggie tray, another for fruit, opened plastic containers of dip, cheese and crackers, pepperoni, and, if that isn't enough, a freaking country ham. I'm pretty sure this is stuff the neighbors must have brought Aunt Bella.

My "birthday" lunch is recycled grief.

Mom tries to hide a pan of pizza rolls under a towel, but I stop her, popping one defiantly into my mouth.

"Ada," begins Aunt Bella, pulling the oven door open and assaulting all of our noses with the smell of pumpkin excrement, "to what do we owe the, um, pleasure of doing this here and now?"

"Yeah," I say through a mouth of fake pepperoni and rubber cheese. "My birthday was on the fifteenth."

Aloysius tugs on my shoelace. *"My water bowl?"*

I go to the sink and grab a small plastic bowl from the drying rack, start to fill it from the faucet.

"It is not your *actual* birthday," says Ada. "It is your *witch* birthday. The night that must be held beneath a blood-ringed moon in which a young witch vows to dedicate herself—themselves—to the laws of the dark world. To its rules, its dangers, and to receive her—their—full power."

"Nice." I punch the syllable to spite her and set the bowl on the floor.

Aloysius dips his paws in and washes them.

"There is a blood ring tonight," Ada continues, "which means we must complete the circle, especially after what happened in town. The child needs to be brought in, even if he *is* a boy."

Mom looks at me. "What happened?"

I open my mouth to explain, but Ada keeps talking. "None of my charts indicated a blood ring tonight. I think it is clear, our patron is calling."

My mother gapes at Ada. "When you phoned, you said you would look out for Dane and teach him how to control his power. That was it. You said nothing about *him.*"

Ada chuckles. "Would you have agreed to it if I had?"

"Of course not!" Mom shouts.

"I'm sorry," I say. "Who is 'him'?"

Mom looks at me, her expression tight. The toad legs or whatever must be wearing off, because her voice has dropped an octave, too. "Mr. Hawthorne."

"That clears it up." Hannah rolls her eyes and stuffs a cupcake into her mouth.

Ada drifts to the table and munches on a kale chip. "I'm sure you've noticed the stench that plagues this town."

My stomach flips. "The blood smell?"

Ada crunches, nods. She swallows and says, "That signature fragrance around town is a distillation of what lies below. The world's underbelly where the spirits dwell. Creatures you don't see every day. And overlording it all is Mr. Hawthorne."

"Satan," says Hannah.

Ada laughs. "Satan. Really. Do you believe in Santa Claus, too? No, dear. Mr. Hawthorne is not the devil. He is our patron. The giver of our powers."

Elena rolls her eyes and crushes the potato chip in her hand to a dusty pile. "Because *of course* we get our power from a straight white guy."

The Reds mutter their agreement, but are silenced by a glare from Ada. "I'll admit, I'm not thrilled with this caveat. Nevertheless, I'm afraid Dane needs to fully join us if we can hope to vanquish that thing in the coffee shop and find out what's been happening here lately." She glances at Aunt Bella apologetically.

"I don't want Dane anywhere near that demon." Mom crosses her arms.

"You made your choice. Dane must make his." Ada looks at me, and I feel myself shrink. "Remember what I told you last night, Craven Kid?"

Goosebumps break out all over my arms. "Join a coven. Catch the killer. Okay. Let's do this first step."

Mom and Aunt Bella look solemnly at each other and Hannah gapes, revealing a pile of mashed cupcake on her tongue. None of them understand. I'm the reason Grant even went out there. If I'm ever going to make it right, if I'm ever going to lay Grant to rest, then I have to figure all of this out.

I look to the Reds—the garden-variety bitch club, as Hannah called them. Elena is still eyeing my hair.

Join a coven. Catch the killer. Get a makeover in the process?

I come downstairs.

The sun has gone down, leaving the room a dim yellow in the light of a singular table lamp, the stretched shadows of the hanging twigs reaching across the walls—an entire forest contained in a box.

I pull at the hem of the dress shirt they made me put on and gesture to the white linen shorts I found waiting on my bed. "Well, I'm ready for the Midsommar reaping."

"We should be so lucky," Hannah mutters in the corner.

Aunt Bella nudges her and shoots her a mom-look.

"We shall take our seats," Ada says, waving her hand to the center of the room.

The couch and armchair have been pushed aside. A glass plate sits on the floor, and six red candles of varying heights wait atop it, unlit.

Ada sits cross-legged on the floor before the plate, and the Reds join.

"Today is a not-a-little-shit day." Mom grabs my hand and pulls me forward. She pushes me down opposite Ada and sits next to me.

Hannah comes to my other side. Elena raises a hand to stop her.

"Not you," she says.

Hannah folds her arms. "I cordially invited myself and—"

Aunt Bella comes behind her and grabs her shoulder. "Not you, honey. Sorry."

She pulls Hannah gently back to the corner of the room. Aloysius scurries up behind me and scratches his paws at the back of my shirt, hoisting himself up to peek over my shoulder. I try not to laugh as he wraps his tail around my upper arm, because he's trying to mimic Louisa, who's still draped around Ada.

Ambrose, Efron, and Caesar all nuzzle themselves next to the Reds.

"So." I give a half grin. "What are we playing? Spin the bottle? Seven minutes in heaven? Drink the Kool-Aid?"

Mom smacks my arm while Aloysius jabs his paw into my shoulder. "Ow!"

Ada clears her throat and slashes a look to me that says, "I will turn you into a newt." I silence.

"In the beginning..." Ada flicks her wrist, and the living room plunges into complete darkness, except for the pentagrams that glow iridescent blues and greens on the walls around us. She lights the tallest candle with a mini lighter. "The soil was wild. The land that had no name was a treacherous fray of spirits, monsters, and magic.

"Buffalo cracked the earth for water, Cumberland waters cut through a gap, and mystical falls flowed with healing and health. The earth provides plenty for fair trade. To give a life, it takes a life.

"Humans are weak with greed. They cut forests, drive our monsters and spirits to retreat into deep woods, caves, lakes, below the ground, lest they too be packaged into cutlets or stuffed and displayed to sticky-mouthed schoolchildren in the Smithsonian."

A snort escapes me. Ada reaches across the candle and grabs at me. I try to dodge her touch, but she grabs my arm, pulling it out over the flame. Mom pulls red ribbon from a spool and starts wrapping it around my wrist.

"We are called to liaison. To keep mortals separate from the dangers of the real world. We are called to protect the Hollow and its soil, stained with blood. For it was this very ground where the mouth of darkness was ripped open for our patron. Praise Tabitha."

"Praise Tabitha," the Reds and Mom repeat in unison, lifting their palms to the ceiling.

"Praise Tabitha," I mutter and roll my eyes.

Mom tosses the spool across the circle. Chloe catches it and wraps ribbon around her own wrist, then takes the lighter from Ada and lights the second-tallest candle. She tosses the spool back over, and Mom does the same, lighting the third-tallest candle. She tosses it back and so it goes, tossing the ribbon and lighter back and forth, until each witch has a ribbon around their wrist, and we are all tethered together. When it reaches Ada she yanks the ribbon back and the silk fabric cuts deeper into my wrist.

Then Ada tosses the spool at me again. The ribbon has formed an abstract star. Ada looks to the remaining candle, the shortest one, and back to me. Tingling sensations warm the fingers on my right hand. I shake my head. "I don't do fire."

Mom looks at me with a tight expression. "It'll be okay this time," she whispers.

Somewhere in the corner, Hannah smacks the wall. "What is happ—"

"Shh." Aunt Bella nudges her.

I take a deep breath. The prints of my fingers burn, every little swirl seeming to ignite itself as I hesitantly reach for the wick of the candle. I think of Photo Grant's ashes upstairs as the coarse wick slides against my fingerprints. I think of the charred bible at the funeral. The little flames in the graveyard.

I think about April.

The burning green door falls on the floor. The fire alarm shrieks like a demonic insect. The word drips on my forehead, glistens under flickering fluorescents. I watch it fade in and out in the mirror reflection behind Grant. Then I cut my eyes to him, feeling the dark smirk pull up on my twitching mouth.

"What are you?" is all he can say.

A drop of blood forces my left eye to squeeze shut. I point at my forehead. "Clearly, you already know."

I take a step from the burning bathroom stall and—

The candle lights itself and I yank my fingers back.

Everyone except for Mom gasps. I look at the floor, unable to face anyone. I can practically feel Hannah's eyes burning into my skull.

The euphoric feeling of righteous destruction tries to climb up into my chest, but I force it back into the dark hole of myself where it belongs. My entire torso shakes.

"Praise Tabitha," says Ada.

"Praise Tabitha," the Reds and Mom repeat.

I stare at the candle. A drop of red wax that reminds me of pig's blood drips onto the plate. The flame changes color. I squeeze my eyes and reopen them to find the flame is back to its normal orange. But I swear, for just a second, it was black.

"Founder of our Under Town, architect of our capital of darkness..." I look up to see Ada's eyes move to the ceiling. "Praise our patron!"

"Praise our patron!" we repeat.

The leaves on the floor start to move. "We stand with our patron."

"We stand with our patron."

"Awaken our sister—no—brother."

"Awaken our brother."

The flames flicker in and out, six orange pearls igniting over and over again. The wax, trickling into blood-colored puddles on the plate, reverses and crawls back up the candles. The leaves blow off the floor and swirl around us in wind I can't even feel.

"Bond us to our brother!"

"Bond us to our brother!"

The shadow of an owl flies across the wall.

"With a crown of skin and bone!"

"With a crown of skin and bone."

"Open your dark kingdom!"

"Open your dark kingdom!"

The owl loses a feather, which falls out of sight.

Ada screams wildly, and soon everyone around me does the same. I turn to look at Hannah, who for the first time in her life looks genuinely scared. Aloysius digs his paws deeper into my shoulder. The leaves blow around us like a cyclone. Our wrists are caught up in the wind, the red ribbon billowing and pulling our arms upward. The fabric pulls tighter, and I feel heat burn through it, deep in my wrist and shooting up my arm. My heart feels like it's melting in the heat.

Everything is leaves and screams and burning as the firelight keeps going in-out-in-out.

And then it stops.

There's the sound of something spinning on the floor. Like a Toss-It ring or a bottle threatening to topple. When it settles, I look down.

A ring of gray and flesh sits in front of me.

My crown of skin and bone.

Mom takes my hand, squeezing tightly.

Ada stares at me, her eyes wide and unblinking. "Happy other birthday." She pulls her wrist from the ribbon. "Now go take a bath."

8

BATH TIME

"I believe you're supposed to wear it," Aloysius clicks when I set the disgusting crown on the toilet lid. I can't bear to touch it anymore. I don't know whose skin and bone this could be made of, and I don't want to know.

"No disrespect to the universe or whatever," I say, "but I'll pass."

Aloysius sighs.

I lean over the bathtub and push the plug into the drain before starting the water. "Couldn't a shower do?"

Aloysius nudges the tub with his paw. *"It is to cleanse you of your mortal energy. Just trust your coven leader and get in."*

"So, it's a baptism."

"Yes, except I'm not allowed to hold you under the water, despite how very much I would like to," clicks Aloysius.

With a sigh I wriggle down the linen shorts and do my usual hopping extravaganza to get them off my ankles. Aloysius tilts his head.

"It's a wonder you can walk with that awkwardness," he muses. *"I can only imagine how you got them on at all."*

"Turn around, or cover your eyes or something."

Aloysius rolls his black button-shaped eyes. *"I'm a raccoon, not a locker-room cohort."*

"You're a *talking* raccoon. There's a difference."

"I've been running around in the nude this entire time, but go right ahead

and be persnickety." He turns and pushes his snoot into the corner with a huff. "Humans."

I pull the shirt over my head and go to the mirror. I turn to the side and poke at my stomach, pull at my skin a little.

"What are you doing?"

I look into the corner's reflection to see my familiar has turned around. I cover my crotch with my hands.

"Judging my body," I say. "You weren't supposed to be looking."

"Good lord, you look fine. Just get in the tub!"

I sigh and pull at the waistband of my boxer briefs.

"I'd keep those on were I you," Aloysius clicks. *"I don't know for sure if anyone else will be showing up."*

I look at him wide-eyed and suddenly feel very watched. To appease whatever might be lurking, I pick up the crown and put it on. It's heavy around my head, and the bones poke into my scalp. Already I'm getting a headache.

I step into the tub and—start jumping.

"Too hot! Too hot!" I spin on the cold tap and stick a lobster-red foot under the running water, then let out a sigh. "Hell's sake, that's good."

"Shh," Aloysius clicks. *"Ease into it and relax."*

Slowly, I lower myself into the tub, letting out a deep exhale in short bursts until I'm completely in. A small drop of sweat, brought on by the steam, slides down my forehead. I know my hair is already frizzing out.

I wonder if there's a spell to keep thick curls from doing that.

I pull at the longer curls in front. *Or turn mud brown into a nice, vivid—*

"Is that relaxing, young man?" Aloysius clicks at me.

I splash him with water and he yelps, retreating to the corner. I laugh and shut my eyes, lean my head against the tiles, and try to chill out. My lower back eases in the hot water. I hadn't realized how tense I was, what with running around and getting the shit scared out of me for the past two days.

The water goes still. Heavy. Like it's not water at all, but a vat of syrup. The air changes, the clean cucumber scent of the bathroom fading to something else. Something old and rotting. It makes my nose itch. I scratch it and when I pull my hand away, I open my eyes to see that it's covered in thick red goo.

Gasping, I sit up and look down into the tub. It's all red, so dark it's almost black. I can't see my own body beneath the surface.

"It's blood—"

The bottom of the tub creaks and falls away, and I drop deeper in. I grab the side of the tub and try to pull myself up as blood spins and splashes around me like the world's most evil whirlpool.

"Hey!" I reach out to Aloysius. "Help!"

He scurries forward and I grab his paw, but my hand slips, sending a string of blood splashing against the floor.

"*Dane!*" he clicks. "*Just relax! It'll be all right!*"

Something grabs my ankle and I scream. A bony hand, somewhere deep down, is tugging me farther in.

Another hand takes my other ankle and yanks. My fingers slip across the edge of the tub. The red streaks on glossy white are the last thing I see before I slip completely under.

I kick, but the bony hands don't give. The crown floats from my head and I reach up, grabbing it like it's going to save me. I should've put Aloysius atop my head instead of *this*.

I can't breathe or see anything, and my brain goes in and out, blackness, red. Blackness—red—

My thoughts go bla—

Images flash. Half seconds at a time. Like a TV changing channels too fast to keep up. There's blood on dirt. A settler cries in the snow. A bald eagle soars above. Head of a buffalo, paraded through a village. Naked women dance, their hair free and wild. A firelit room. A woman in a black hoopskirt wiggles her finger at me. *Join me. Join us.*

Mangy dog howls in the woods. Copperhead slithers on hot limestone. A mouse crawls straight into its jaws and the copperhead clamps down. It opens its mouth and the mouse crawls backward out, then walks in again.

A witch hangs from a tree in front of an orange sunset. The witch rides a man on a downy featherbed. A man rides a man on the downy featherbed. The witch eats cake and runs her fingers along an oily broomstick. I run my fingers along an oily broomstick. I lie with man on downy featherbed. I hang from tree.

The earth is a mother.

I am dead. I am all right with that.

I break the surface of the bloody black water and gasp for sweet life. I go to grab the side of the bathtub, but my hand hits grassy earth instead. My fingernails scrape through dirt. Was there ever a bathroom?

I'm in a bubbling hot spring. A tiny, black spring in the woods, hazy with steam. A bottomless puddle.

If a Dane falls through the earth and comes out in hell, does he even burn? No, that's not the phrase. *If a tree falls on Dane and nobody makes paper from the tree*—that's not right, either.

I pull myself out of the spring and find that the crown of skin and bone has made it here first. It waits on the bank, dripping red and black. The magnetic pull in my bones forces my arm out before I think to move it. My hand grabs the crown and places it back on my head.

I push myself onto my feet and take in the dark woods around me, the trees encased in cobwebs, dust falling from their limbs like spring blossoms. Beyond them, a fire burns. The fire wants to meet me. I want to meet the fire. The fire is the light on home's porch. Mother's open arms.

Oxygen drifts into my pounding brain. *If a tree falls in the forest and nobody is around*—that's what it is!

The flames do not burn alone. There are many who join it, and here I am in blood-soaked boxer briefs heading straight toward them. I hug myself and focus on the trees.

I come through them and out to the fire, where a hundred iris-less faces turn and stare at me. Before them, in front of the fire, stands a man. A three-cornered hat adorns his head. He eyes me proudly as I come forward.

He is tall, elegantly handsome, with high cheekbones and a striking jawline. He's ethereal, with large dark eyes that feel as though they can cut right into my soul, and a complexion so pale that his skin is almost translucent. As though it hasn't seen the sun in hundreds of years. His body is long and lanky, yet strong, as though his muscles are made of thick vines and willowy boughs.

Closer now, I can see that his hat and the rest of his clothing—a long coat that goes down to his boots, a waistcoat, and breeches, like that of an early explorer—aren't made of any fabric I've seen before.

When I was in fifth grade, our class took a trip to the 4-H conservation camp. There, we learned about all kinds of birds. Cardinals, blue jays, you name it. We learned about their feathers, how to tell which is which. How am I remembering this, especially right now? But I do remember standing out on the observation deck, looking for birds. I remember feeling watched then. I remember finding an owl feather as it fell from the sky, seemingly into my hand. I remember feeling proud.

And that's how I know that this man's clothes are made from the feathers of horned owls.

He opens his arms.

"Mr. Craven," he says, his voice as smooth and deep as an undisturbed sea.

I let him take my shoulders. I look past him, studying the others around the bonfire. A woman stands at the front, all in black. Her face is covered with a long veil. She lifts it and smiles at me from behind foggy-tea eyes.

Praise Tabitha.

Witches with broken necks and witches without gather behind her. And behind them, ghosts, five hundred or so. Movement passes through the trees behind them. Ruffles of fur. Small pairs of violet eyes peer out through the darkness, and bats flap above the dusty treetops.

The man in the explorer's hat moves his hand farther around me, his fingers digging into my shoulder blades, and he pulls me into a hug. I wince as his fingernails cut the skin of my back.

"I have been waiting for you," he says in my ear. "For that black flame to flicker and alert me of your homecoming at last. Are you ready to join me?"

"Yes," I whisper, feeling the wicked righteousness tingling in my arms once more.

"Are you willing to do my bidding," the man continues, "to follow the path I've laid for you?"

"Wh-what?"

Tabitha saunters around the fire. The man releases me, and I stumble a few steps backward. Tabitha comes to me, takes my hand, and pierces my finger with a stone knife. I cry out as blood drips from the wound. She forces my finger to my chest and uses it to draw a dripping-red X over my heart.

"Will you serve your patron," says the man, "as a vessel, to let my monsters and spirits run free and wild?"

What does that even mean?

"Ada said nothing about that." My voice trembles. "She said you just give them their full power."

"You will do as your patron pleases." The man ignores me. He doesn't blink as he takes my hand. Blood smears his palms from the gash in my finger. "For this is the power I give unto you."

"That doesn't make sense," I manage, my throat tight.

"What are you?" is all Grant can say.

"Clearly, you already know."

The feeling I've known since April, to destroy, to disturb, to cause pain in return for pain, crawls up from my gut and into my heart. The feelings I've been pushing down. The flames deep inside, hiding beneath a mask of sarcasm, begging to come out.

Are you a good witch or a bad witch?

I scan the crowd of ghostly faces, looking for one in particular. But he's not among them. Where is Grant? He would never accept death and move to the other side so casually. Actually, he'd take an astronomical amount of pleasure in haunting me for the rest of my life. It hits me like a semi. *Grant's not dead, you idiot. Three others were missing, and they buried the wrong asshole.*

My eyes dart up to the man's.

He could tell me everything, but he's not going to. Not unless I give him what he wants.

Are you a good witch, or a bad witch?

The man puts his cold, cadaver-like fingers under my chin.

"Boy," he says, "do you join me at last?"

I count to three in my head, force the dark, wicked tingling to subside. "You're a liar."

The man's eyes harden, and he pulls his hand away. His lips, closed tight, seem for a moment like they'll smile. But he doesn't.

"What did you just say?"

My legs tremble. My hand shakes as it lifts to my chest to smear the bloody X. "I don't think you give anyone power. I think you're just a user."

The man gapes at me, looks to Tabitha, then glances back at the other ghosts. When he casts his eyes back on me, his irises are even darker than they already were.

"My dear boy, I urge you to reconsider." His voice is even, yet tense, the undisturbed sea before the hurricane.

Are you a good witch, or a bad witch?

"Why?" I ask. "What can I do that you need so badly?"

The man blinks, and I think I can see a slight trembling in his jaw as he grinds his teeth. "I did not bring you here so you could annoy me."

"Oh, I can be *very* annoying." I secretly enjoy the gasps of all the dead people around us. "Where's Grant Allen?"

"Join me first." The man reaches out his long, skeleton-thin fingers to grab me.

I stumble backward, raising my hand to protect myself and—

The bonfire explodes behind him.

Ghosts scream and the man shields his eyes. My arms feel like they're on fire. Something deep down next to the magnets feels like it's *thanking* me for letting it out.

The man gasps at the bonfire and hurries to recompose himself. He turns back to me, his eyes huge and proud. "However did you manage that?"

"If you gave it to me, then you'd know."

I run. I run as fast as I can, fleeing the mob of ghosts on my trail. Are they really following me or is it my imagination? I don't risk looking back.

I skid past the trees, tumble through the dirt, and look out for the surface of the hot spring. Yards away, steam rises in a plume to mark the spot.

"Dane Craven!" I can hear the man shouting.

I don't look back. I run to the spring, and with a deep breath, I jump in, hoping that this is the way back to Aunt Bella's house. Back to the coven. I have to tell them, and we have to find him. A relieved sob pushes out of my lungs and a mouthful of blood pours into my throat. But I don't care.

Because this coven is being lied to. And because Grant. Is. Not. Dead.

THE HOLLOW: RABBITS

ot safe.

Grant's head jerks sideways and he's awake. How long was he out this time? A few minutes? An hour? The whole night?

He stares at the rotting wooden ceiling above him and tries to string time together. A glance to the window tells him it's early morning, the view covered in a milk-colored fog.

What day is this? Thirteen…fourteen? He can't remember. *Has anyone been looking for me?*

He rotates his ankle, the one the rabbit-masked man twisted. It's stiff, turned inward, but it's usable.

Grant pushes himself onto his elbows and wills his legs to swing over the edge of the long wooden table. He moves like syrup, his muscles long unused. Blood geysers into his head. His temples pulse with vague memories. A bony hand shoving spoonfuls of greasy woodland meat into his mouth, from a rusted skillet.

Finally, the blood settles and Grant is able to see again. He looks down at the floor, strewn with dead leaves.

With a silent breath, Grant lowers his feet to the floor, and his bare toes drag ten tiny streaks into the dust. His ankle burns, threatening to give out under him as he attempts to stand. Slowly, he lets go of the table and holds his arms out for balance. He looks to the ceiling, expecting footfalls at any second.

One minute passes. Two minutes.

Grant looks at his legs and finds that someone has put him in threadbare pants. Faded plaid. The sundress lies in a wadded pile in the corner, next to the refuse bucket the rabbit-masked man's been helping him to use.

The damned dress. He wouldn't have had to wear it if he hadn't—

With silent, hesitant steps, Grant inches his way to the window. Through the fog he can make out the woods, surrounding the cabin on all sides. How far out are they?

Grant hobbles to the door as silently as he can, and peers into the dank, unlit common room of the cabin. It's empty, except for the wood-burning stove and a greasy, blackened skillet. Steep stairs ascend to a second floor.

He goes to the door, places his hand on the knob. Swatches of fur brush past his feet and he claps his hand to his mouth to keep from crying out, but it's too late.

Three gaunt rabbits hop around him.

Above, a footstep thuds. Then another.

Grant yanks the knob. The door attempts to open, but its latch is aged and stuck. He looks over his shoulder to see the feet of the rabbit-masked man at the top of the steps, the yellow plaid trousers.

Pull! Grant silently screams. *Pull, you jackass!*

He jerks the knob with both hands as hard as he can. The door swings back and knocks into him. He pushes his way around it and hobbles onto the porch.

Just twenty feet, maybe thirty, and then the woods will hide him. He supports his weight against the porch rail, descending the steps as fast as he can.

His feet hit dirt and he runs, ignoring the fire in the meat of his foot.

He rounds the side of the cabin, coming upon a nearly collapsed chicken coop.

He slides in arms first, curls up, and waits.

Hannah used to like this game. Seeing what small spaces they could fit into and waiting for someone to find them. Grant's good at it. Heavy footfalls grow louder. Grant peeks through the slats of the coop. The man moves in no hurry around the corner of the cabin and past him without even looking at his hiding spot.

Outside the coop is a stump, covered in the dried, probably hundred-year-old blood of unfortunate chickens. An axe is wedged into it, rusted and dulled with time.

That'll do.

Grant slaps his face, like he used to before a wrestling match. He beats his head, breathes heavy. *Time to fight. No choice.* He bolts from the coop, and by the time the man is turning back to the noise, Grant is gripping the axe, holding it in position like a baseball bat.

"Hey, motherfucker!" he shouts. "Over here!"

The man comes for him, arms outstretched, moaning something unintelligible.

Grant swings the axe. It chops into the man's rib cage. The man falls to the ground with a shriek. Grant pulls the axe out and brings it down again. And again. And again, until the man is a pile of yellow plaid, rabbit fur, and fresh, bloody pulp.

Grant stumbles backward, taking in the sight of what he's done. He drops the axe to the ground and sobs. He falls to his knees and buries his face in his arms.

He takes three slow breaths. Then he looks back at the pulp.

It's gone. Something strikes the back of his head. A firework blinds his vision, and everything goes black.

9

CODE BLACK

My eyes shoot open and I gasp for air when I reach the surface of the bloody spring. I find, however, that I'm in my bed in Aunt Bella's upper-floor guest room. I don't remember getting here. I don't remember climbing out of the tub. But it's definitely morning because sunlight slices the avocado-green wall and turns it yellow.

My head pounds and forces my eyes shut again.

A furry snoot pushes along my forehead, sniffing, and paws tug at one of my curls.

"*Dane?*" Aloysius clicks. His little paw raps on my pulsing cranium. "*Are you awake?*"

My hand jerks up from beneath the comforter and shoves his paw off me. "Shh. Let me die in peace."

A barely audible whimper escapes Aloysius and he scurries to my side. I open one eye to see him staring back with great concern.

"*Never fear. I shall nurse you myself, and you'll feel tip-top in no time at all.*"

I groan and close my eyes again.

Was I ever really in the woods? My hands sweep along my legs and feel the polyester plain weave of my gym shorts. A Spider-Man T-shirt covers my torso.

It was all a dream.

The door opens, banging against the wall.

"Be gentle!" Aunt Bella shouts from the hall. "I repainted last year!"

I force my eyes back open, burrowing deeper beneath the comforter as Ada sweeps into the room and heads straight for me. Louisa wraps around her left arm, her head swaying over Ada's wrist. When she spots me, she hisses.

"What is the matter with you?!" Ada demands. I think she relishes the wince that her shouting provokes, and I rub my temples. "Have you no dignity? Have you no sense of pride?"

I grumble and roll over. "Have *you* no ibuprofen?"

The Reds file into the room. They've changed out of their white dresses. How long have I been out?

"No!" I say. "It's Monday! You have school!"

They laugh and Chloe folds her arms. "Fall break, baby boy."

I never want to see these girls again, but I know that at this rate I'm probably never getting anything I want.

Mom pushes past them and grabs Ada's snake-free arm, spinning her around. "Calm down."

"Calm down? Calm down?!" Ada laughs hysterically. "Your spawn just offended *Mr. Hawthorne*. How could I possibly calm down?"

Mom folds her arms. "Did you know that he was going to show up and talk to my son? Because that definitely is not the usual."

"Of course I didn't know," says Ada. "Usually, it's just Tabitha with a book to sign. I would have shouted it from the rooftops if I'd known our patron himself was going to—"

"Now, I'm not blaming you—"

"I'd hope not! I had nothing to do with this obscene—"

"However—"

"There is no *however*—"

"*However*," Mom shouts, "at the end of the day, that is Dane's choice!"

I manage a weak smile. "Go Mom."

"I won't have my son used by some ghost-devil," she continues.

"Ghost! That's it!" I push myself up onto my elbows. "I saw all the ghosts in the Hollow last night. At least, I think it was all of them. And I didn't see Grant."

Aunt Bella's face drops. "What?"

"He wasn't there," I say. "Like, at all."

Hannah peeks into the room, and Aunt Bella turns to her. They look at each other wide-eyed, their chests swelling with the unmistakable gasp of hope. Mom takes Aunt Bella's hand.

"That might not mean anything," says Elena. "He could have passed."

Aunt Bella fights a tear in her left eye. "But there's a chance. Right?"

"Poppycock and huff-huff," says Ada, and I fight back the laugh about to blast from my pursed lips. I just love weird-ass words. "Don't be distracted, ladies. Let's not forget that Dane has *refused* Mr. Hawthorne. It's only a matter of time before he punishes us, and I will not allow some *male* to destroy my coven!"

"I won't," I say, "because I won't be in your coven."

Ada leans over the bed and slams her hands deep into the mattress. She locks her eyes with mine. "You're joining us, you brat, or I'll burn you at the stake myself before Mr. H has us all for breakfast!"

I wink at her. "I like it hot."

Ada stands straight, holding her hands up in surprise. She looks to Mom. "Don't you ever want to hit this kid?"

"All the time," Mom says. "But he's his mother's gay son, and I respect that. I suggest a compromise. Dane, you already joined the coven last night"—she ignores my groan—"so, you do your *part*. But he doesn't have to accept anything from Mr. Hawthorne. Not until he's ready."

"He will never allow it," says Ada.

"He will this time."

"How can you know that?"

Mom shrugs in response.

Ada considers, looking at me like I'm a spider she's squashed with her shoe that she's dismayed to see is still alive. Finally, she waves her hands as if flinging the whole ordeal away. "I suppose it'll do."

I lay my head back on the pillow. "I get the vibe that I did you a favor. This patron of yours seems as trustworthy as a snake oil salesman."

Elena raises her eyebrows and looks at her fellow Reds like she just solved a crime. "Hm! An old guy telling a bunch of powerful young women he owns them is a load of bull! Who was it that called that out? Oh yeah, it was me. You're welcome!"

Ada raises her finger but whatever she's going to say is cut off by the phone buzzing inside her robe. The Monkees' theme song plays. She pulls the phone from a pocket and her eyes light up. "Nobody move. I'll be right back."

When she leaves the room, Aloysius crawls onto my lap. *"No matter what, I'm on your side."*

Ada sweeps back into the room, her mouth gaping and her eyebrows knitted. "We have to go, Reds. Now. You too, Craven Kid."

"Why?" asks Mom.

Ada stops, barely looking over her shoulder. "That was Mayor Kowalski. They've found something in the woods. A Code Black."

She sweeps out of the room. Aloysius hops to the floor and I drag myself from the bed.

"What is a Code Black?" I call after the Reds as they exit. My eyes fall on Mom.

"Murder," she says.

Ada leads us through the backyard, toward the woods I was in yesterday morning. It feels like we're moving in slow motion as we near the tree line. Hours ago there was nothing, and now there's a Code Black. *Murder.*

I stuff my hands inside my hoodie pocket and fight against the cold chill sweeping up my spine. The Reds are leading me toward something I'd rather not see. I glance over my shoulder and nod slightly to Mom and Aunt Bella, to Hannah. The three of them are standing on the deck, watching us go. I wish they could come, but Ada said the mayor was specific—only Ada and her girls are allowed to see. I guess I'm a girl now.

Aloysius scampers beside me, not nearly as poised as the cats ahead of him. Passing the first line of trees and the rock walls near the very spot he scurried toward me yesterday, I can't help but smirk.

"Aw, it's where we met," I joke.

"Feels like only yesterday," he clicks.

We trek farther into the woods, and the dirt softens into packed mud beneath my sneakers. The birds chirp their shrill melodies. Perhaps it's a warning, for what we're about to see. Another piece of Grant's body? A dirty white sundress?

It didn't work yesterday, but I reach out to a wilted piece of brush as we pass, hoping to read something, anything, on it.

"Don't touch anything!" Ada snaps and I jump. "This is a crime scene."

I nod as fast as I can. Ada resumes walking and we follow.

Ahead, the woods open into a clearing, the treetops ascending and meeting like the dome of a state building. Two people stand before it like gatekeepers. I squint to make out their features, but can't discern anything.

Maybe it's Mr. Hawthorne and Tabitha, back already for round 2. I shiver.

Ada stops walking. The Reds halt and I nearly bump into Elena, but I catch myself, my sneaker sticking in a patch of mud with a nasty sucking sound.

"Ladies," a woman says, her voice tight but cordial.

"Madame Mayor." Ada nods and steps forward.

Now I can see the woman. She's tall, in a dark-gray pantsuit with shoulder-length black hair, hands pushed deep into her pockets. Her eyes fall on me and she sighs, sliding her gaze to Madelaine.

"Tell me it's not so. Madelaine, if you don't give him back and stop—"

"Of all the boys in the Hollow, you really think I'd kidnap *him*?" Madelaine asks.

Chloe glances at me and smiles. "I would. He's cute."

My face gets hot. "Uh, thanks?"

Ada raises her hand toward us, a professional way of telling us to zip it. "He's with us. This is our newest member, Dane Craven. You know, Robyn's child."

She gestures to me and I step forward. "Dane," she says, "this is Mayor Bridget Kowalski."

The woman smiles tersely and extends her hand. I take it absently and shake. I realize my mouth is hanging open, so I clamp it shut.

"You look surprised," she says. "Expecting some curmudgeonly old man?"

"Not an old man," I say. "Oh, I mean—not curmudgeonly, either. I mean—"

I feel shorter and shorter with each icy blink of the mayor's eyes. She nods at me with a tight smile. I nod in return. She nods again. That's when I realize she's done with me, so I throw my arm across my waist and bow. Yep. I bow, as though she's the bloody queen of England and I've offered my coat for her to walk on.

I stumble backward, nearly tripping over twigs and rocks, and take my place with the other peasants.

Mayor Kowalski shakes her head and blinks, clearly dumbfounded. She turns to Ada. "Sheriff Doyle and I came the minute he was tipped off, but there's not much to go on. I thought all of you might be a little more useful."

She gestures to the second figure, the sheriff who stopped us the other night. I remember hearing him ask about codes, all different colors, and wondering about their meanings. I tilt my head and pry open his mind.

"*The little prick looks just like his father. Curly headed punk bitch.*" I shut his mental notebook and look away just as he makes eye contact. Must be feeling the invisible insects crawling on him. I don't think I'll like this guy very much. I pull my hood on and resist the urge to yank it completely over my eyes.

"Todd." Ada nods.

"Adaline," Sheriff Doyle responds.

Ada looks back to the mayor. "We'll see what we can do. What do you think?"

Mayor Kowalski turns and walks through the brush into the clearing. "Whatever it was that did this, we doubt it was human. But take a deep breath before you look."

Elena's face twists up like she just snorted cayenne. "How can we breathe at all?"

I retch and push the neck of my hoodie over my nose. The stench of blood over the town was bad enough, but I would gladly inhale that over this. This reeks of rotten flesh and muscle, human chemicals and waste.

Mayor Kowalski steps aside, finally revealing what she called us to see. Acid pushes up from my stomach and I swallow it back down, pressing the cotton harder against my nose and mouth. Chloe leans on a tree and dry heaves. Only Madelaine and Ada seem undisturbed.

The last time I felt like this was when Mom told me Grant was missing— that feeling of your heart splatting through your entrails and dropping into the earth's core. It takes me a moment to not just look at it but *see* it.

Bones and skin that must've been rotting out in the open for weeks. Two skeletal bodies strung together, arms laced around each other's ankles to form a circle. What's left of their bodies anyways. They're missing fingers, toes. One's lost a whole foot.

Their heads are only half there, half their faces gone, sitting at the center of the flesh-and-bone circle. Entrails wrap around them, crossing back and forth, forming the shape of a star.

"Four missin'," Sheriff Doyle begins, "one buried, and now two found."

"So, we're paranormal detectives?" I whisper to Chloe.

Chloe nods. "Basically."

"Is that what Mr. Hawthorne wants us for?"

"Who?" Mayor Kowalski raises an eyebrow at me.

Ada shrugs and forces a laugh. "My date the other night. You can't trust kids with anything personal, can you?"

I purse my lips and try to focus my attention on the trees instead of looking at the sight again, but they're splattered with what has to be dried blood, so I stare down at my muddy sneakers instead.

"Well," says Ada, "definitely Code Black. As for what did it, I think we can rule out Code Scarlet. Vampires are much neater."

My eyes feel like they're going to pop out of my skull at *this* piece of information.

"Code Green?" Chloe shrugs with her palms up, a hopeful smile breaking across her lips, as though she just wants to win the game and get out of here pronto.

But Ada shakes her head. "No. A zombie would never leave this much brain."

"What about Code Silver?" Madelaine pipes up, and everyone turns to her. Her eyebrows are drawn together in worry.

Mayor Kowalski lets out a small grunt and rolls her eyes.

Ada shakes her head, and sounds almost comforting when she says, "No, dear. Werewolves are too impulsive for something so obviously premeditated, and they're far too rare in this region."

Madelaine nods, like she's relieved. I narrow my eyes at her, but she turns around and walks to the other side of the clearing. I hope someday *I* can mention werewolves and zombies with a straight face and not feel like a lunatic.

"It's a serial killer," Elena announces, throwing her hands up like an unimpressed CIA agent on TV. "None of this is exclusively *X-Files* material."

"That's possible, of course," Mayor Kowalski says. "But I guess I'm just really hoping it's something you can take care of."

"Regardless," says Ada, "I'm sure we can solve it."

"I suggest you do so as quickly as possible," Mayor Kowalski says. "We can only cover up a murdering spree for so long."

Ada nods solemnly. "Of course. Do you mind sharing how you discovered this? You said you received a tip, so how *are* you covering this up?"

To this Mayor Kowalski smirks. "Lucky for us, my nephew broke the rules and came hiking out here. Speaking of which, I told him not to wander." She turns to the woods and calls, "EJ!"

I can't believe my ears. It has to be some other EJ No way. No how. Nope.

The EJ, the one with the eyes, cuts through the bushes to my right and steps into the clearing, brushing dirt from his blue flannel shirt. He's wearing hiking boots, and his tight, brown hiking pants make me wanna—

"You?" I spit the word out, and any sexual desire I might have been feeling is pushed away by confusion.

EJ spots me and his face drops. "Oh. Hi."

"You all know my nephew, EJ," Mayor Kowalski turns to him. "Where were you?"

"Just having a look," he says. "But I haven't found anything else."

Across the clearing, Madelaine folds her arms. "I thought I told you to leave the witch shit to us."

EJ raises his eyebrows at her. "I didn't know hiking was exclusively for witches."

"Manners." Mayor Kowalski gives EJ a look. "I suggest we have a closer look, now that we're all here."

Ada holds her hands up. "Safety in numbers! Split into groups of three and fan out."

"That would leave a group of two," says Elena.

Ada shrugs. "I do spells, not math. Sheriff, Madame Mayor, shall we?"

She turns and disappears through an opening in the brush. Mayor Kowalski motions for Sheriff Doyle. He tips his hat to us, gives me an unsure glance, and follows them away.

"I'll go with you, Dane," Madelaine steps quickly to me and grabs my arm before I can pull it away.

"No way," Elena crinkles her nose toward EJ. "Reds together."

"Dane's a Red," Madelaine argues.

I'm almost touched. If I weren't so suspicious of her motives, I'd thank her.

"Reds. Together," says Elena.

Madelaine looks at me, her mouth twisting into a frown. She walks to Chloe and Elena, looking at EJ like she wants to kick him. The Reds disappear into the trees, their cats in tow. EJ sighs with relief as though he just avoided having the crap slapped out of him. Then he turns to me, his cheeks turning bright pink.

"So..." I tap my fingers against my thumb quickly to pat out any hint of fire running through them. "You're in on all of this?"

"Uh, yeah," he says. "And you're a...a witch."

My stomach drops a little. The way he says it, it's almost like an insult. "Yeah, uh, I guess I am."

"Cool." He folds one arm into his elbow and uses his free hand to scratch the back of his neck. I guess he's just as uncomfortable as I am. For me, it's because I'm alone with him. But for him, it's because he's alone with the witch.

"That thing in the coffee shop..." I start. "Do you think it's what did this?"

EJ shrugs. "I have no idea."

"You lunged at it." I point out. "Do you know what it was, at least?"

"No." He shakes his head and shrugs again. "I have no idea."

"Then why'd you lunge at it?"

"Fight or flight?" He dares a look at me. "And plus, I thought it was going to lunge at you first."

Someone get me a biscuit, because I am now a pool of clarified butter. I should *not* be tossing my boxer shorts at a boy right now. I'm standing next to an insanely disturbing murder scene. I stuff my hands in my hoodie pocket and drum my fingers against my stomach. *Pat out the fires.*

"Well, thanks." What else can I say? I don't know if he meant that the way my fantasies just took it. Without thinking, I tilt my head, and his arms instantly shoot up.

"Stay out of my head!"

My jaw drops and I stammer. "Wait! No. No, sorry. I didn't mean to—"

"I don't like it."

"I'm sorry."

His expression darkens to a scowl, and he looks away with a sigh. "It's fine. Whatever."

Great. Now he's even *more* uncomfortable being alone with me. "I'm sorry. I didn't mean to start doing that. It's hard to control when I'm—when I'm nervous."

EJ licks his lips and half smiles. "It's fine. I accept your apology." Then he slides his eyes to me, and the half smile becomes a full grin. "You get flustered around me. You can't help it."

Before he can see my megablush, I beeline to a random tree. "I'm gonna look over here."

"I'm kidding!" he calls out.

Aloysius scurries up and swats my ankle with his paw. *"Not everyone is out to make a fool of you."*

"Stop listening in!"

"What?" EJ calls.

"Nothing!" I sigh through a wince. "But I'm sorry. I won't read your mind again, I promise."

EJ nods. "Thank you."

I set about trying to read in on the leaves, hoping that maybe since they're this close to something it will be a different story. But nothing.

"So," I start slowly, "what does EJ stand for?"

His breath catches for a moment, and I glance at him. He's full-on blushing now, and I can hardly stand what it does to me. I want to grab his face and feel the heat of his cheeks as they grow redder and redder. He squeezes his eyes shut. "Elton John."

I laugh. Hard. "No way."

"Yeah. My parents were weird."

Were? "Oh, I'm sorry."

"No, it's okay. But yeah. Elton John Kowalski."

I shrug. "My middle name is Yuletide."

"*That's* weird."

We laugh, but when I glance past him, something catches the light near a tree. I move toward the object. Some sort of broken glass, cracked into coarse shards. When I'm close enough to see what it is, all breath leaves my body.

A cell phone.

I stoop and reach down, taking the phone in my hand. Glass crumbles from the screen and falls to the ground. I try to click the power button, but it's stuck. I push my thumb against it even harder.

The atoms of the phone explode into my mind before I can—

"Rabbit Skins, Rabbit Skins."

A flash of a face. A blond with bloodshot red eyes, grinning at me as he raises a fist.

The image changes.

I'm wearing a white sundress. I'm on the ground. "I'm in the woods, my name is Grant Allen, I'm seventeen—"

"Here to cleanse you of your sins."

The man in the rabbit-skin mask peers at me with his dead eyes. Is he smiling at me under there? Worms and insects crawl across his plaid suit. The fresh bodies of three boys a little older than me surround us in a pulpy, mushy mess. One of them was blond too.

The rabbit man's hand twists my ankle, and he drags me deeper into the woods.

I scream.

"Drags you down, and eats your bones..."

"No!"

"Keeps you for his very own."

I kick and punch the air, screaming with every drop of oxygen in my body, clawing at the dirt. Other arms grab mine, hands push my legs down, and I'm lying in the dirt, the same piece of earth where Grant was taken. I can't let the phone go, as much as I want to.

My gaze tosses back and forth, between the faces of Ada, EJ, and the Reds all looking down at me.

And I can't stop screaming.

10

TO WALK A MILE IN ONE'S DRESS

"Eat this." Ada thrusts a leathery wad into my palm.

I crinkle my nose and sink deeper into the stiff, wine-colored upholstery of the sofa. "I will not."

She rolls her eyes. "It's beef jerky."

Slowly, I nibble at it. It's tough, salty, and fibers of it stick in my teeth. Aloysius perches on my lap, staring at me with the mournful eyes of a mother watching her baby get its first shot. We're in the parlor of Collingwood Hall, and I avoid looking at the looming portrait of Tabitha staring icy daggers at me.

Finally, I mash down the jerky and swallow.

"How do you feel?" asks Ada.

My headache eases up a bit, and the salt is alerting my brain that it's about to be okay. "A bit better."

Ada glances at the Reds. "Magic hangover." She turns to me. "The salt helps."

"So..." begins Elena. "What the hell just happened?"

I've already told them what I saw, even though I didn't want to talk about it. I'd rather never see it again. Or hear it. That morbid nursery rhyme rings in my ears.

"I don't know," I say, tearing off another piece of jerky with my teeth. "His phone was on the ground, I grabbed it, and then bam: 4D cinema with me in the role of Grant."

Ada stands with arched eyebrows. I swing my leg over to where she was sitting, glad to finally stretch out. She paces around the back of the sofa, tapping her fingertips together as she thinks.

"You mean you—but that's psychometry!"

"Gesundheit," I say.

"Objects showing you their histories," she explains. "The things that have happened near them."

"Yeah," I say, "that. I've been doing it for like"—I count the months on my fingers—"half a year now?"

"Interesting."

"Usually, it's just things that were said or done around the object, but that's twice now that an object gave me the emotions of the owner."

Ada beelines to the bookcase next to the fireplace. She runs a finger across the spines of the leather volumes. "Mhm," she says. "Sometimes emotions become trapped, in times of great stress or trauma. I'd say your cousin had quite a few emotions to spill into that phone."

Madelaine looks at Ada like she just sold her an imitation designer purse. "How can he do that and we can't?"

"We all have our talents, Madelaine." Ada pulls a book from the shelf and cracks it open, rifling through its pages. "I have my way with the stars and the moon. Robyn has her potions. Elena is the best at control, and you"—Ada cuts her eyes to Madelaine, as though challenging her to reply—"seem to like light bulbs."

I think of Hallow Bean, when Madelaine turned the power back on without touching anything. Did she flip the lights during the ritual, too?

Chloe sticks her hand out to me. "I have a talent, too. Take my hand!"

"Not now, Chloe!" Elena claps at her and Chloe whimpers like a puppy, folding her arms.

"But to get into the *emotions*," Ada continues, returning to her page, "that's pretty advanced, Craven Kid."

I roll my eyes and sit up. "You just said it was just their stress or whatever."

"It's one thing to pick up on their emotion," Ada says. "To possess them, even in memory, is another. It's incredibly rare. I've only ever heard of one other witch able to do such a thing. I remember the night you were born." Ada finally finds her page. "There was a blood ring then, too. Around a beast moon, I believe. Which is odd in its own right. But that's how I knew what you'd be."

A single *boom* thumps in my chest. I think of the black flame. The bonfire exploding.

"*What are you?*"

"Clearly, you already know."

Are you a good witch or a bad witch?

"What do you mean?" I half whisper.

"That you'd have a way with monsters," says Ada, and I let out the breath I've been holding.

At this, Madelaine exchanges a smirk with Elena and looks to me. "Noted."

I glare back at them. Great, another theme party in the making. Let me guess, we do "The Monster Mash" with Frankenstein's monster over at the pool hall? "Back to what's really happening. The man pulling me—Grant, I mean. It was the same man at the coffee shop."

"Are you sure?" Madelaine asks.

"Same plaid suit," I say, feeling a bit queasy. "Same rabbit mask."

"I don't like that." Chloe takes a step back. "I don't wanna know."

Elena side-eyes Chloe with a frustrated grunt. "You already saw him. The coffee shop?"

"I'm blocking it out."

Ada sighs and grabs my ankle. I pull away from her touch fast, and she sits down. "Yes, the man in the rabbit-skin mask. Curious thing."

"Curious?" I raise my eyebrows. "The man had his own theme song."

"The theme to *The Munsters*?" Elena challenges.

Ada shakes her head. "I know it well. It's a local legend. If you'd put your damned smartphones down every once in a while, you'd probably have heard of it, too."

"What was that?" I stare at her.

Ada takes a breath. "Rabbit Skins. That's what they called him. He was a serial killer over a hundred years ago, known to stalk the woods and the outskirts of town, wearing the furs of, well, you know."

I have an inkling that morbid Hannah knows all about this freak.

"He'd leave the victims almost unrecognizable at the edge of the woods, just as he did the body your family buried. He'd take their faces."

Chloe cringes. "Why?"

"I don't remember. But I imagine it had to do with what's *under* the mask."

"How horrifically extra." Elena pulls up her phone and scrolls, clearly over this.

My mind zeros in on what Ada said. *The body my family buried.* It couldn't be. "You mean—"

"You said it yourself." A gleam brightens Ada's irises. "Four went missing. We all saw it, there were two in the woods. Your cousin was dragged away. That leaves the body with remnants of blond hair that was found a week and a half later."

I shake my head. I've wanted it to be true, but I don't think I can let myself believe it yet. "Aunt Bella identified the body."

"She wouldn't have been in her right mind," Ada says. "And if she identified him, they wouldn't have pushed it further. This is a small-town police force, not *NCIS: Los Angeles*."

"So, he's alive," I say.

Ada takes a deep breath. "I wouldn't go that far. I only mean that another's body was buried, and that Grant Allen is elsewhere, alive *or* dead."

I pull my legs out from behind Ada and stand. "Well, let's go! We have a killer to catch, and an asshole to find, and I can't wait to call him that to his face."

"Hold up!" Ada stands. "We can't just waltz out into the woods—"

"We already did—"

"—and vanquish a killer ghost—"

"But I can read objects—"

"—and bring your cousin home before din-din!" Ada drowns me out. "This is dangerous, and I'm not sending any of my witches out unprepared. The first step is for me to get back to Mayor Kowalski and Sheriff Doyle. Then, I need to research this Rabbit Skins, and meanwhile, you need to hone your powers."

I roll my eyes. If she only knew what I was capable of...what I did six months ago...

"All right." Ada paces. "We have a lead, then. Girls and Craven Kid, go home. I'm going to call up Kowalski to relay this information and spitball ideas on how to cover it up. There are more bodies to bury and identify, and it's a messy process. Rest up. Once that's all taken care of, I want us all to get back together and do a few practice spells."

"Not all of us *need* practice," protests Elena.

Ada stops pacing and glares at her, an eyebrow raised. "Oh yes, you do. None of you have ever fought a serial killer from beyond the grave."

With a grunt, I follow the Reds through the foyer and onto the veranda of Collingwood Hall. In the daylight, the yard isn't so creepy, though the gate at the end of the winding drive still weirds me out with its black iron cats. In the fresh air, I take a deep breath and immediately regret it as the stink of blood sweeps into my lungs.

"Do you ever get used to the smell?" I cough out.

"Yeah, but it comes back sometimes." Chloe pats my back, like I'm a child choking on a hot dog.

Madelaine goes down the veranda steps, heading for her pink car. "Let's get out of here."

I stare at the back of her head as I follow, imagining each perfectly laid strand of hair parting like a curtain to reveal her thoughts, and her plans for me. She whirls herself around and asks, "What the hell do you think you're doing?"

Oh shit. I lean back, my head shaking involuntarily. "Sorry—"

"You can't read our minds," she shouts. "It's not allowed."

"You read *mine* all the time."

Chloe smirks. "Because you think too loudly."

Madelaine blinks a few times, like she's combating an eye roll, and beelines to the car. "Keep building that wall, then. Could you imagine if we were all reading each other's thoughts all the time?"

"We'd kill each other," admits Elena.

Madelaine responds by sliding into the driver's seat and slamming the door shut behind her.

Aloysius scampers up behind me and brushes his body against my ankle. *"Since you're heading home, I think I shall go find a nice tree to nap in. I am a nocturnal creature, you see, but if you've any trouble, call to me in your soul."*

"Like queso," I nod, and Aloysius waddles across the yard, toward the cluster of trees that stand between the hall and a horse field. I'm a little sad to see him go—I don't want to be alone with my coven after accidentally breaking the rules. I fall in step next to Chloe.

"I'm really sorry," I mumble. "I didn't mean to piss anyone off."

Chloe smiles. "Eh, we all try it at some point. You're good. Don't mind Madelaine *too* much. She's been really out of it since she was, like, fifteen. When her brother went missing."

Madelaine rolls the window down and sticks her head out. "You broadcasting an episode of *20/20*, Chloe?"

Chloe snaps her attention to Madelaine. "Oh, I just—"

Madelaine casts her eyes to me. "It was two years ago. I'm fine. We'll never know what happened to him, and I've moved on."

I swallow. "I know how you feel."

"I've moved on!" Madelaine repeats. But this time there's a darker undertone in her voice. Like a violent cry is punching at her insides, desperately trying to escape. "Jason was seventeen. We were out in the woods at night. I couldn't see what was happening." She thrusts her hand toward the dashboard and the headlights flicker and flash before fading out again. "That's why I like keeping the lights on and got good at it."

A shudder erupts across the back of my neck, and I recall the first time I read in on an object. Back in the spring when I wasn't sure any room I entered would be safe. It was someone's key chain, a gift from an ex-boyfriend, discarded in the dirt during the breakup.

Elena shrugs. "I learned to use control to my advantage when we moved here from Arizona in fourth grade and redneck kids kept calling me names. One boy couldn't move his jaw at all for three days. I hope he liked thin soup."

I look to Chloe. "What's your talent?"

"Take my hand!"

"Not now!" Madelaine shouts and the car horn honks itself. Chloe whimpers. "Come on. It's almost dark, and we have something else to show you."

Elena laughs, as though she's remembered some private joke, and walks toward me with an expression that can only say, "You're not gonna like this." I hear Chloe humming behind me, fiddling with some sort of fabric.

"Um," I look at Madelaine, wide-eyed. "So. What are you showing me?"

"Feeding time," says Elena.

Before I can respond, Chloe covers my eyes with a red scarf.

11

INITIATION

"h, I was just kidding about stealing boys." I mimic Madelaine's voice, my vision completely blackened under the red scarf. "Now hold still while I break your kneecaps."

Madelaine laughs. "I don't break boys' kneecaps."

I sigh.

"I castrate them."

I cross my legs. Where is Aloysius? I've been screaming into my soul, I think, since before they tossed me in the back seat. Madelaine zooms over a speed bump and the top of my head hits the roof of the car.

"Hey!" I cry out. "Take it easy, I'm not a toy!"

"Zip it," says Elena.

The car comes to a hard stop, and my face smacks against the back of Elena's headrest. Chloe's hand digs into the knot at the back of the scarf and it comes undone. As it falls away, I blink out the window to see that it's dark already. We've stopped in the parking lot of a park, the playground sprawling before us under a white floodlight. Beyond that, up the hillside, stands a large red-brick building, alone and silent behind brambles of dead bushes. If lightning struck right now in the distance, I wouldn't be surprised.

"What is it?" I whisper.

Chloe leans toward me. "The old hospital. It opened as an asylum in 1910. Then, in the '50s"—her eyes light up—"it was converted to house patients with tuberculosis."

"Out," says Madelaine.

"You know," I say, "your whole 'kidnap-out-kidnap-out' routine really leaves a lot to be desired."

Madelaine turns in her seat and smiles at me like an impatient retail worker. "I'll be sure to log those complaints for you. Now, out."

I slide out of the car and join Chloe in the cold air, stuffing my hands in my hoodie. Madelaine slinks around the car toward me. "Ever been here before?"

"No," I say.

"Good." She smiles. "It's a Jasper Hollow rite of passage to—at some point, preferably during childhood—touch the front door."

"You want me to touch a door?" I challenge her.

Madelaine nods. "Yup."

"Yeah. Okay. Sure." I start walking.

Madelaine grabs my arm and I yank it from her grip. "I want proof. A rock. Or a twig or something. Don't cheat and just grab something close by. I'll be able to tell."

Ambrose scurries out of the darkness and paws at Madelaine's ankle.

"There you are, baby." She bends down and picks up the cat, whispering something in his ear and kissing his forehead.

"Ambrose is coming with you." She throws the cat, and it latches onto my chest, stabbing my collarbone. I jump and wave my arms. The cat is hanging from my hoodie.

"Don't hurt him!" Madelaine shouts over the most genuine laugh we've gotten from Elena yet. Ambrose lets go and falls to the ground. "Not you, I was talking to Dane."

Ambrose points his nose in the air and makes his way toward the playground. My head is still hurting a little from reading Grant's phone, and I'd rather be at home. Maybe force Hannah to make me pancakes for dinner and bop around to show tunes. What I definitely don't want to do is follow a magical cat into an abandoned hospital. I don't know what I fear most, ghosts, squatters, or gowns that don't close in the back.

"*It sounds to me,*" Ambrose meows, his voice in my inner ear velvety and deep, "*that you mostly fear the unknown.*"

I double-take. "You can talk to me?"

"*Of course,*" he meows. "*We can communicate with other witches if we so please. Now hush and follow.*"

I amble after him, looking over my shoulder with almost every step. I'm scared some sort of ghoul is going to pop up behind me if I look away. Maybe there's no reason to be scared. Maybe it's going to be okay. Maybe I'm—"Ow!"— face-planting against the front door of the old hospital.

"*There's a door there,*" Ambrose meows.

"Yeah," I say. "I sensed that. I've touched the damn door, come on."

He meows again. "*The rock?*"

"Oh. Right."

I squat and fumble by the door for something. A pebble could do. Then I hear a meow. "*Come on.*" Ambrose jumps through a shattered window, disappearing inside the hospital.

"No!"

Pulling out my phone, I switch on the flashlight and head to the window, already catching a strong whiff of the blood stench inside. If I don't puke up every bite I've taken in the last day, it will be a regular Christmas miracle—in October, no less!

With a deep breath, I stick my head through the opening. The light from my phone cuts across a large room. Must have been the foyer. Water-stained wallpaper peels off the graffiti-covered walls. The floor is caked in dust and leaves.

Looks like a great place for a killer to hide out with their victims...

"Ambrose!" I call breathlessly. A gust of stench pushes into my nose and I gag. I take one slight suck of air. "Here kitty kitty—"

I breathe out. Big mistake. The smell in here is *not* just iron and rot. It is iron, covered in saliva, coated in rot, dipped in excrement and bodily fluids, *then* left to marinate for over half a century. Vomit chokes up the back of my throat. I swallow.

In the dark of the room, golden eyes catch the glow of the flashlight.

"Here, kitty kitty—"

"*Do you honestly think that will work? Come here.*" Ambrose purrs. I shake my head. "*Come here, foolish mortal.*"

With a sigh, I heave myself over the windowsill, but overshoot myself and tumble to the floor. My hand lands on some unseen object.

"*There is nothing to fret about, Mr. West,*" a voice taunts in my ear. "*Your fantasies, as you call them, are entirely treatable.*"

I yank my hand away before I can find out exactly why Mr. West should fret and see that I've landed on an old lighter.

"*Try to be careful,*" the cat meows. "*And follow me.*"

Ambrose stalks halfway up the stairs. I push myself to my feet and stumble after him, cramming my free hand into my pocket, terrified of brushing against anything else.

I reach the bottom of the stairs and take a step. The floorboard groans under my foot.

"Why are we going up here?" I whisper as I take step after groaning step.

"Ask me no questions, and I'll tell you no fibsies."

"I believe the phrase is, 'I'll tell you no lies.'"

"Silence, foolish mortal," the cat meows.

Finally, we reach the second floor. I tilt my head back to see the stairs continuing to wind up three or four more floors. A window at the end of the corridor lets the moonlight in, and lime-green graffiti radiates from the blue flowered wallpaper. Ambrose turns down the corridor, and I follow. We make our way past a torn mattress, piles of stuffing, a door half off its hinges. I step over an overturned bathtub that I assume must've been used for hydrotherapy. I shudder, realizing that if I'd been born at the wrong time, I could've been in it— that historical asylums aren't just a cheesy Halloween theme. They were places for people who didn't fit. Where they thought they could change people like me.

"If I'm a witch, then *am* I a mortal?" I ask, shaking my mind back to the present.

"Considering you could drop dead at any moment?" Ambrose brushes his tail against my leg. *"Yes, you foolish mortal."*

I open my mouth to respond, but Ambrose cocks his head back and lets out the loudest, most obnoxious meow that he can. I rush to shush him but am cut off by a noise on the floor above us. I freeze, my eyes scanning the ceiling. For a moment, I thought I heard a growl. Something scrapes the ceiling. Scratching. Clawing. Growing louder. Then, another growl.

I run. I run so fast that if I ran backward, it would be tomorrow again. I bolt down the groaning stairs and slam into the door. Ambrose scurries past me and out the shattered window.

"Bon appétit!" he meows and is gone.

I turn. Red eyes glow in the dark at the top of the stairs. The shadow of something monstrous begins its descent. I point the flashlight from my phone at it, the pool of light catching on huge paws. I gasp. It *is* a monster, with pale flesh and a gaunt rib cage poking out between patches of gray-and-brown fur.

Shit-shit-shit—

The head of a wolf stares me down, licking its lips as reaches the last stair.

I take half a breath, pushing my back to the door. "Hey, what is this? Virgin sacrifice?"

The beast halts. Blinks. A smile seems to form on its lips. *Can monsters smile?*

It takes a step toward me, then another, lowering its head like it's bowing. I smell blood on its breath.

Maybe it's the fear, but my brain scans my memories for something, *anything* to get me out of here. I picture Judy Garland in her blue gingham dress and ruby slippers, and the cowardly lion getting all up in her face.

Smack!

I bitch-slap the hell out of the monster's nose.

I don't wait to see what kind of slap it can return. I run, and just like that fabled cowardly lion, I spring out the window, away from Oz the Great and Terrible.

12

RABBIT TRAILS

"You're all sick!" I struggle as Elena pushes me toward the back seat of the car. "Demented. Psycho!"

"Flattery gets you everywhere." Elena pokes her finger between my shoulder blades.

Madelaine rubs her cheek against Ambrose's head as she reaches into her jacket and pulls out a treat. The cat licks it from her palm and purrs. "Good Ambrose."

"*Good Ambrose*??!" My voice climbs an octave. "He left me to get eaten by a monster! You may as well have wrapped me in paper and called me a Crispy McDane!"

Madelaine shrugs. "You ran fast."

I shake my head, as though it'll jiggle the logic into place. My mind is smothered with awful images from the day—mutilated corpses, visions in phones, and now whatever that *thing* was. I feel like I can't run back to Lexington fast enough. "What even *was* that?"

Chloe, who's busied herself with taking selfies, glances at me. "A monster."

"Golly." I sound a yokel chuckle. "You don't say!"

Madelaine struts to the driver door, opens it, and tosses Ambrose inside. "Jesus, relax. It doesn't eat people. Just woodland animals."

"You're a regular zoologist, I see." I raise an eyebrow. "Been tracking its migration patterns?"

"Yes."

I blink at her. "Why would you send me in there without knowing?"

Madelaine smiles and shrugs. "Ada said you'd have a way with monsters. Thought we'd get you started. It was just an initiation, chill out."

Frantic scurrying kicks up mulch on the playground and I whirl, my heart leaping. It's coming after us! I'm going to die.

A fat fur ball leaps through the dark and slams into my legs.

"*Come on, put up your dukes,*" Aloysius clicks, putting his paws up like a street fighter and bouncing toward Elena. "*I'm fortunate not to have rabies, but in this moment, I wish I did!*"

Elena puts her hands on her hips. "Dance, trash panda, dance."

Aloysius stops jumping and drops his paws. With a frustrated whimper he scurries back to me. I pick him up and demand, "Where have *you* been?"

"*I've been trying to catch up! That girl is a speed demon.*" Aloysius points at Madelaine. "*Whew. All that running has me famished. Perchance, have you any snacks?*"

There's a jack-o'-lantern on Aunt Bella's porch. I huff for the entire car to hear. Not only have these psychos subjected me to an array of terrifying things, they've made me miss my favorite autumn thing. I love to slice and dice pumpkins until they grin like a demented cat.

"We'll pick you up at one tomorrow." Madelaine looks at me in the rearview.

I shake my head. "I have to do online school. Not all of us get fall breaks."

Chloe looks over at me like she might cry. "You're homeschooled? That's why you're such a dork! Oh, baby boy!"

She tries to hug me, so I hold up Aloysius like a shield. "Not till this semester."

Elena turns in her seat and looks back at me. "You know a really awesome thing witches can do? Homework. Snap of the fingers and there's an instant A. Add a few Bs, just to keep them off the trail."

"I'm already a dork." I push the car door open. "Don't want to be a dumbass, too."

"Cute," says Madelaine. "We'll pick you up at one. And remember, not a word to anyone about today. You know nothing."

"But they deserve to know—"

"These aren't middle-school secrets!" Elena takes over, sounding a frustrated groan. "One, it's a murder investigation. Two, it's a murder investigation involving a government cover-up. Three, Igor isn't one of us. She can't know everything."

A gnarly ball forms in my stomach. I didn't realize throughout all of this that I wouldn't be allowed to talk about it. I remember Aunt Bella's face this morning when we realized there's a chance Grant's still alive. And now I have to look her in the eyes and *not* tell her that we buried someone other than her son? I feel disgusting already.

Madelaine shoots a close-lipped smile at me in the rearview. She'd probably rather reach back and rip my hair out—use it to build a nest for her thunderbird or something. "One. Be waiting."

I'd like to tell her to sit and spin, but instead I get out of the car and put Aloysius on the ground. I grab the door in a fit of anger, but I stop myself from slamming it, instead closing it just hard enough to send the message. Madelaine reverses the car and spins it around onto the road, then speeds out of sight.

"I smell food." Aloysius scampers to the porch.

When we're inside, I'm hit with the smell of Italian seasoning. Following Aloysius into the kitchen, I'm happy to find Hannah in her sunshine-yellow apron again. She chants "Dirty Deeds Done Dirt Cheap" under her breath and whisks a pot of Alfredo sauce.

Balanced on the counter is a pan of garlic bread. I reach around her and grab a piece, stuff half of it into my mouth with one bite, and groan. "Oh god."

Hannah spins around, waving her whisk at me, sending droplets of sauce onto my face. "Back it up! It's not time."

I swallow. "God, I'm starving."

Aloysius reaches up and tugs the leg of my gym shorts. *"Water bowl, please?"*

"I wasn't ready to serve that," says Hannah.

I take a bowl from the cabinet and hold it under the faucet. "I'm sorry. Do you want it back?"

"You're a jackass." She turns back to her sauce.

I set the bowl on the floor and reach to the pan for another piece of bread. Without looking over, Hannah swats the back of my hand with the whisk.

"Ow!" I rub at the sting. "It was for Aloysius!"

"It's. Not. Ready."

Aloysius clicks softly. *"Garlic doesn't sit well with us raccoons, Dane. Might I just have some plain pasta and, perhaps, are there still any of those delectable pretzels from last night?"*

I quietly pull the pretzels from the cabinet and sprinkle some on the floor. By the time I've done that, Hannah's breath has grown louder, and she still refuses to look at me. I fold my arms and lean against the counter. "I saw you didn't wait for me to carve the pumpkin."

Hannah stiffens, but still doesn't look at me. "Well, I had to do *something* while you ran around with the three-bitch circus. Strainer, please."

I sigh, bending to the lower cabinet and pulling out a metal strainer. I set it in the sink for her. "I'm sorry. I didn't really have a choice."

Hannah grabs a boiling pot and carries it over to the sink. She sloshes it all into the strainer, revealing fettuccine. "It's whatever. I don't care."

Yet you cared enough to make my favorite dinner.

We stand in silence while Hannah shakes the strainer to dry the pasta. I'm tempted to steal another piece of bread, but she'd probably chop off my pinkie with the butcher knife, so I shove my hands in my hoodie pocket instead.

"So," Hannah breaks the silence, her voice quiet, "what was out there?"

I bite down on the inside of my cheek. Madelaine wouldn't know if I told her and swore her to secrecy, would she? The magnets pull inside my bones, and I immediately feel guilty just thinking about it. I should tell her *something*, though.

"You could just lie and say you don't know," she answers for me.

"It's not like that—"

"Dinner!" Hannah screams. She jerks open a drawer and tosses a fistful of silverware at me. "Be useful and set the table."

Aunt Bella sits in her chair, her face tense as she watches Hannah scoop pasta onto her plate.

"You know," she says with caution, "we don't have to be formal. We could just eat in the living room and watch something."

"We are a family, Mother." Hannah finishes with Aunt Bella's plate and goes to Mom's. "A family that eats at the table together is statistically proven to stay in contact and be less likely to kill each other—it probably prevents cancer, too."

"I'd like to see your research." Aunt Bella rubs the space between her eyes.

Hannah fills Mom's plate and saunters near me, avoiding my gaze. I lean back like an obedient Sunday school student for her to serve it, but she just drops the pot in front of me and slides into her own seat.

I rub my left temple, totally wiped out from today. The last thing I need is for Hannah to be mad at me. Especially since it's not even *my* fault I've been gone all day.

Mom purses her lips and inhales deeply through her nostrils. "Well, this looks delicious." She takes a bite and makes a big show of loving it.

Hannah shrugs, keeping her eyes on her own plate. "I mean, I'm no potion master, but I can open a jar of Classico."

Aunt Bella holds up her fork and for a split second I think she's going to stab Hannah in the jugular. "Room."

Hannah looks almost relieved as she stands and disappears into the living room, the thud of her combat boots banging up the staircase. Above us, a door is slammed.

Aunt Bella sighs. "I'm sorry. She's hit the same phase that I did. The I'm-not-a-witch-and-I-feel-left-out phase. Plus she's—we're dealing with a lot."

"Don't be sorry." Mom eyes Aunt Bella with a sisterly look. "I remember that phase well."

Aunt Bella nods and forces a smirk. "I've turned into our mother."

"Stop now before you have a stroke."

Forcing a snort, Aunt Bella turns her attention to me and takes a steadying breath. "I know you can't tell me anything." I stiffen. "But...any sign of? Any clues?"

I chew the inside of my lip. "I..."

"Or at least any idea of"—she blinks back a tear—"of what he might have been doing out there?"

"No," I whisper.

Liar.

"Nothing?"

"Not that we found."

You're a dirty liar, Dane Craven.

"I don't think I'll ever unsee it." I push my palms against my eyes, burrowing my head deeper into the pillow.

"*Try not to dwell on it.*" Aloysius rests his head on my foot.

I've pushed the bed against the window, and I'm looking out at the backyard, to the edge of the woods. The moon is shining full and white above the trees.

"There's a lot of shit out there," I mutter, "isn't there."

"*There are more things in heaven and earth, Horatio, than are dreamt of in your philosophy,*" Aloysius clicks proudly. "*Shakespeare.*"

"My god, you're definitely a gay's familiar." I grunt. "I wish I could tell her a little bit. She's really freaking mad at me right now."

"I know it is difficult, to not be able to share your entire life with your loved ones. But that is why you have me."

I sit up and scratch his head. "And I'm glad to have you, but it's different. Plus, you know how into this stuff she is. She probably knows something about it."

The killer's nursery rhyme, if you can even call it that, echoes in my thoughts. *Rabbit Skins. Rabbit Skins. Here to cleanse you of your sins.*

I recall a lot of weird stories growing up. Things they tell you to scare you when you're little. Hell, things *Hannah* tried to scare me with when we were little. The cat man singing in the Red River Gorge. The goat man under the bridge. The hook-handed man in the park. But a rabbit man is news to me.

"You aren't suggesting you break coven code and tell her?" Aloysius presses his paw into my foot. *"You were told in no uncertain terms—"*

"Are you my familiar, or my conscience?"

"Both, as a matter of fact!"

I pull my foot from under him and get off the bed. "Well, no one in the coven has a relative's life at stake. I can't just lie here and 'not dwell on it.'"

I leave the room, shutting the door behind me so Aloysius can't follow me out.

"Foul play!" he calls from inside the room. *"Let me out!"*

I follow the screams of Ozzy Osbourne down the hall to Hannah's door, and I have to pound it before she can hear me.

"Who dares disturb my worship?!" she yells.

I push the door open and find her lying on her purple-and-black bedspread, limbs splayed like she's making snow angels. Her eyes are puffed and red, her cheeks a little wet. I've never known Hannah to cry.

"The hell do you want?"

"I need to talk to you!" I shout back.

"What?"

"TURN IT DOWN!"

She shuts the speaker off just as I scream.

"Jesus, does your mom not care about hearing her own thoughts?"

"Not anymore," she says coolly. "What do you want? Come to gloat about being the skinny boner prince of the land of Lalaloopsy?"

"*Skin* and *bone*, and no."

"What then?"

I have to be careful with what I tell her, and how I go about it. If I tell her everything, the Reds will know somehow. And they are right about one thing: a murder investigation hangs in the balance.

"A name came up today." I settle on. "And I know you know a lot of freaky stuff from the area."

Hannah nods like a flattered mob boss. "If *Ghost Adventures* would take my calls, we'd be a very famous town."

I link my index fingers together and try to sound casual. "Well, given everything that's happening, I'm developing an interest in serial killers."

"Ah!" Hannah looks delighted as she sits up and crisscrosses her legs. "You've come to just the right place, dear boy. Who would you like to hear about first? Jeffrey Dahmer? Night Stalker? Ted Cruz?"

"I was thinking about one called Rabbit Skins."

For a moment, Hannah is quiet. "Why would he come up?"

"Just a name-drop." *You liar.* "But still. It's an interesting name."

Hannah folds her arms and twists her lips back and forth in thought. "He's Jasper Hollow's very own serial killer. But like, back in the early 1900s or something. He killed like three or four people."

"Okay," I say. "But who *is* he."

"I think I know why he came up." She pulls out her phone and starts clicking.

A minute later she's thrusting the screen under my chin. I look down at a website for locating graves.

"What's this?" I take the phone, my stomach flipping at what I see. I'm staring at the Tell No Tales Tree, next to an aged and familiar headstone marked Charles Frederick. "You don't mean—"

Hannah grunts to cut me off. "You and Grant had your 'girls have cooties' time or whatever there, right? That's his grave, believe it or not."

"So, this Charles guy…" I fumble for words.

"Is Rabbit Skins," Hannah says.

My hands tremble and I almost drop Hannah's phone. My mind flashes to the remnants of our thumbprints. Our secrets, sealed with blood. I remember it raining when we did that. Droplets washing down into the soil.

The ghost will rise and kill whoever breaks the pact.

My heart skips a beat and I have to sit down. Am I next?

You didn't answer the phone.

"What's wrong with you?" Hannah comes to me and tries to grab my shoulders, but I pull away from her grasp.

"I have to find him," I say.

Hannah shakes her head. "He's six feet under, unless a freak robbed his grave and sold him for parts on the black market.”

I pick the phone back up and type *Rabbit Skins* into the search bar, but all I get is the same vague information over and over again. Serial killer, four estimated victims (five in some results), and a fur mask.

“So much for the Information Age.” I set the phone back down.

“I read all about him at the library,” says Hannah. “They have a shit ton of old newspapers, and when I was, like, ten I followed the case after school while Mom was working and Grant was playing soccer. I don’t remember most of it, but it’s probably still there.”

“I need it.”

Hannah gasps and her eyes light up, like a light bulb has suddenly flipped on. Shit, she’s figured it out. Now the Reds *will* make pink milkshakes with my brains.

“You don’t think we have a copycat, do you?”

I sigh. “I don’t know, okay?”

“I knew it!” Hannah’s voice gets tight. “This has to do with Grant, and you aren’t telling me a damn thing. Holier-than-thou witch shit.”

“I’d tell you everything if I could,” I say as sincerely as I can. Hannah just raises an eyebrow. “But I’m kind of at the mercy of a demon man living in the netherworld of our bathtub and his army of Polly Pockets, remember?”

“Or do you think he’s come back from the dead?” Hannah’s eyes light up again. I stay silent and widen my eyes to secretly confirm. She gasps and fights a grin. “Oh, shit! A killer zombie ghost is stalking the streets, and you’re going full *Ghostbusters* on his pervy ass!”

“I’m not busting anyone’s pervy ass.”

“So, you’re a bottom.” Hannah nods. “I wanted to ask, but I wasn’t going to force it out of you.”

I gag. “Oh my god! No! Just no. I mean—Jesus H., I don’t know yet. Back to the point, I need information on the rabbit man. Can your mom help me get that?”

“Help you get what?”

We turn to the door to see Aunt Bella holding a steaming purple mug. She darts her eyes between us. Moms always do that when they want you to think they’re on to you.

Hannah folds her arms. “Oh, you’re speaking to me again.”

Aunt Bella raises her eyebrows and holds the mug out to Hannah. “For now. I brought hot chocolate as a peace offering. It’s a triple.”

Hannah takes the mug and nods like the mob boss again. “Your tribute is accepted.”

Mom slides around Aunt Bella, carrying a teal mug.

"Do I get hot chocolate, too?" I ask.

With a subtle shake of her head, Mom holds the mug out. "No, it's to help you get some sleep after these past few days."

I take the mug and look in it, expecting to see melted chocolate. What I'm looking at, however, is a gray liquid with flecks of purple floating in it. "Um." I try to give Mom the mug back. "I'm full but thank you."

"Drink."

I take a tiny sip, and drool immediately pools onto my tongue. It tastes like white chocolate, peanut butter, and oh—is that caramel?

"What do you need help with?" Aunt Bella looks at me and Hannah.

"Some old newspapers from the library," says Hannah. "Reading material."

"What kind of material?"

Hannah starts to respond, but whatever it is I'm drinking fully relaxes my shoulders, and I feel my censor cut off. "Serial killers."

Mom and Aunt Bella both raise their eyebrows, and for a second I think I'm having double vision. I blink.

"This wouldn't have anything to do with what you saw out there, would it?" Mom asks.

I take another little sip. "See, I can withhold important information, too."

"Dane Yuletide."

"Ha-*ppy* holidays!" I take another sip.

Aunt Bella moves over to the bed and sits on Hannah's other side. "Honey, I don't think it's wise to expose you to any more death. It's just going to mess with your mind right now."

Mom comes over and sits on my free side as I lap up the white-chocolate-caramel-peanut-butter heaven in my mug. "What did you learn?" she whispers.

"That you're a liar," I giggle. "Just like me."

She takes the mug from me. "You've had enough."

"Mom!" Hannah stands, snapping my attention to her. "Dane has a mission."

Aunt Bella stands. "I can't give you the information, even if I wanted to. We gave those articles away years ago."

"Who has 'em?" I slur.

"The city," says Aunt Bella. "Something about historical preservation, I don't know. Probably so they can hide their cover-ups easier. But it's not like you could just walk in and ask for it, so I would forget the whole thing. Ada can get them if the coven needs them."

"This isn't fair," Hannah scoffs. "Serial killers are my comfort and joy. You can't take them from me."

"I would rather you focus on your cooking hobby." Aunt Bella heads out of the room.

Mom nudges my shoulder. "Bedtime."

I rub my eyes with my fists. "I can't sleep. My planet needs me."

Hannah, meanwhile, stares daggers at me. "Too bad we don't know *someone* linked to the courthouse."

A light bulb brightens in my head, and I nod to her as Mom forces me to stand and leads me from the room.

"How was that peanut butter so peanutty?" I bump into the walls of the hallway.

Mom sounds like she takes great pleasure in telling me, "That wasn't peanut butter. It was dried eye of possum."

"Hold on"—I gag—"I gotta go puke."

Mom pushes open the door to the guest room and Aloysius immediately runs to me. "Bed."

She closes the door behind me.

"*Dane,*" Aloysius clicks, "*I have quite a large bone to pick with you. You mustn't lock me in here.*"

"Shh," I fumble for my phone in the dark. "I gotta see a man about a ghost."

I fall back on the bed, typing furiously on my phone screen. I click Send and set the phone down.

"Shit!" I sit up, grab the phone, and furiously go into my messages to reread what I just sent to EJ in his Instagram DMs, hoping to god I imagined it.

You top or bottom?

I scream with my mouth shut, and my face feels like it's going to burst into flames. I rush to type out an explanation, but the dried eye of possum kicks in completely, and my eyes droop shut.

13

IN WHICH THEY FIND MY HIDDEN BODY

NOPE. Then, **That was meant for my friend.** And then, **Laugh emoji, laugh emoji, peach.** And then, **The peach was a typo,** followed by my phone number.

I sent all of this to EJ this morning, the second I woke up from my peanut-butter-impostor potion. It's now almost two and he hasn't responded. I can't even excuse him in my mind because there is no school this week and no way would Hallow Bean be that busy, if he's even working.

Smooth, D-Frizzle. Just smooth.

"What's so fascinating?" Chloe leans over and I shut my screen off and slip the phone into the pocket of my gym shorts before she can read anything.

"Mindless scrolling," I lie. "Hands dropping a potato, and it's magically diced. Political rants. Recommendations for a pet spa. America's favorite pastime, baby."

"You're acting weird," she says. "But like, beyond your usual."

"Thanks."

Chloe breaks out a grin and pulls her hands up to her chest like a demented meerkat. "Boy trouble?"

Elena, who has been scrolling through men's hairstyle after hairstyle, graces me with a cocked eyebrow. "Whatever she advises, do the opposite."

Madelaine stops pawing the shirts on the rack and eyes me.

I shake my head. "No boys, no trouble."

"Now *that* I can get behind." Elena nods to me with respect and Madelaine, thankfully, turns back to the clothes.

I'd been trying to focus on schoolwork, and failing, when they pulled up. Hannah, who'd been watching some true crime show or other, saw them first and alerted me of their arrival by shouting "The bitches are coming! The bitches are coming!" like Paul Revere before proceeding to shove the couch in front of the door.

I didn't even fight them this time. What's the point? I wish Aloysius had been awake when they came, though. He'd at least have some advice about the EJ problem. But raccoons aren't allowed inside the mall.

When we'd sped past the Jasper Hollow city limits toward Lexington, I couldn't help but hope they were taking me home. Like they finally realized I'm a lost cause and gave up.

Now I'm following them like a lost dog, watching Madelaine choose my wardrobe.

"Shouldn't I be picking these?" I ask. "You don't even know my size."

Chloe laughs. "That's the first thing about you that I read."

"And I think you have enough gym clothes," says Madelaine, "for someone who doesn't even work out."

I stuff my hands in my hoodie pocket. "Just want to be comfortable."

"Do you realize how ridiculous you'll look in a red jacket with gym shorts? In the cold?" Madelaine starts sorting through jeans and chinos, but when she picks up a lime-green pair of men's capris, I tear them from her polished nails and toss them over my shoulder.

"Who said anything about me wearing a red jacket?" I ask.

"I'm pretty sure that was decided when we made a cyclone in your living room and you got a snazzy birthday-boy crown," Elena says.

I fold my arms. "I have no intention of singing backup for Madelaine and the Stop Signs."

"You have to wear the jacket," says Madelaine. "It's tradition. Some witches wear pointy hats. We have jackets. Red is the most visible color. It helps those from the supernatural world to identify us."

"Is it really a good idea for me to wear a target?" I ask. "What with an owl man and a rabbit man around?"

Madelaine shakes her head. "Mr. H doesn't need any help recognizing you. Now let's find a fitting room."

She whirls me around and leads me to the back of the store where an overly smiley college-aged girl assigns me to a stall at the end of the row. Elena shoves a pile of clothes into my arms and I make my way. Chloe tries to follow.

"You can't go in together," the girl chirps.

"God bless you," I say and shut myself in the stall.

I drop the heap of shirts and pants onto the little bench and make a point of not looking in the mirror while I try on the different items. I don't remember the last time—other than at the funeral—that I wore "real" pants, and the denim feels scratchy against my legs as I pull up a pair of black jeans. I pair them with a random cable knit sweater and take a deep breath, forcing myself to finally look at my reflection.

I hardly recognize who looks back, but I knew him once.

I look like I did this time last year. Long before there was a cut on my thumb to seal a pact. Before I stayed in bed for a month and had to switch to online school.

Maybe I'm a bit paler, though. A little thinner. My hair hasn't seen product in over six months.

But it's me.

Okay, maybe the Reds are good for something, because I never would have been able to put these clothes together on my own. And they make me feel good about myself, too.

That's kinda new.

"Okay, so I was fifteen," says Chloe as she emerges from a changing stall and looks at herself in the three-way mirror. "I used to hang out with my grandma after school. She'd sing songs that were big when she was my age, and we'd talk about boys."

I stop sipping my iced coffee and look up at her. "But how did you find out you were a witch?"

Chloe laughs. "Oh! My grandma died when I was seven. How do these look?"

I sit quietly and sip my drink, but neither Madelaine nor Elena say anything. When I glance back up, they're all watching me.

"Oh." I swallow my coffee. "Um. They're blue." None of them laugh. I roll my eyes. "Werk, hunty."

Chloe claps and flits back into the stall. I try to push my free hand into my hoodie out of habit, but it's gone. My poor dear gray friend now rests in peace in a food court trash can, and I'm stuck in a black jean jacket that I'm not convinced I pull off, but they all swear I do. The elbows crinkle every time I move.

"You're being a buzzkill," says Madelaine. I look up at her, confused.

"You realize we change things, right? Not just talk to ghosts and zap Igor. Okay, look."

She gestures across the store to a teen guy with perfect hair and sunglasses. He walks down the aisle like he owns the place. Guys like him always made my life hell. I become tense in spite of myself.

"Don't you just hate douches?" Madelaine asks.

"Sure, but—"

Madelaine looks at the guy and snaps her fingers.

The guy bends his elbows, bringing his hands to his armpits. He flaps his bent arms like wings and caws like a crow, jumping up and down three times. The Reds fall into fits of laughter. Elena twirls her finger, and he starts to spin around while doing the Chicken Dance.

Madelaine snaps her fingers, and he stops and straightens. Face as red as the girls' jackets, he looks around, pulls his glasses down to make sure no one saw, then walks on, a little more quickly than before.

"That was cruel!" I say through a snort.

"No." Madelaine grins. "It was fun. Imagine the revenge you could pull on people who've hurt you."

I guess it *would* feel a little safer to go to school, knowing I have the power to protect myself. I check my phone again, and picture EJ in this jacket. On a motorbike. Carrying me to freedom. Anything that blocks the memories from getting in.

"Why are you blushing?" asks Elena.

I snap the phone screen off and pocket it again. Still no response. "No reason."

"You know, I love your hair." She reaches her fingers toward my curls, but I pull back.

If someone's not making fun of my hair, they're petting it without consent. The price of boy-curls.

"Thank you."

"Can I style it for you?"

I put my hand on top of my head instinctively. I've heard that before, too. "I don't think so."

"I promise it'll look amazing."

Madelaine tosses her own hair and dips down, threatening to swat me with her coiled mane. "She did mine."

Ah, so Elena is the pixie with the magical salon. I feel like I owe Elena a little something. She did convince the cashier that my easily four-hundred-dollar clothing total was an even twenty by snapping her fingers and sliding a gift card across the counter. I kept my mouth shut when I saw the card was actually her driver's license. At least I paid *something*?

"Okay, fine," I huff. "But no new colors. No frosted tips. No mohawks. No man buns. No shaving the side of my head—"

Elena thrusts her phone screen toward me, and I gape at myself in the reverse camera view. Something changed while I was listing my rules. I grab the phone to get a closer look. The frizz is gone. Entirely. I have perfect, movie-camera-ready hair. The sides and back are trim, not balling up in little puffs of hair balls like they tend to do over the course of a day. The color is the same, but richer—a nice mahogany instead of mud.

It's just what I'd thought about in the bathtub the other night. "How did you do that?"

"Magic." Elena holds up her hands and wiggles her fingers.

"Okay, but how?" I press.

Elena sits on the floor. "Close your eyes, and just feel it. Picture it with everything you have. Don't stop until you can just barely feel those hairs tickling your brain."

I shut my eyes tight and try to feel it. I imagine thick, coarse hair, black, sticking every which way. I focus on each individual strand. My hands tingle and my heart skips a beat as whatever it is deep inside me starts to work. A flash of warm, golden light fills my vision, and the hairs bristle along my frontal cortex.

"Agh!" Elena cries out. "Stop it!"

I open my eyes and nearly fall on my back from laughing. Elena scowls at me from behind a thick curly black mustache. Madelaine can hardly breathe as she holds her phone up to take a picture, but Elena shields her face.

"No!" she shouts. "I look like my Uncle Arturo!"

Chloe comes running out of her stall. She stops and doubles over when she sees Elena. "Oh my god, you do!"

"Take it back!" Elena orders me.

I'm still laughing. "I don't know how!"

"Just think about it in reverse!" Elena's face glows red hot under the mustache. I think if she gets any madder, steam is going to shoot from her ears.

I close my eyes and try to quiet my laughter as I think about the bristles leaving the front of my brain, think of the little hairs retreating, falling off, and vanishing entirely. The warm light ignites my eyes and tingles as it works its way down, back into my gut. After a few moments, I open my eyes to see that Elena no longer has the mustache, but she's kept the scowl.

"I'm really sorry," I say, a few more chuckles escaping me.

"Do it again," Elena says, "and I'll make you bald."

"Okay, okay." I take a breath through the residual laughter. "I won't."

My phone buzzes in my pocket. I pull it out as fast as I can to see a new number lighting up the screen. I shoot to my feet and walk away. "Gotta pee."

"Mhm," says Madelaine. "Care to share with the class?"

"I can give you a beard, you know."

"I *was* a beard," she says. "It's a hairy situation."

Ducking around a clothes rack, I open the text and read:

Sorry, I was hiking again, no service. But I think the better question is, drunk or high? (This is EJ) There's a laughing emoji at the end.

I sigh with relief and smirk as I type my response:

Sleeping potion from my mom, actually. Please forget I ever asked that.

Asked what? with a winking emoji.

I type furiously before the Reds come looking for me:

Actually, I do have a real question.

Go for it.

Would you want to break the law with me tonight?

A moment of quiet. My chest tightens. Then, three dots.

I thought you'd never ask.

14

BUMPS IN THE NIGHT

"We're supposed to meet here." I zip my jean jacket to brace against the October night. "Any minute now."

I wait with Hannah and Aloysius by the side door of the old courthouse. Aloysius nods but Hannah doesn't respond. She hasn't said much to me since I got home wearing this outfit and carrying an armload of shopping bags. She told me I look like "prep central." I can't say it didn't hurt a little. But I'm not going to let it ruin how I feel.

Above us, the clock on the dome of the courthouse tolls midnight. I pull my phone out, but nothing from EJ.

Aloysius scurries back and forth like a watchdog. *"Are you certain he's coming?"*

Hannah scrunches her nose at him. "What's he saying?"

"Yes, I'm sure he's coming," I say to translate.

Headlights appear down the street and we both make a point of scrolling on our phones, as though we're just waiting for our parents to pick us up. The car slows down as it pulls past. Thankfully, it picks up speed and disappears around the corner.

"We can't stand here much longer," says Hannah. "I think that was an unmarked cop."

"Dane!" Aloysius scurries to my ankles. *"Someone is coming!"*

I step back into the shadows, pulling Hannah with me. I look at her and force a laugh to appear normal, like we're a couple of random kids who just *happen* to be loitering around the courthouse late at night. Footsteps round the building and stop.

"Is this where the party is?"

I look over and catch the silhouette of EJ, half-illuminated by the blue glow of the streetlights, and try to ignore the instant flutter in my stomach.

"Yes," I say. "Welcome to my heist."

"If we get caught, I'm telling them you kidnapped me."

Hannah leans against the wall of the courthouse, eyeing us suspiciously. "What's going on here?"

"You pointed out we need someone with access to this place," I explain. "So naturally, I asked EJ to break into the courthouse and get those newspapers for me."

Hannah widens her eyes. "Dane, I was kidding! You can't just break into government buildings, I don't care *how* fun it's going to be to drive the getaway car."

"*For* you?" EJ knits his eyebrows at me. "Who said I'm doing it *for* you?"

I fumble for a response. "But you said—"

"I'm not doing it alone." EJ pulls a key from his pocket, dangling it so that it catches the light. "Let's go, Godfather, before my aunt realizes her key has been switched with a Yoshi mini-ornament."

Hannah grabs my wrist, gently pulling me back. "I talk a lot of talk, but come on, Dane. This is too far. We're talking jail time and criminal records."

"I know." I pull my wrist away. "But they have the information I need! Besides, this was partially your idea, and I thought you wanted to be included."

"I do." Hannah darts her eyes between me, EJ, and the door, her lips twisted as she considers. Finally, she tosses her hands up. "Fine, let's do it. But you owe me so much after this."

"Hold on, we can't *all* go," I say. "Too risky."

With a shrug, Hannah reaches for the key. "Looks like you're the lookout, EJ."

I feel myself blush. "He knows the layout, though, and can lie his way out of it more easily if we get caught."

"My aunt is putty in my tragic orphan hands." EJ winks. He *winks* at me.

Hannah bites her lip, and I can tell she's pissed off now by the way her breathing has gotten louder. "All right then. What do I even do?"

"Be a lookout," I say, trying to punch the word so that it sounds like the best job ever. "If you see anyone coming, send a signal to Aloysius."

"*And I'll call to* you." Aloysius stands on his hind legs and places a paw over his heart, like a tiny hero.

"And you," EJ locks eyes with me, "be stealthy. You aren't the most discreet witch I've ever met."

"McScuse me?" I scowl.

EJ cringes. "Did you just say 'McScuse me'?"

Hannah laughs. "Okay, I like you."

Me too, I let myself think, but quickly lock the thought down into my emotional vault.

EJ pulls the door open. It creaks loudly and I cringe, checking around me to make sure no one is watching, but the streets are deserted.

Holding the door open, EJ bows. "After you."

I hold my head high in an attempt to hide my nerves as I pass EJ and cross the threshold. The light that briefly flowed into the darkened courthouse is sliced into oblivion as EJ follows, the door shutting behind him. Just us, the darkness, and the smell of polished wood.

"Are you sure this'll be okay?" I ask, my courage gone. It sounded so simple when I was texting him earlier. Sneak into a government building, get information on Rabbit Skins, leave, find Grant. As though I were just stopping by the dollar store for movie-night snacks. "I don't want this on my record."

"You have a record?"

"Well," I force a smirk, "I *did* anchor the school news, so I'm pretty famous."

"That's not a record, that's a résumé bullet point for your first fast-food job." EJ walks past me in the darkness. "This way, please. Keep your hands and feet inside the tram at all times, and no flash photography."

EJ leads me toward a narrow door on the left, our footsteps echoing against the marbled floor. A red Exit sign glows ahead, casting the hall in blood-colored light. I allow my fingertips to brush along the walls. One thousand old conversations jaunt through my mind.

"What has this city come to—"

"I'm tellin' ya, ain't got nut' agin'—"

"Man, screw jury duty."

I wonder if Rabbit Skins himself ever walked through here. Or Mr. Hawthorne.

EJ pulls open the narrow door. I squint through the red dark to see that it's a small, old-fashioned elevator with an accordion fence. Pulling it back, he rattles it into place.

"Going down?" EJ asks and flicks on an aged yellow light bulb that hangs from the cage's ceiling.

It's tiny, barely enough room for two people. Also, it looks like it hasn't been used for thirty years, and I don't fancy the idea of plummeting to my death in front of the only cute boy that's ever bothered to learn my name.

"That is a creepy-ass elevator," I spit out. "Can't we just take the stairs?"

"I mean, we could." EJ shrugs. "But they're worse."

With an I-don't-care-either-way roll of my eyes, I step inside. EJ squeezes in next to me, and I try not to stiffen up as his shoulder brushes firmly against mine in the tight space.

I'm trying to remember if I put on deodorant when his scent fills my nostrils. Oh god, what *is* his bodywash? It's springtime, and May breezes, and making out near an open window, and soft, clean laundry, and—I force myself to stop inhaling. Now, if Jasper Hollow smelled like *this*, I'd have always lived here.

EJ looks me over as he pulls the door shut. "That a new outfit?"

"I ran out of sweats," I say.

He pushes the lowest button, and it glows a garish orange. The entire elevator rattles. EJ side-eyes me, his eyebrows drawn together. "Uh, you okay?"

"Yeah. Why?"

He points at the narrow space between us, and I see now that I've grabbed the hem of his jacket.

"Oh my god." I let go, the fabric slipping between my thumb and forefinger. Fire scorches my cheeks. Oh, that I could burst into flames right now. "I am so sorry. I don't know why I did that."

EJ chuckles, shaking his head. "You're totally fine."

I kind of want to do it again, but I'm *not* about to tell him that.

The elevator finally begins its descent, slowly, until at last it stops with a rattle. An unseen bell dings, but the door doesn't open.

"Holy shit!" My breath picks up speed. "We're trapped!"

EJ reaches his arm across me and pushes at the bars on my side. I slowly look to him, where his eyes have already met mine. "You open it yourself."

My face boils red as I sling back the gate and push open the door, stepping into the darkness of the basement. "We're taking the stairs back up."

"Aye-aye." EJ follows me out and slides a hand along the wall, until finally he flips a switch.

Fluorescent bulbs flicker in and out above us. Tall shelves run in rows down the long concrete room, each one filled with boxes and the spines of scrapbooks.

EJ heads toward the far end. "The stuff we want would be at the back."

I amble along, folding my arms. It's a lot colder down here, and the sound of dripping pipes make it decidedly creepier. A chill breaks through me. I step over a fat cockroach and continue on.

"How do you know where it is?" I call to EJ.

"Because I know things," he calls back. "I'm smart like that."

"Fine," I pick up speed as he rounds the corner of a shelf. "But how do you know *these* things?"

"My aunt might be able to keep things from the town, but she has a helluva time keeping them from me."

I turn the corner. EJ scans over the highest shelves.

"So, guessing you live with her, then?" I dare to ask.

"Yeah." His voice drops in volume. "My parents died in a wreck when I was twelve."

"Sorry."

EJ shrugs. "I'm okay. So, you? Staying with your aunt, I mean?"

"For now." I shrug. "While everything that's going on...goes on. Mom's worked from home since I was ten, and I've been doing online school, so, we're just wherever I guess."

"Where's your dad?"

Now *I'm* the one scanning the shelves, though I can still feel his eyes watching me. "All I know is that his name is Luke, and that he lives in New York State now. When Mom left the Hollow with me, he left too, but in the other direction. Apparently, I have his hair."

I suddenly realize that he probably left because of the whole witch thing.

"Oh, that sucks."

"Eh, he was probably a dick," I say. "He got Mom to have me in his Laundromat."

I risk a glance at EJ. He raises an eyebrow. "A Laundromat?"

"Yeah. Here in town, actually. Probably didn't want to risk any magic shit at the hospital. Messed up, right?"

The left side of his mouth tilts in a sympathetic smile and he sighs. "Yeah, that's messed up. Sorry to hear that."

I turn back to the shelves. "Eh, I don't remember it."

EJ knocks on the wood of the shelf and walks. "Not here. Must be on the other side."

He turns the corner and I follow.

"So, guessing you don't have a lot of vacation plans if you're bored enough to break and enter with me." I fish some more as EJ climbs a shelf.

"I'm bad at making friends," he grunts, pulling a thick leather volume from its perch on the top shelf.

"Same! Not that it's been stopping me. And...I guess you're out of girls to date in school, too?"

He squints down at me. "No. Actually, I'm out of boys to date."

Oh... *Oh!*

"Catch!" He drops the volume, and it lands at my feet.

I stare up at him with a neutral face. "I don't catch."

EJ lets out an amused chuckle and climbs down. I kneel and grab the book, turning it to look at the spine. The title is *Women in Terrible Cahoots Here.*

I snort. "That's the best fake title they could come up with? What'll they call it now that I'm here? *Homos and Hexes?*"

"That could be the title of your memoir."

"The title of my memoir will be *Dane: The Man. The Mystery. The Bottomless Queso Dip.*"

I crack open the spine and sit on the floor. The first page shows the sketch of a woman, and I recognize her immediately as Tabitha Collingwood. There's a snippet of a diary entry written by her husband Lester. He suspects her of having an affair in their smokehouse and vows to find out. The next page is an account of how he was found dead, slashed by a suspected antiabolitionist.

I flip through the pages, coming across a crinkled and faded photograph of women in hoopskirts and veils who stare expressionlessly at some unseen corner of the room. A note scribbled on the bottom details that the veils were red.

Turning the page, I stop at a newspaper article from 1915. The story tells of a wild dog wandering into the town one night. Apparently, the thing was massive and rabid, and attacked citizens. It was shot down by a young woman named Rebecca Wednesday. The article also notes she was in a fashionable red hat.

"Madelaine's ancestor?" I point at the photograph.

She's beautiful, even by today's standards, with large dark eyes and lips in a perfect bow. I reread the part about the dog, where the journalist describes its wolfish appearance and muses that wolves don't tend to live around this state, and something clicks. The Wednesday women seem to have a habit of dealing with werewolves.

I remember Madelaine's worry that the killer would be a Code Silver. She'd seemed so concerned, and then Ada was so comforting. I remember her talking about her brother.

"Did you know Madelaine has a brother somewhere?" I ask offhandedly.

"Mhm," is all EJ says.

I flip farther through the book. When I hit a page toward the back, I almost drop it and crawl out of my skin. A sketch of a rabbit head, with the body of a man, stares back at me.

The headline above it says, in three-inch type, "Rabbit Skins Evades Capture."

I peer at the article, my hands trembling.

10 May. 1901.

The body of Miss Emily Black, aged sixteen, was discovered in the early hours of 9 May by Earl Townsend along Elgin Creek. This is the second killing by the alleged murderer, the first being fourteen-year-old Zeke Adler. The victim's face was partially removed, making identification difficult. A rabbit paw was left on the corpse of the victim, the calling card of the killer, who the town has come to know as Rabbit Skins, after a brief sighting of the masked man by seventy-year-old Martha Duncan. A note, scribbled in crude script, was left in the hand of the victim.

Below is a photograph of the note, and a chill sweeps up my spine as I squint to make out the words.

I need them fresh.

On the next page, there's an article about the victim named Zeke, who was found in the woods two weeks before. He was also missing half of his face and held a similar note.

"He's a maniac," I whisper, turning the page furiously. "Here's another one."

"Read it to me," says EJ.

I suck in a breath, my heart quickening as I hold the paper to the light.

"'Rabbit Trails Lead to the Woods.' The police feel confident that the capture of Rabbit Skins is imminent. The man who has terrorized our Hollow for nearly two months has left a bloody trail into the woods, following the abduction of fifteen-year-old Thomas Emmerson..."

"What happened?" EJ asks.

I'm about to turn the page again when I hear a furious clicking in my inner ear. I jump to my feet.

"Aloysius is contacting me," I say. "I think someone's coming."

"Shit." EJ pushes himself up. "Hide that!"

He points to the scrapbook in my hands, and I shove it under my jacket. We bolt from the stacks, and EJ runs toward the far corner opposite the elevator. I follow, but knock into him as he stops abruptly.

"They're on the stairs." He turns and pushes his hands against my shoulders. "Go back to where we were!"

I do as he says, and he runs back to the other end of the room. I kneel against one of the shelves, and the entire room goes black. EJ cut off the lights.

My heart hammers in my chest, and I breathe as quietly as I can, listening to the dripping of the pipes above me.

A hand grabs my shoulder and I startle.

"Shh!" EJ whispers. "Just me."

"Oh my god."

He breathes out. I can sense his face near mine. That soapy, fresh smell. "Gotta love adrenaline."

"Tell me again why you agreed to this?" I lean in a little and drop my voice even lower, the footsteps growing louder as they come down the stairs.

"I thought it was obvious," he whispers, and his knuckles brush the back of my hand.

Before I let myself think twice, I turn my wrist and lace my fingers between his. He returns the contact, folding his fingers around mine. I shouldn't be focused on this right now. We're about to get caught. But this is the first time I've held another boy's hand. Ever.

And it feels so right.

God, I want to kiss him. I want to kiss him so freakin' badly, but that would be weird. You're not supposed to make out when someone's about to catch you breaking the law, correct?

We wait in the dark, but nothing makes a sound. No one comes into the basement.

"I guess it was a false alarm," EJ sighs, pulling out his phone and tapping the flashlight on. "Shall we?"

My hands nearly burst into flames and my heart climbs into my throat.

In the blue light of EJ's phone, Rabbit Skins stands. He raises a decomposed hand as though to wave, but the light glints against metal and I squint. He's waving a knife between us, as though deciding who to kill first. My heart feels like it's stopped in time, no blood moving through me as sweat breaks out and rushes down my head, leaving my face wet and cold.

"Run!" EJ screams, but he falls against the shelf when Rabbit Skins thrusts a palm toward him.

I reach for EJ's hand, but freeze mid-way, unable to move anymore. Hands outstretched, I stand like a statue in the dark basement. Why won't my arms move? I push every muscle in my body to keep myself moving, but I have no control over them. I can't move. Why can't I—

Ahead of me, Rabbit Skins stands with one hand, the one holding a knife, out toward me, as though he's keeping me here. He's not even touching me. How can—

My heart turns to ice in my chest as I remember Grant's memories, preserved in the cell phone. This man killed those three other boys. Slammed them against the trees, and he didn't touch them then, either.

I can blink at least. And I blink over and over, my brain forging connections and filling in blanks. Rabbit Skins is—was—just like me. Charles Frederick was a *witch*.

15

VANDAL

My brain feels like it's going to melt from my skull.

Rabbit Skins takes EJ by the ear. EJ, who also seems to be frozen and can't fight against the killer, flashes his wild blue eyes between me and the ghost.

Oh, hell no. This is the closest I've ever come to first base with a boy. A demon witch-ghost is *not* ruining this for me.

My body burns, grilling itself with flames that want to—*need* to—come out. My muscles shake, my bones rattle, and within my right fist, between my tightly coiled fingers, smoke rises.

So, this man was—*is*—a witch, and clearly a bad one. My arms burn even hotter at just the thought that me and this monster have something in common. But if Hawthorne's reaction to my power is any clue, Rabbit Skins is about to find out just how wicked *I* might be.

My thumb twitches, and then my index finger. Onward, one at a time, the fingers become loose, letting go of plume after plume of hot, thick smoke. Tiny orange flames ignite from my fingerprints.

I blink and my vision goes red for a moment, like I'm seeing the world through a colored gel, then the flames take over.

Fire pours from my hands, lighting them entirely, but my skin doesn't broil. Unfrozen, I lift my arms, heaving the air that sizzles in my lugs. EJ's terrified eyes land on me as I step toward him and the killer, my head low. All of my instincts say, *"Kill. Kill. Kill."*

The flames climb higher from my hands, setting off the fire alarm. The sprinklers rain down on my head, exhausting the flames, leaving only steam in their wake. The fire alarm screeches and the lights of the basement flip on. Rabbit Skins vanishes in the same instant.

It's as though he was never here.

"Dane?"

I force myself to meet EJ's gaze. His eyes bore into me, glancing between me and my hands. He looks terrified, his bottom lip quivering.

"What are you?"

"Clearly you already know."

Metal clangs by the stairs and my eyes fall through the rain of the sprinklers and on Sheriff Doyle. Over the screams of the alarm, he shouts, "Hands where I can see them, boys!"

After narrowly escaping an undead serial killer hell-bent on carving me up like a jack-o'-lantern, getting arrested isn't so scary. Still, these handcuffs holding me to the chair are tight, and my right wrist does not appreciate it. Despite being soaked and shivering, my body tingles with fire while something dark ebbs its way through my stomach.

Doyle peers at me from across his desk, arms folded, with a smug expression. I slide my eyes left, to EJ, who won't stop bouncing his leg anxiously, and then to Hannah, who's still staring at me with narrowed eyes and twisted lips, silently telling me, "I freakin' told you so."

"So, who's gonna talk first?" Doyle lazily swivels left and right in his chair. "Or do I need to throw you in jail for the night?"

"I'm pretty sure that would be illegal," I say tiredly, not in the mood for this adventure anymore. My arms *really* want to melt these handcuffs. "Considering we're minors, and you have yet to call our parents, or tell us exactly what you want us to talk about."

"Stay silent," Hannah whispers. "That's our only loophole."

Doyle stands so fast that I think he's going to lunge across the desk. I lean back as his face thrusts toward me. "You got a hell of a lot of nerve, kid. First you break in, then you act like I came in here and snatched you out of bed. Definitely Robyn's boy."

I tilt my head and focus on his forehead. *"Curly headed punk bitch. Looks like his sorry excuse of a—"*

He points a finger at me. "If you don't stay out of my head, I'll tase you."

Hannah reaches a cuffed hand into her pocket and pulls out her cell phone, frantically swiping for the camera. "Yeah, I'll bet that's *exactly* what Jasper Hollow wants to be known for once that hits social."

Doyle swivels his stare to her. "Use that phone, I don't give a damn, because I ain't going to do anything. Ever hear of getting scared straight?"

"That won't work on Dane."

EJ snorts. At least it's *something*. He hasn't said one word to me, just glanced at me every now and then with a look I've seen before. I saw it on Grant's face in April. He's seen my flames and he's afraid of me.

He's afraid of the bad witch.

Doyle sighs. "Let's try this again. Just what were you doin' in the basement?"

I need to think, and fast. Having a record before I even get a driver's license is no way to start out in life, and Mom is already going to kill me, whether she has to wait a prison sentence or not. "I was getting witch records for Ada."

Doyle cocks his head. "Oh, that so?"

"Yes," I say, staring at his badge in lieu of eye contact. "We needed the backstory on a town legend. Rabbit Skins."

"Oh, I know," says the sheriff. "That's what she told me when we talked earlier."

I dare to look him in the eye. "Oh, you talked to her?"

Doyle nods. "I was going to get them to her tomorrow. But I'm enjoying that hole you're digging, so carry on."

I roll my eyes to the ceiling. "No, I think that's all I had, sir."

To my surprise, the sheriff chuckles. "You act just like your mom. Used to drag me into trouble all the time and half-ass her way out of it."

I can build on this. "Yep, runs in the family, I guess. So, you understand. Well, I suppose we'll all have a good laugh about this someday. If you could just undo these handcuffs, we'll—"

Doyle shakes his head. "No sir. And I *did* call your parents. They're on the way."

EJ's eyes bug out. "You mean you—"

Doyle looks at him like he's a mouse, and he can't wait to spring the trap and snap his neck. "Called her first, buddy boy."

A grumble falls from EJ's mouth as Doyle leans back in the chair, satisfied. "While we're all waiting, I'd like to ask you a couple of questions."

Hannah looks left and right. "Do you see my lawyer present?"

"They fall out of regular jurisdiction." Doyle looks to me. "So, why're you three vandalizing the old graveyard?"

I look at Hannah, then to EJ, but both of them look back at me with the same confused expression. "Er, what?"

Doyle reaches for his phone and thumbs through it a minute before sliding it across the desk. "I just came from the old graveyard before I got the report on Miss Allen loitering outside. Care to explain it?"

The three of us look forward and down at the screen. It's a blurred picture taken at night, but the flash reveals the Tell No Tales Tree. I stiffen. "What about it?"

Doyle presses his thumb and forefinger to the picture and zooms in. An upside-down star is carved deep into the bark. "See it now?"

"Yeah. I see it. But I don't know what it is."

Doyle scans my face, then Hannah's. Finally, he turns his attention to EJ. "Where were *you* before you came here?"

"At home!" EJ's eyes are bugged. "Seriously. Aunt Bridget saw me before I left. It would've been ten minutes to midnight. I told her I was going to Walmart."

"And he did come right after midnight," I say, but more to myself. I hate that for a split second even I suspected him, but I'm so confused about what I'm looking at. That's Grant's and my tree. Someone's messing with our spot. It's too eerie to be a coincidence.

"I'll stop this right now," Hannah half-shouts, and I jump at her sudden volume. "I don't fuck with that shit."

"Language," says Doyle.

"I don't mess with that stuff. I read tarot and I play with a Ouija board sometimes, but I stay away from the dark things."

Nodding, I say, "And I—"

"No need," Doyle raises his hand. "Ada's already cleared the coven. She wasn't sure about it, either. No, I think a nonwitch did this. Somebody's messing with things they don't understand, and now we've got four dead boys."

Silence fills the space between my ears. "Do you think whoever did this is behind the ghost of Rabbit Skins coming back?"

"That's why I gotta know who it is," says Doyle. "We *adults* who *handle these things* have a few questions for them."

THE HOLLOW: LUCKY CHARMS

They'd sealed the secret with blood. Now the ghost has him.

Grant's mind bobs in and out, coming and going between memories and the present, neither of which he wants around. His eyes squeeze tighter, but the memory only becomes more vivid.

A technicolor Dane stands with a pricked thumb before a headstone in the old cemetery.

"It's done," he says. "The ghost will rise and kill whoever breaks the pact."

"I won't tell anyone," Grant replies. "What about Hannah?"

"I'll tell her when I'm ready."

A drop of rain hits the Easter lilies growing around the headstone. Easter lilies make Grant think of that stupid bunny song.

"There is this one guy," Dane says, his face blushing red, "in my class."

"Oh?"

"Jordan. But that's not going anywhere."

"Maybe he's hoping you're—"

"No."

"No offense, dude, but like, I'm not surprised or anything. You aren't very dude-ish."

"Shut up."

They stand while sporadic raindrops become spring drizzle, but it doesn't wash the blood off the headstone. It only waters the Easter lilies.

Hippity-hoppity. Hippity-hoppity.

Grant mumbles a few of the song lyrics, his raw voice breaking on the quiet notes. The scorching throbs in his head keep time with the music.

Grant's eyes open and he's alone in that rotted room. The long table is hard beneath his back. He's lain here for so long. His foot throbs and pulses, hanging just over the edge. *What day is this?*

He's lost track.

Turning his stiff neck, Grant looks to the door, left ajar.

He lies silent and listens for Rabbit Skins somewhere in the cabin. Lurking and waiting for Grant to try to run again.

Hippity-hoppity. Down the bunny trail.

Grant pushes himself onto his elbows, and his head instantly begs for him to lie back down. He's barely able to swing his good leg off the table and slide his weight onto it.

He stares at the door and hesitates.

All is quiet. Grant hobbles forward, holding his arms out for balance as he reaches for the doorknob to hold him up. He lets out a grunt as he topples forward, grips the doorframe, and tries with everything to hold himself upright.

The main room of the cabin isn't the same as it was last time. It's been decorated.

Grant's stomach heaves as he looks at the ceiling.

Body parts hang by strings, dangling above Grant like tinsel. Hands, fingers, ears, feet. Pools of blood have dried across the floor of the room where they've dripped, staining the amber-colored wood. On a table near the wood-burning stove, there's skin and stitches and Grant doesn't need to look further to know that they are faces, made into masks.

They must be pieces of those guys in the woods. The burnouts. Little trophies of his victims. They died quick. But Rabbit Skins seems to want Grant to go slow.

Pushing himself off the frame, Grant hops to the front door. He turns the knob and pulls as hard as he can. It won't open. He'll have to break the lock.

He scans the room for tools, but all he sees are that greasy skillet and needles threaded with black string. No sign of the dull axe.

Grant turns back to the door, lets his forehead fall against it in defeat.

Raspy breaths mere feet behind him tell Grant he is not alone. He whirls, ready to attack his kidnapper, to find Rabbit Skins' face inches from his own. Grant raises his fists to fight, but they freeze mid strike.

"What the—"

Rabbit Skins' hand covers Grant's face, and he squeezes, as though feeling a melon for ripeness.

"Mustn't," he rasps. "Not ready."
He escorts Grant back to his room.
Run! Grant thinks. *Turn and run! Why can't I—*
With Grant tucked away in the room, Rabbit Skins shuts the door.
Hippity-hoppity. Hippity-hoppity.

16

SPELL THE T, HONEY

When I'm pulled off the fuzzy sofa by Madelaine and told I can't tell Hannah what I'm about to learn, I add it to the pile of crap I have to sit with and hope no one notices as I slide my phone out of my pocket and check for texts. Nothing.

Great. EJ probably won't want to talk to me anymore after last night. His aunt's probably already killed him and stuffed his body in a crawl space with lime slices. I need to apologize, and thoroughly—that is, if he'll even talk to me after what he saw. He looked so afraid of me. Like I'm some sort of supervillain that can zap him into a pile of debris.

Once again, I've been stolen from my schoolwork on this fine afternoon and brought to Collingwood Hall for what Madelaine calls "Red School." I'm guessing this is where we'll rehearse darting our eyes in unison like possessed do.

Ada descends the stairs in a technicolor rainbow of a robe that makes her look like Joseph and his technicolor dreamcoat. There's a thick old book in her hands, and when she reaches the bottom of the stairs, she tosses it to the far end of the room where Chloe just happens to be standing.

Chloe ducks and narrowly misses the hit. "What did *I* do?"

Pacing back and forth, Ada swishes her robe. "There is a page ripped out of that book! A spell that I need. A spell we *all* need. And it's gone! *Rip!* Which one of you did it?"

"Maybe you rolled a joint with it and forgot," Madelaine says. "Might have been when you picked that outfit." Ada glares at her and Madelaine sits on the couch, crossing her legs like a docile schoolgirl. "I'm joking. God."

Chloe holds up her hands in surrender. "Don't look at me! I only steal gum and dates!"

Ada looks at Elena, who folds her arms and stares back at Ada as if to say, "I dare you."

Ada turns to me.

"I only steal hearts." I bat my eyelashes and ignore the Reds' snorting. I mentally slap the memory of EJ's hand in mine out of my head and reinforce the inner wall I've been building to keep them from hearing my thoughts.

"*And* government documents," she notes.

I do my Muppet move. "I'm *sorry!*"

Life's been a hellscape since last night. First, I got yelled at by Mom, and then by Ada. I'm grounded until I'm old enough to need dentures, except for Reds-related business. Hannah isn't allowed to drive anywhere, and I heard her scream her head off this morning when she discovered the new parental control on Netflix. You can feel as bad as you want and say sorry as much as you want, but adults still *love* to watch you suffer.

Finally, Ada sighs and waves her hands. "Fine. Well, if anyone sees a random page with an ancient spell just *blowing* around, please let me know! In the meantime, we must practice control!"

"Wait what?" my heartbeat picks up speed.

Aloysius scampers down the stairs, licking his lips, the cats following. *"She gave me the most wonderful snack!"* He pokes at my shoe. *"Do you think your mother could run to the market and fetch something called an 'Os-car May-er Bologna'?"*

I quiet him with a headshake. The memory of Rabbit Skins freezing me in place, of feeling every muscle unable to move, of watching EJ barely able to even panic, replays in my mind and sends a chill down my spine. "I don't know if I'm up for that, to be honest. Can I just sit this one out?"

"Sorry, but no dice. It's necessary for your own protection." Ada breezes to the record player. "Line up, ladies. And male. Across from your familiars."

"This is pointless," Elena says as she drags her feet to the middle of the floor, Caesar taking his place across from her. "I don't have to practice this. I'm the best at it."

Madelaine tosses her hair over her shoulder and stands next to her, scooting Ambrose into place. "For now."

The record player crackles on and silences us. The lead singer of the Smiths informs us he is the son and heir of nothing in particular.

Ada slowly lifts her hands, like a bad symphony conductor, and closes her eyes. "Focus on your prey. *Feel* your prey. *Be* your prey. And think of them doing as you want them to. We'll start simple. Make them cover their ears."

Next to me, Chloe tilts her head a little and stares at Efron. Down the line, Elena snaps her fingers and Caesar immediately bows his head, pressing his paws against his ears.

My stomach is in knots. I was already scared my abilities were some kind of evil, but the idea of forcing someone to do something, now that it's been done to me, feels like a whole new level of wrong. How can they not see how this isn't acceptable?

"Dane," Ada urges me.

"I really don't want to," I say through gritted teeth.

"You'll be glad you can later."

All eyes bore into me. With a sharp inhale, I tilt my head and imagine Aloysius putting his little black paws over his ears. I imagine I *am* Aloysius, imagine what my fur must feel like to the touch.

I snap my fingers. Aloysius covers his ears. A wave crashes deep in my stomach; tingles break out over my chest and down through my arms. My lip twitches.

Go on. You know you want to.

I blink and Aloysius falls back with a whimper. He struggles against my invisible force, but he remains on the floor, batting his paws as the darker side of me crawls out of my soul and pushes him harder against the floor.

Stop!

I squeeze my eyes shut.

Grant can't breathe. He struggles against invisible hands that hold him under water. Don't want him to get up. I want him to struggle until he can't hurt me.

"Stop!" I pull my eyes open and stumble backward, falling onto the couch. I bury my face in my hands and breathe deep, as the darker part of me slinks away, back down to where it came from.

Are you a good witch, or a bad witch?

When I finally look up, everyone's staring at me like I just kicked a dog.

Aloysius rights himself and stares at me with his teddy bear eyes. *"It's all right,"* he clicks. *"I know you didn't mean to."*

"No, it's not all right. You're my familiar, as in friend. Not a lab rat. And I'm not doing this," I say. "I'm not controlling anyone."

Ada opens her mouth to respond, but I shake my head.

The Reds look to her, probably hoping she'll let me have it. But Ada only nods and flicks her wrist. The record player screeches to a stop.

"I suppose if you already know how to do it, I won't waste your time."

Her gaze locks onto mine. "Though I don't know *how* you could master it so easily."

"I get it," I say, my voice shaking. "I do things. But how is this helping us find my cousin before it's too late?"

"Fair enough." Ada raises an eyebrow.

I reach under the couch, where I stuffed my backpack, and pull it out. "I have something."

My hands tremble as I unzip the bag and pull out the scrapbook from the courthouse archives.

"Where did you—"

"Doyle let me keep it." I open the scrapbook and flip to the back, where the Rabbit Skins articles are. "Just figured it would be easier if I had it, I guess."

"You need to be more patient," says Ada. "I could have—"

"I don't know how much time I have!" I snap. I know I'm being dramatic, but Jesus H., he's been gone since mid-September. I can't leave him any longer.

He's probably dead by now. Even if he wasn't when—
Shut up.

I come to the first article and thrust the scrapbook into Ada's hands. She looks over it, reading parts of it out loud to the room.

Every now and then Chloe shudders and takes a step back. "I don't like that," she announces when Ada has finished with the first article.

"None of the victims had faces," I say. "The bodies we found? Yeah, where was the face skin? The one we buried? No face."

Ada barely nods, turning the page. "He's repeating the past."

She reads the next two articles quietly, but I read those with Hannah last night when we got home.

"What is it?" Madelaine asks.

"A boy named Thomas went missing, but his blood trailed into the woods. They found a two-story cabin way out there, and when they entered, armed, they found Thomas dead on a table, his face cut off. Rabbit Skins was kneeling on the floor, wearing the boy's face, and eating a live rabbit. Its heart was still beating."

Chloe plugs her ears with her fingers. "Nope. Don't like this!"

"Once they apprehended him and tore off the mask, that's when they could see the right side of his face was completely burned. The other half, they recognized, was Charles Frederick. He was a pastor who was removed from the church for suspicious behavior. He skipped town in the dead of night two months before the murders began."

"Yeah," says Elena. "So, he could build his murder house. But what kind of suspicious behavior?"

"He was a witch," I eject. Everyone gapes, and Ada shakes her head, already dismissing me. "When he showed up at the courthouse, he held EJ and me in place. Without touching us."

"Okay," says Madelaine, connecting the dots, "but he was also a preacher, or reverend or whatever?"

Elena cocks an eyebrow. "I'm not surprised he went berserk, then."

Ada skims over the final article. "He claimed a dark spirit drove him to it by melting his face with its hand. I imagine when you're in the woods and there isn't much material to cover your missing face, well, a rabbit will do. That is, until you find a new face."

This makes my arms tingle again. Just hearing it, thinking about it. Could the spirit have been a wicked witch? And were they a Craven, somewhere down the line?

"In jail, he confessed to preferring the flesh of children," Ada reads on, "because they were more, as he said, 'fresh.'"

Elena folds her arms. "And then what happened?"

"He was found in his jail cell covered in cuts, an inverted pentagram carved into his chest, and his throat slit. No one knows how he got a blade to do it. On the wall, written in blood like finger paint, was a message. 'Gone Home.'"

"Nope!" Chloe plugs her ears again.

I rub my temples. "Last night, Doyle showed me a picture from the old graveyard. Someone carved that same symbol into the tree next to Rabbit Skins' headstone. Someone's messing with ghosts. Maybe I should try to read in on the tree, or—"

"Can you?" Ada asks.

My face drops. "No. I've tried, but I never get anything."

Ada nods. "I thought so. Trees tend to have their own guards against that sort of thing. And a headstone is already sacred. Besides, it's hallowed ground."

"So what, then?" I'm getting impatient. "Someone who is *not* a witch may have brought Rabbit Skins back and is manipulating this whole thing."

"Dark necromancy," Ada mutters. "Far darker than what we do, talking to spirits and such. You're suggesting a complete return from the grave."

"I guess."

Ada shakes her head. "Then I really do need that missing spell. When a person is purposefully brought back after they're buried...let's just say it's no longer a simple ghost. Its soul has been stripped of any humanity and is much harder to put back into the ground. We can't just hum and send him back down.

No. We have to bind him."

"Now that we're all in a fantastic mood," Madelaine breaks our silence as we come up the stairs into the dining room of Collingwood Hall, "I have a surprise."

I groan. "I can't take any more surprises."

"You'll like this."

Elena nudges me forward, and I go farther into the dining room, shoving my hands in my pockets. Aloysius rubs his body along my leg.

"It really is all right, you know," he clicks. *"It's part of my duty as your familiar."*

"It shouldn't be!" I whisper. "I feel awful about it and I'm sorry. That practice will be retired, I'll make sure of it."

I feel bad about the whole controlling him thing. About the ghost of a serial killer dragging Grant into the woods. And about EJ and Hannah getting into trouble for me.

Is it time to go home and eat my feelings yet?

Madelaine opens a drawer of the dining room sideboard and pulls out a large box. It's tied with a bow, with the logo of some shop that we didn't go into yesterday printed on it.

"When you were getting your coffee," says Madelaine, "I saw this and just *knew* it was you."

I raise my eyebrows. "I think if I come home with one more piece of preppy clothing, Hannah is going to gouge my eyes out with a corkscrew."

Elena rolls her eyes. "Jealous little Igor."

"Go put it on," Madelaine says. "It's a surprise for all of us."

She looks at me like she's in on some private joke with herself. I take the box and go into the parlor alone. Tabitha Collingwood's painted eyes stare me down as I set the box on the sofa and undo the bow. Slowly, I lift the lid to reveal a square of blood-colored fabric nestled in a cushion of black tissue paper.

I grab it and lift it, the folds giving way to reveal the jacket in full.

Involuntarily, I take a deep breath. The magnets stir in my bones, forcing me to hug the jacket, to embrace the soft fabric rubbing along my cheek, as though I'm welcoming a close friend. I smooth the large lapel and the high collar with my fingertips, then slip it on. It's a long peacoat that runs halfway down my thighs, double breasted and slim fitting. I button the eight gold buttons that run down the front.

Madelaine was right. It's very me. As I clasp the final button, my chest swells and I stand erect, the black lining settling against my back, as though all this time I've been a mixed-up puzzle, and now the pieces are finally snapping into place. My hands drift down my sides, my fingers making the plunge into the pockets. But they don't make it, instead sliding right past the flaps and hanging loosely at my sides. I'm taller than I thought I was.

"Ooh!" Chloe coos, flouncing into the room.

"I look like a traffic light," I say before she can see me smiling.

"A *sexy* traffic light," she says.

Elena snaps her fingers repeatedly as she enters with Madelaine, and I tense up for a moment before I realize that she's just applauding poetry-slam style, not casting a spell.

"Okay, now I can be seen with you in public," Madelaine says.

I roll my eyes and go back into the dining room to look in the mirror. I halt and stare at myself.

Whoa. I look good in red.

17

TOP OF THE WORLD

n Main Street, I stop in front of the shop window next to Hallow Bean to make sure my coat is smooth and my hair looks just as good as when Elena first perfected it.

My stomach is a breeding ground for butterflies, and every now and then they fly up beneath my heart and make it lift with a boom. I don't know why I didn't just text EJ. I don't even know if he's working, or if his aunt would even let him work when he's grounded. For a second, I consider fleeing. I could call Hannah and make her pick me up, let her see me in this jacket first. She might kill me on sight and then I won't have to worry if whatever this is with EJ is happening.

But I already lied to the Reds and told them I was meeting Hannah down here. I decided that I've never looked cuter and now would be an excellent time for me to show up for coffee.

I beeline to the door of Hallow Bean and duck inside without even counting to three first. When the bells sound my arrival, a barista older than me, probably midtwenties or so with short black hair and a purple streak, startles behind the register and drops whatever they were fiddling with on the countertop. The butterflies become still and I can't decide if their stillness is from disappointment or relief that EJ isn't here.

"Hi there!" The barista grabs the object they'd been studying, some sort of wooden spike, likely a broken piece of a chair or table leg and shoves it under the counter. "I'm Scout Sadow, and my pronouns are they/them. What can I get for you today?"

"Uh— a cinnamon roll latte, please," I say and reach into my inner pocket for my wallet.

Scout nods, tapping the screen of the register. "By the way, *love* your jacket."

This makes me smile. "Thank you."

"What's the name on the order?"

"Dane."

Their finger halts above the screen and they look at me with a gleam in their eyes.

"Oh," they say. I try to hand them a five-dollar bill, but they just shake their head. "Don't worry about it."

"I'm sorry?"

"Just a sec."

Scout walks back to the kitchen, and a moment later EJ is pushed through the doorway. His face is scarlet, and his eyes double in size when he sees me. They glance over my jacket as he hesitates.

My heart speeds again, pulsing in my ears.

"Hi," he says.

Okay, butterflies, knock it off.

"Howdy," I offer, and wince. *Howdy? Really? Are you Woody the Cowboy?*

"Sorry." He keeps his eyes on the register. "I made the mistake of telling Scout about you and they think they're my big sibling."

His face becomes even more red, and I try to ignore the butterflies in my stomach performing aerial ballet.

After a moment of silence, he says, "Nice jacket."

"Oh, this old thing?" I look down at it. "I've had it for minutes."

I give a socialite laugh and EJ looks at me like I've peed on his lawn. "Nice."

He grabs a steel pitcher, reaches into the refrigerator under the counter, and pulls out a carton of half-and-half.

He remembered—shut up.

"So." He pours the half-and-half into the pitcher and drops in a thermostat. "About last night."

"Oh, no worries!" My heart skips a beat.

He looks up at me as he plunges the steam wand into the pitcher. "What?"

"I got you in deep shit and your aunt won't let you talk to me anymore." I give a big shrug. "I get that."

"What? You're being so awkward." He grins.

I can't help but laugh. "Well, I didn't think you'd want to lay eyes on me again after that," I confess and grab a wooden stirrer, twirling it nervously between my fingers. "But I didn't hear from you, so I just wanted to check."

EJ cringes. "Yeah. I'm sorry. I just needed to think a little. I don't break into government buildings for just *anyone*."

"Oh, really now?" I feel my face light up. "I'm *special*?"

"Oh my god, shut up." He spins on the steam and pushes the shots button.

I bolt down the counter and peer around the espresso machine to face him.

"McScuse me? Shut up?"

"I don't mean *shut up*, I mean"—he shakes his head and an embarrassed smile pulls across his lips—"you're driving me wild."

I raise my eyebrows. "Say what now?"

"You heard me."

"I'm sorry, I can't hear you." I fold my arms and smirk at him. "It's really steamy back there."

"*Stahp.*" He spins off the steam and pours the hot half-and-half along with my shots into a large to-go cup. He pushes it across the counter. "No worries, I'm not *that* in trouble. Aunt Bridget isn't really great at keeping me under lock and key. And I... I just like you, okay?"

If his voice gets any more constricted, I think it will snap in half. He keeps his eyes on my cup.

"Impossible," I say, the butterflies bursting into flames and rising as little baby phoenixes of confidence. "Because I like *you*... Therefore, you don't like me back. Teen angst. It's a roller coaster."

"Oh god, not the angst!" EJ says in horror, still staring at the cup. "Shit, I forgot the cinnamon roll." He reaches back for the syrup pump and starts shooting it into my cup as fast as he can. "I'm sorry."

I snort. "It's okay. Seriously. I'm still going to tip you."

EJ laughs and looks away for a moment, then bites his lip.

Don't bite your lip, that's my job. I gulp.

"I'm off in half an hour," he says. "Would you want to go somewhere? Are you grounded?"

"I am, yeah," I say. "But I'm already out of the house..."

Scout marches from the back and swats EJ's shoulder with a rag as they pass. "Take your tips and get lost. I don't want your hormones flavoring the coffee."

"Okay, then," EJ says, glaring at them like he doesn't know if he'd rather trip them or hug them. He turns to me. "Would you want to go somewhere *now*, then?"

My heart trips over itself and the words lodge in my throat. *Go somewhere! Just do it!*

"Where?"

He shrugs. "Do you trust me?"

"Did you just quote *Aladdin*?"

"I did."

Scout plunges their arm into the tip jar and throws a wad of cash at EJ. "Out! Now!"

"You're a psycho, aren't you?" I say as EJ stops the car near a thicket of trees.

EJ smirks and shakes his head. "I'm not taking you to the woods, it's the back edge of the park."

"You didn't answer whether you're a psycho or not."

"You're related to Hannah Allen." He smiles at me. "I think you can handle my weirdness."

"Fair enough."

We get out of the car. The air is crisp now that the sun has started its slow dip to the horizon. I button the front of my jacket and try not to notice that EJ is staring at it, shoving his hands into the pockets of his blue puffy coat.

"A walk in the park?"

"Don't judge me," EJ chuckles. "I threw this together last minute."

He heads for an opening in the trees, the start of a trail. I almost have to run to keep up with him. My arm bumps against his. I want to hold his hand. Rest my cheek on his shoulder.

It's too soon for that, right?

As we near the end of the trail, my breath has grown short. It's deceivingly steep, but EJ doesn't seem fazed at all. I believe every time he mentioned hiking now. He must have calf muscles that could death-kick a mountain lion.

We come to the crest of a hill. At its top stands a small picnic shelter with a weathered table and benches beneath a metal roof.

EJ points over my shoulder, away from the hill. "Look."

I turn my head and stop walking, then suck in my breath.

We're looking out over a rolling sea of treetops and hillsides. Below, Jasper Hollow stands like a miniature Christmas village, a bowl of steeples and streetlights. The dome of the courthouse pierces its center.

"Wow," is all I can say.

"This is the highest point in town." EJ heads toward the picnic shelter. "Not a lot of people will make the walk up here. I get it to myself pretty much every time."

He hitches his leg up on the tabletop and hoists himself. Lifting his arms, he closes his eyes and breathes in, the setting sunlight coloring his face.

I follow him over, debating whether or not I'll join him, already feeling awkward that I'm not tall enough to glide up there like that. But when I step closer, he bends, offering his hand.

Pursing my lips, I look up at him, his eyes silently asking the question, and I'm reminded of *Aladdin* again. EJ on his magic carpet. *"Do you trust me?"*

My hand slides over his, his warm palm wraps around mine, and he helps me step onto the table. Red jacket brushes blue coat. Our hands stay clasped, and I catch myself studying his knuckles, bent over my own. I swivel my face to the view.

"It looks normal from up here," I say. "Like there *aren't* ghosts and killers and shit waiting for me."

"This is my thinking spot." EJ's fingertips sweep over mine. "I come here when I want things to be pretty and nice. No one knows I do."

"So, I'm the first person you've brought here?"

He steals a glance at me. "Well, I thought the view could stand to be a *little* better." He winces. "That was really douchey. Please ignore—"

I kiss him, my hand grabbing the back of his head. It isn't graceful, our lips barely meet on the right spot and my nose pushes into the side of his, but I don't care. My heart is drowning in overwhelming feelings, and I have to let them out.

My first kiss.

Our bodies turn instinctively and press against one another, our lips staying locked. His tongue dares to go against mine, and I let it. My hands move to his back and squeeze tight as his arms take my waist and pull me closer.

Finally, I pull my head back for air. "Are you sure about this? Because I get it if you gotta think about it."

"Shh." EJ lowers his lips to my ear, where he kisses the side of my neck. "I'm positive."

"I've never made out before," I say. *Stop the words!*

"That's okay," he barely mumbles, his mouth finding its way back to mine, and I lose myself in his kiss once again.

"What are you?"

"Clearly, you already know."

"Stop!" I push EJ back and step off the table. Images of Grant's face that night, of my reflection in the bathroom mirror, the slur dripping down my forehead, flood my mind. The dark urges deep down flare up and my arms tingle. The fire begging me to let it out for just a second. I shake my arms, trying to force it back down. "Sorry. I... I need a minute."

"I'm sorry." EJ wipes his mouth. "I shouldn't—I'm sorry."

"It's not you!" I hold my hands up. "Not you. It's... I shouldn't be this happy right now. He's out there somewhere, and I'm—"

"No worries." EJ nods. He jumps off the table and takes a few steps toward me. "I get it."

I shake my head and turn to the view. "No. You don't. If you did, you wouldn't have brought me here."

"What?" EJ moves next to me, and I step away from him. "Don't be ridiculous, of course I'd—"

"No." The darkness pulls at me, drags me down deeper with it. I fold my arms and hug them tight around myself. "I'm not as good as you think I am."

EJ searches my face for my meaning, his eyebrows drawn tight. He stares at my jacket for a moment, before dragging his gaze back to mine. "No one's perfect, and I'm sure—"

"Don't you get it?" *Stop the words. Stop. The. Words.* "I *hated* Grant by the end. He was a homophobic fuckface who outed me and made really, really bad shit happen to me. I feel guilty, sure. I feel bad for my aunt and Hannah."

EJ comes another step closer, and I take another step back. "Okay Dane, I need you to breathe for me."

But I can't breathe. I can't even think about breathing. The word-vomit is pouring out, and with each word I get louder, and louder, as though my heart will burst from my chest if I don't get rid of the words.

"Sit down. I'm going to tell you exactly what happened. I'm going to tell you what happened in April."

18

APRIL

"**H**eads up, D-Frizzle!" The words are shouted in a voice forced two octaves lower. *Why do straight guys do that?*

The paper wad hits the back of my head an instant later and I flinch forward, my face almost plunging into my locker. Snorting and hollering continue in surround sound before melting in with the rest of the hallway rush. I take a deep breath, ignore whoever it was.

I hate the whole D-Frizzle thing. I don't know why I ever started that. Jesus, I was a freshman when I came up with it. I was young and stupid.

Grabbing my backpack off its hook, I shut my locker and jump to see Katelyn Bradley waiting behind the door. The logo announcing that our school is proudly presenting *My Fair Lady* pulls across her shirt.

"Scared me," I mutter and slam the locker shut.

She thrusts a card into my hand. "Sign this," she orders. "It's for Mrs. Elliott. We're going to give it to her onstage tonight."

Please and thank you? I think, holding the open card to the locker and pulling a pen from my pocket. Most of the cast has already signed, most of them extra-large, leaving me a tiny corner. I scribble a quick *thanks* with my name, and hand Katelyn the card back.

"Aw, thanks, doll baby!"

"No problem." I tilt my head and smirk at her.

"God, he's so awkward and tragic."

I straighten my neck and stop reading in on her as she disappears into the crowd of the hallway.

Slinging the backpack over my shoulder, I go downstream with everyone else trying to get out of this godforsaken building until Monday, except for those of us who are in this year's musical. Tonight and tomorrow at seven, parents and grandparents will be subjected to a tortuous rendition of *My Fair Lady* just in time to ruin their Easter, complete with unnatural pauses and the world's most spectacularly long scene changes. Joseph Franklin has been practicing his curtain pulling for three months and he *will* be a star by the time this is done, damn it.

I push my way along.

"Sex." "None of this matters, the world's ending anyways." "Sex." "I hate everything." "Sex." "The ableism is strong here."

I stumble through the front door of the school and rush down the steps as fast as I can. I cut between the buses and to the parking lot, where I instantly spot two heads of bright blond hair catching the sun.

"Hurry up, bitch ass!" Grant shouts when he spots me, leaning on the doorframe to the driver's side. I bound toward them.

"Grant"—Hannah doesn't look away from fixing her blonde ponytail in the side-view mirror—"don't talk to yourself in public."

Grant cringes at her. "What're you doing out, anyway? Doesn't the sun make you burst into flames or something?"

Hannah pulls down her black-rimmed sunglasses, in the shape of two big hearts, and smiles at her twin. "You should jerk off more often. Turn those navy-blue balls a nice bright shade of teal. You'd be less of an aggressive dickhead."

"Mommy, Daddy, please don't fight." I wave my hands at them.

Hannah's eyes slide to me, giving my outfit a once-over. She shoves her sunglasses back up and hides her eyes. "You're too preppy to ride in *my* carriage. Both of you. Start walking."

"It's *my* car," Grant says.

"But I get it if you die," Hannah deadpans.

"*You* drive like a maniac."

I pull at the hem of my blue plaid button-down. "It's *sort* of like flannel."

Hannah laughs mockingly and shakes her head. "You'll never be my punk princess."

She slides into the front passenger seat. I toss my backpack across the back seat, onto the pile of their overnight crap for the weekend.

"I think it's demented that your school is out an hour after ours," Hannah says as Grant starts the car and pulls in line with everyone else trying to book it out of here.

I shrug. "But I get to go in later."

"Driver," Hannah says like an old woman, "taketh me to the nearest drive-through. I need a chocolate shake."

"No," says Grant. "This town has Starbucks. I'm in need."

"I don't think that barista you want to bang is on the clock yet," Hannah argues. "School *just* let out."

Grant turns to her. "She's in *college*, though."

"You are *such* a stain."

He halts the car when we fall into the line of others waiting to exit the parking lot. I tense up as Jordan Green appears between the cars, walking with his friend Liam.

Grant glances at me in the rearview. "Yo, isn't that—"

I loudly sing scales. Hannah plugs her ears.

"The hell is wrong with you?"

"Warming up for my award-winning performance as Street Person Number Five," I say, not breaking eye contact with Grant.

"Fine." Hannah waves her hands. "Go to Star-*butts*. I'll read our tarot while we chill."

"Ugh, that witch shit is so gay"—Grant glances at me again—"I mean. Stupid."

I force a chuckle. "Yeah."

Grant turns on the radio and clicks on his phone before a loud pulse fills the car. "This weekend has officially begun!"

He floors the gas and whips around the line of cars as Hannah screams with delight out the window and I whoop toward the skylight.

"It does *not* say that." I take a sip of my three-shot cinnamon concoction over ice.

Hannah stares intently at the cards. "I swear. I predict you holding a baby. Also, you have a cute dog in the future."

"Infants smell like wet animal crackers, and dogs smell like death on a stick." I set my cup down. "No thanks."

With a grunt, Hannah pushes the cards together, lays them on the rest of the stack, and hands it off to Grant. "Your turn. Shuffle."

"I don't need cards to tell me I'm awesome," he says, but obeys.

A woman across the Starbucks patio gives us a subtle but disapproving look as she gets up and makes her way to the door. Her eyes lock on mine for just a moment, and I tilt my head.

"God, they're everywhere these days."

I look away as she goes inside.

The April breeze picks up just as Grant starts to lay out his cards, and three of them blow off the table and skid across the concrete. Hannah rushes to pick them up. She looks at them on her way back to the table, her eyebrows dipping down behind the rim of her sunglasses, her lips tight.

"Shuffle again." She thrusts them at Grant. "These don't make sense."

Grant sighs, but shuffles. I glance at Hannah and note that in the dim area behind her sunglasses, her eyes are darting back and forth between us.

"Sex," "I'm 'bout to bust—" "Sex." "Who took my vodka?" "Sex." "Should I tell her that her nose is running, or—"

"Whose house is this?" Hannah leans next to me.

"Her name's Katelyn," I say, tipping the red solo cup to my lips and forcing another sip of…whatever it is. It stings my throat as I swallow. "Her parents don't believe in *no* or some other shit, so they buy her all the liquor she wants."

With a gag, Hannah takes a sip of her own drink, which she made sure to tell me is Sprite because she's driving so Grant can get smashed. "Wasn't she the one screeching for three hours?"

"She played Eliza, yes."

"Yeah." Hannah takes another drink. "I wanted to cut her throat out."

"Sex." "Te-qui-la."

I look out at the party. Really, *orgy* feels like the appropriate word here, because most of my castmates have devolved into grinding on each other in a human-centipede formation.

I'm having to focus on Hannah when she talks because my ears aren't just filled with the bass of the music. They're also filled with the cacophony of people's thoughts, and I can't seem to turn them off in the haze of the alcohol I've downed.

I wasn't even going to come, but when Hannah and Grant came up to me in the hall after the musical, Jessica Spier made a beeline over to introduce herself and invited them. I think she was checking Grant out, but I didn't feel like reading in on *that*.

So naturally, Grant had to get in on it, and now Hannah and I are the wallflowers of my own cast party. We even hoped that Mom and Aunt Bella would shut us down, but I think they saw the golden opportunity to go clubbing together.

I empty my cup. "Hey, there's a hole in my glass!" I snort. "I heard that in an old movie once."

"You're so weird." Hannah shakes her head.

"Uno momento," I say and push myself from the wall, braving the grinding heap of bodies blocking the way to the kitchen.

"Sex." "Ew, my pimple just popped." "I want Taco Bell."

I enter the kitchen and stagger to the island counter, trying hard to seem sober as I pick up a random bottle of something, pour it into my cup, and mix it with some sort of juice. I take a sip, and it tastes like citrusy vomit, but eh. Whatever. I slosh it down.

Across the kitchen, I spot Jordan Green with his back to me. He's laughing about something and waving around a beer bottle. He steps to the side and now I see that he's talking to Grant.

Heat crosses my face and I stumble forward, pretending I don't see Jordan or his green eyes as I glare at Grant.

"Hey, cuz!" he says and slaps me on the shoulder.

"Sup, bruh?" I spit out and take a sip.

"This is awkward." Jordan chugs his beer then gasps. "Shit, I need more. BRB. This guy's really cool, Dane."

I watch Jordan go to the refrigerator, then snap back to Grant, who's making a drunken kissy face at me. "Aw, he knows your name."

"What have you said to him?" I ask, my words starting to slur.

Grant shrugs. "Shootin' the shit."

I tighten my grip around the cup, shaking my head. "Well, don't shoot *my* shit."

"I won't tell him you're in love with him."

My face feels like it's on fire. "I'm *not*. I just think he's cute."

Grant narrows his eyes and slides them to Jordan across the room. "I agree. Did you know he and his family raise pigs?" Then he scowls and chugs from his cup. I reach out for his shoulder, and he pushes my hand away. "Don't touch me."

"Seriously." I harden my glare at him. "Don't say *anything*."

"Yeah, 'course," Grant says and takes a drink from his cup. "Stop acting like a scared queer."

"Mc*Scuse* me?" I hiccup.

"Dane!" Katelyn grabs my arm from behind and spins me around. "Thank god! I need your help."

She smells like alcohol and cigarette smoke as she grips both of my shoulders.

"What?" I ask.

"He's always so nice." "Just come be with me for a second. Skylar Clark won't leave me alone and I need him to think I'm taken for a sec."

Before I can agree, she's yanking on my arm and pulling me into the kitchen and through the sliding door onto the deck. A handful of people are out here vaping, smoking cigarettes, and stamping their feet, laughing at some obscene joke I missed.

She takes me toward the stairs. "Down here," she says.

We go down the stairs and into the dark night, but no one else is here. I look around, taking a sip from my cup awkwardly.

"You look pretty safe to me," I note.

"Yeah." Katelyn crouches by a trash can and grabs something in the dark. "I couldn't say it up there or everyone will want it."

A flame flickers in the dark as Katelyn lights a bowl. She takes a deep hit and coughs, tries to pass it to me.

"No," I say. "My mom would kill me."

"Aw, that's cute." Katelyn lets out a wheezy laugh. "Mine left it for me."

I nod. We stand in silence for a minute, and I swivel my cup in my hand, looking down at the alcohol spinning in a tiny whirlpool.

"I love your hair," she says.

"Thanks," I say, not looking up. "I need to get it cut."

"So, you're gay, right?"

I dart my eyes to her. "What?"

"Sorry," she laughs, picking up the bowl. "This is good shit."

I turn and bolt up the deck stairs.

"No, seriously!" she shouts. "I'm sorry!"

My hands tremble on the stairwell as I fumble for excuses. *She's drunk. She's high. It'll be fine.* I beeline across the deck and back into the kitchen.

Hannah has made her way there and is concocting some sort of red drink while a girl watches in wide-eyed amazement, her elbows propped on the counter.

"And there you go." Hannah slides the cup to the girl. "Just don't blame me if your liver cuts itself out of you and flees."

The girl giggles and dances away with the cup. I go to Hannah.

"Can we leave?" I ask. "This isn't fun."

"Hell yes. I'm about to go postal. Where's golden boy?"

He's left the kitchen, so I make my way to the living room. Someone spots me and whispers to another person. A pair of eyes on me becomes twenty.

The bass pulses in my ears, the track getting littered with unspoken words.

"Gay." "Didn't know." "I mean, I figured." "Gay." "Better not touch me—"

My cup crumples in my grip as I look at all of them, my face growing even hotter and my heart sounding *boom* after *boom* as my pulse takes over my ears. Something deep inside me stirs. I've never felt it before. That urgent longing to light the room on fire and vanish into white flames.

"Gay." "Dane's gay." "Dane's—"

My eyes fall on Grant, who sits on his ass in the corner, drunk and half passed out.

I sit in the tub, clothes on and wrists clamped between my legs, staring at the ceiling.

I'm out of tears. No energy left to punch the side of the tub. My head hurts from slapping myself for being so naive as to trust that it would stay secret.

Even if we sealed it in blood.

Even with the threat of murder.

My mind is stained with the look on Jordan's face as I stayed silent and bolted out of Katelyn's house before they could see me react. The look I've always dreaded. Fear. Like I'm a predator.

My phone wouldn't stop buzzing with notifications of messages on my social accounts. Ones from people who were there, telling me they don't care. Ones from people who weren't there, telling me to keep away. Texts from Hannah begging me to come out of the bathroom.

I shut my phone off and threw it at the door an hour ago.

I wish this tub would open and swallow me whole. Just drag me into the sewer where darkness lives. Because it's all I can feel now.

The lights over the sink extinguish. All that's around me is blackness and the heavy falls of my breath. I pull my hands from between my knees, reach up, and—

A spark shoots across the room. I flinch, but it misses me. Pulling my hand closer to my face, I squint through the dark. A burning sensation breaks out over my index finger, and I wince as a tiny orange flame lights itself from beneath my fingernail.

With a cry, I flip on the tub faucet and duck my hand under, shudder at the sizzling sound of the flame exhausting.

That's new.

Mom and Aunt Bella haven't returned from their big night out yet. This is one of the first times I actually wish my mom knew. About me being able to read minds and now apparently shoot flames from my fingertips. I wish I'd already come out to her about being gay as well.

I grab my forehead as a sharp pulse shoots through a vein. *I'm never drinking again.*

A soft knock drums against the door.

"No," I say hoarsely.

The doorknob jiggles and the door swings open. I sit up as Grant enters, flipping the lights back on and waving a thin metal stick.

"Y'all need to do a better job of hiding your skeleton keys." He tosses it into the sink and shuts the door behind him. "Above the door? Really?"

"Get out."

"Let's talk—"

"No!" I raise my voice. "Anything I say you're just going to repeat."

Grant leans against the door, sloppily, and folds his arms. His words are still slurred from the alcohol. "I was drunk, man. And then it just slipped out."

"Slipped out!" I grip the side of the tub. "That doesn't just *slip* out."

"You were being a little bitch." He hiccups.

My teeth grit behind my trembling lips. The muscles in my left eye twitch, trying to push out tears that aren't there anymore. "So, you outed me to my entire school?!"

Grant shuts his eyes. "Look, it's fine. No one cares."

My fist pounds the side of the tub. The candle on the back of the toilet lights itself. My voice raises to a volume I didn't know I could reach. "*I* care! It's *my* decision! *My* timing!"

Grant's looking at the candle that's now burning and melting vanilla wax. "Was that lit a second ago?"

"I'm talking to you!" I pound my fist again. "Hey, asshole! Look at me!"

But Grant keeps staring at the candle.

A second later, he's thrust against the door. It nearly buckles under his weight as he struggles against the invisible force holding him. His legs kick, hovering five inches off the ground. He grabs at his throat, looking at me with bugged eyes, choking.

I glance down at my outstretched arm, fingers splayed.

That's new, too.

With a gasp, I release my hand and Grant tumbles to the ground. He catches himself on the doorknob and can't twist it fast enough.

"You're a freak!" he says. "You're a fucking freak!"

He bolts from the room. And I'm left staring at my hand.

Man, I hate *My Fair Lady*.

I wait alone in the wings while Seth Mullins shout-sings "With a Little Bit o' Luck" at the audience. His wailing is about to make me explode. I haven't slept or eaten since last night, and the sooner this tragedy is over the better. It's been bad enough to sit in the greenroom with the rest of the cast, who'd rather whisper about me than talk to me. But waiting to make an entrance in a musical somehow makes this whole out-of-the-closet moment a little *too* on the nose. Even if all I'm supposed to do is sit in the back and look amused for ten seconds before the song ends. If I ever get the urge to participate in theater again instead of just watching it, I'll throw myself down the stairs.

Someone grabs me from behind and stuffs a cloth into my mouth.

"Hold him still!"

"He's coming undone."

"Well, tighten it!"

Ropes cut into my wrists behind me as I scream into the bandanna that slices against my mouth. They've torn the cravat from my costume off my neck and tied it around my eyes, blocking out any light.

Fingers rub against my forehead. Something sticky, pulpy, and congealed runs down as fingers paint on me.

It smells like iron and rot.

Smells like Jasper Hollow.

Someone clicks their phone camera, and the *click* of the flash goes off five times.

I try to kick at my attackers but miss. There's three of them. Six hands carried me wherever we are. One of the voices belongs to Jordan, I know that. The other is a friend of his, Colin. But the third person hasn't spoken yet.

Shouts and protests tear from my throat, but they're strained, unintelligible sounds, my words unable to pass through the gag.

"Oh, he ain't getting away from that," Colin snorts.

"Come on," says Jordan. "Fight!"

A fist slams into my stomach. I double over.

A hand takes my hair and pulls my face up. A sob pushes through my gag as lips brush against my ear.

"What was that you did last night?" a voice whispers, and my blood ices over. Grant, my own cousin, is doing this.

Grant tightens his grip on my hair and shakes me before flinging me back.

"That's what I thought," he says. His footsteps die away.

Get them. Something silky and inviting slides across the gravel at the bottom of my soul and slithers its way up. My arms tingle. *Get them all.*

Jordan and Colin burst with laughter. A door slams in front of me, the metallic scrape of a lock soon following.

I let a few more sobs escape as the anger continues its climb. My wrists burn, so hot I think they're on fire.

The ropes fall away. I don't question how as I tug at the gag and blindfold. They've locked me in a stall of the boys' second-floor bathroom. No one can hear us. Help is at the other end of the school, watching the play.

I look below me where the ropes have fallen at the base of the toilet. The ends are charred. I squeeze my eyes shut, the anger broiling my chest, my neck, shooting down my arms in white-hot pulses that tell me to fight. To get away.

And if necessary, to kill.

I pound on the door of the stall. "Let me out!"

"How did he—"

"Goddamn it, motherfuckers!" I keep pounding. "Let me out!"

"Shut up!" Grant belts back. "This is what you get!"

"Let me out!" I scream, slamming punch after punch into the door, not caring about the pain it causes me. My brain feels like it's going to explode, it's so hot. Sticky goo drips down my forehead. I wipe a finger above my eyebrow. Dark-red liquid stains my fingertip and a whiff of the scent shoots up into my nostrils. They've put real blood on me.

With a scream, I pound the door of the stall again. My fists can't take it anymore and I push my palms against the green-coated wood, heave as the unquenchable anger shoots down my arms, igniting my fingertips.

I close my eyes and force myself to take three deep breaths.

On the third, I inhale the scent of smoke. I open my eyes as the door bursts into flames.

"What the fuck!" Colin screams.

"Get out!" Jordan's footsteps fade from the bathroom. "Fire! Get out!"

"Dude, come on!" Colin calls, before he too flees.

The fire alarm goes off. I stumble backward, watching it with amazement. But I don't feel any fear. Because I made that happen.

Grant releases a stunned breath.

My eyes dart to the hinges of the door. One by one, they rip themselves off the frame.

The burning green door falls on the floor. The fire alarm shrieks like a demonic insect.

Grant stares back at me, his eyes wide, his arms stiffly at his sides. My reflection glares back at me in the mirror behind him. The word *fag* drips down my forehead.

"Where'd you get it?" I ask, not looking away from myself.

"P-pigs," he stammers. "You know, like in Stephen King... I'm s-sorry."

The slur glistens under flickering fluorescents. I watch it fade in and out in my reflection. The whites of my eyes are bright red, almost glowing. I turn my stare to him, feeling a dark smirk pull on the corners of my twitching mouth.

"What are you?" is all he can say.

Blood drips into my left eye, forcing it shut. I point at my forehead. "Clearly, you already know."

I take a step from the burning bathroom stall and the flames part to provide me a path. Grant watches with amazement, not noticing that the sink he leans against is plugged and filling up with water.

"It was," Grant says, "j-just a prank, m-man. We good?"

I lift an eyebrow. Shake my head. The sink overflows, and Grant glances at it. He seems to realize now that I'm ever so slightly urging him to step toward it, and his knees shake.

"You were safe," he tries again. "Jus-jus-just a prank. Like a—"

I smile. "Like a practical joke."

"Yeah!" Grant nods. "Exactly! So we're all cool. We cool?"

The darkness takes over completely and I force his face down into the full sink without touching him.

Maybe someday I'll regret how much I enjoy watching him struggle for air. But right now, I relish the sight of him kicking, grabbing at the sides of the sink, pawing at the faucet, unable to turn it off.

And when he passes out and collapses to the floor, I cackle.

19

ONE GIANT LEAP FOR DANE, ONE MASSIVE KICK IN THE ASS TO MANKIND

"It isn't *your* fault," EJ says, his face only half-visible in the darkening sunset. "You know that, right?"

Next to him on the dewy grass, I tighten my grip around my knees and stare down at Jasper Hollow. The lights twinkle in the twilight like a haze of stars, and I pull myself back to the present. "Mhm."

"Dane." EJ leans closer. "You aren't the reason he's dead."

"I could be." I slowly let my breath out. "Part of me wanted him dead. Whatever part it is, the part that lives way down, it wanted to kill him." I think of Mr. Hawthorne, looking at me with desperation, expecting me to join him. My chin trembles and I turn to EJ. "What if that's who I really am? What if I'm evil?"

"You're not evil." EJ puts his hand on mine and for a second, I think of pulling away. But I make myself keep it there and embrace the soft squeeze of his grip. "You were pushed. And you did not kill Grant."

"What if I made Rabbit Skins do it?" I shiver.

"What?"

"I wanted Grant to die." My face twists up and a tear runs from each eye. "I wanted so badly for him to hurt as much as he hurt me. What if, without even realizing it, I summoned him and brought him back?"

"You heard Doyle." EJ tightens his grip. "Someone was messing around near that grave. Unless you carved a star into a tree, it's not you."

I shake my head. "I don't know."

"If you weren't sitting here worrying whether or not you're evil," he whispers, "then maybe you would be. But evil people don't care if they are or not. I should know. I watch a *lot* of superhero movies."

"Stop being perfect for me." I pull my hand away and push myself to my feet. "Aren't there other gay kids around here? You know I could cast a spell on you and turn you into a living robot, right?"

"You won't, though."

"How do you know?"

EJ stands up and faces me. "Because you aren't a bad witch."

I bite my lip and look down. "You don't know that."

"All I know right now"—he slips his fingers through mine—"is that you look like you need a break."

I squeeze my eyes and more tears fall.

"You want queso?"

My eyes fling open, and I stare at him, surprised. Then I cry even harder. His eyes widen. "Oh, I'm sorry! I was thinking about your memoir title. If you don't like that, we can get something else! Dane? Are you okay?"

"Shh," I say. "Say that again."

"Dane, are you okay?"

"No." I smile and hate myself for the mess I am. "The part where you offered me queso."

"There's no way you're enjoying this."

EJ stops biting my ear and squints at me through the darkness of the car with a dopey grin. "What?"

"I've had queso and a stick of spearmint gum. Not a good combination."

"Your breath is just minty!" He laughs. "I swear."

I lunge across the middle console and grab his face, planting a hard kiss on his lips.

"Nights like this shouldn't be allowed to end," I grumble.

EJ lifts my hand and kisses my knuckles. "I'll let you go inside," he says. "But I don't want to."

I pout at him. "No, this is the part where you suggest running away."

EJ drops his jaw and raises an eyebrow, scandalized. "Why, Mr. Craven, what kind of cad do you take me for?"

"One that I like," I say and force my hand onto the handle of the passenger door. "Okay, okay, I'm going."

"Real quick," EJ says. He runs a hand along his seat belt. "Are you going to tell anyone? About us?"

My heart drops a few inches, but I force a shrug. "We don't have to."

"It's just that there's a couple of people," he mumbles, his voice tight, "that I don't think would like it, is all."

I tilt my head back, mouth open in a silent *oh*. "You mean the Reds."

EJ shrugs. "Well, Madelaine specifically. She'd probably rally an angry mob."

I shake my head. "Why don't you two like each other?"

"It's stupid, really. She just doesn't like that I know things. And also, she hasn't been super nice to me since we were freshmen." Even in the dark of the car, I can see his face has turned pink. I lean forward to interrogate him, but he answers before I can. "We were a *thing* then."

My eyes widen. I chew the inside of my lip, trying to find something to say.

"Obviously, that was a long time ago," EJ says in response to my silence. "We were, like, fourteen or fifteen, and I hadn't accepted everything. Sorry, I should have told you outright that I'm bisexual." He stares at me expectantly, but I can't stop picturing him and Madelaine kissing. That's not an image I like. A nervous twitch pulls at his lip. "I hope that's not a problem?"

I shake my head to snap out of my blank stupor and say, "I don't care that you're bi, I'm just surprised you dated her, is all. That's a long time to hold a grudge."

"You don't know Madelaine Wednesday like I do," he says, a dark undercurrent in the gravel of his voice.

I fling my hands up and shake them. "Okay," I say. "Back to sappy, happy stuff."

"Can I text you tonight?"

I look up at him and wiggle my eyebrows. "You can do anything you want."

EJ purses his lips and grabs my shoulders, shaking me gently. "I. Can't. Deal!"

We kiss one more time before I forcefully eject myself from the car. I lean down and look at him one last time.

"Good night," I say.

"Good night." He grins.

Another urge to smash his lips with mine shoots through me, so I shut the car door and take a few steps back before it overtakes me. EJ backs out of the driveway. I let my fingers graze my lips as I watch his car shrink in the distance.

When I came to Jasper Hollow, I didn't think I'd ever be liked by anyone. Not in a town like this. But, holy shit, I might have a guy. A guy to share my secrets with, who doesn't care that I have some dark power threatening to rip up my insides. Who knows why I jump back and shut down sometimes, and can pull me out of it with a hug and a cup of melted cheese—

"Good lord, son!" Mom shouts and I scream. "You're giving me diabetes with all that sap!"

I spin around to see my mother sitting on the porch swing with her arms folded. A red ember glows between her fingers as she takes a drag of a cigarette. I bolt up the porch steps.

"How long have you been there?"

"Long enough to get four cavities listening to that." She takes another puff.

I stare at the cigarette. "You don't smoke."

Mom watches the smoke pluming, a little embarrassed as she flicks ashes from the cigarette. "Well, they're from Bella's weekend stash. Don't tell Hannah. But yeah, a lot of old habits seem to be coming back lately. I've been stressed."

"Me too." I reach out my hand. "Give me that."

"Nice try." Mom stubs the cigarette out and sets the blackened butt on the rail, where I can see a little pile adding up. "Okay, I'll stop again. Come sit."

I'd rather run upstairs and scribble *Mr. Dane Kowalski* in a notebook, but I trudge over to the swing and sit next to Mom, who puts her arm around me and tips me over so that I'm lying with my head on her lap.

"The hell are you doing?" I ask.

Mom pats my head. "Shh. I've waited for this moment all of my mothering life."

"Have you been drinking potions again?"

"No," she says. "Red wine."

I grunt.

The way her hand runs across my hair reminds me of April. After it was all done and I was home, sitting in the bathtub with my clothes on again, Mom pinching my chin while she wiped my forehead with a wet cloth.

"Who did this to you?"

I wouldn't tell her. Just stared back at her, thinking of random things like TV shows and books. Not even on purpose, my brain just focused on literally anything other than what had happened.

"*What, are you afraid I'll kill them?*"

I just stared and blinked at her in response to each question.

"*Because I would.*"

That was the most she ever said about my sexuality. For the longest time after that, I kept thinking, *Say something. Anything, to confirm, well, anything.* But I understand her intention. I know she was normalizing everything. But still. Like the witch stuff, I wish she'd just said *something*.

"What's his name?" she asks, pulling me from my memory.

"EJ." I mumble.

"Isn't that the one you broke into the courthouse with?"

"I was let in. He had a key."

Mom sighs. "You remember that you're grounded, right?"

I lace my fingers through hers. "See, I was hoping that you *didn't* remember. Considering I *have* to leave the house to run around with my peers. It's kind of my job now."

After a moment of thought, Mom waves a hand. "I guess the cause was noble, even if the method left something to be desired."

"Thanks."

"Is he nice to you?"

"Yeah?"

"He wasn't given to you by the Reds, was he?"

I open my eyes and sit up. "What?"

"Just making sure!" Mom reaches for the pack of cigarettes and the lighter.

"No, he was not *given* to me."

"Good!" she smiles at me as she lights a cigarette. "I want to meet him."

"Mom—"

"If you're going to make out with him in a dark car, I need to meet him."

I stand up. "I'm going inside."

"You can't hide him forever!"

"Good night, Mother!" I swing the front door open and go inside.

Upstairs, someone screams.

I bolt up the steps. Another scream rings out. It's coming from Hannah's room. I run to her door and push it open. She's sprawled on her bed, lit by the pale-blue glow from the TV, a ravaged bag of Halloween candy piled on her stomach. Aloysius curls up next to her, peeking out from between his paws.

On the screen, a woman in black and white runs through a foggy forest, screaming her head off.

I let out a sigh. "Really? What are you *doing*?"

"Entertaining ourselves." Hannah keeps her eyes glued to the screen. "Private club for rejects. You aren't allowed."

"No matter how many times I tell her to turn it off, she doesn't understand!" clicks Aloysius, trembling. *"And no matter how many times I shout, 'Don't go in there!' the girl does go in there!"*

"Why are you terrorizing my familiar?" I ask.

"Told you." Hannah bites into a Reese's Pumpkin. "Private club. What are you wearing?"

"A jacket," I say.

"That's it!" Hannah sits up, candy tumbling off her, and presses pause on the remote as hard as she can. She flips the bedside light on and stands up, points at me with that Sicilian curse finger.

"What's wrong with you?" I ask.

"No, not what's wrong with me. What's wrong with *you*?"

"I like your jacket." Aloysius gives me a polite nod. *"Very much."*

"I never see you," says Hannah. "You're always going around with *them*. You're keeping secrets with *them*. And now you're walking around looking like a Ken doll. Dane, you are turning into one of *them*!"

"I am not."

"Then what are you doing?"

"I'm working with *them* to find your brother!" I shout, and instantly regret it.

Hannah's face drops. She sinks onto the bed, gripping the comforter. Aloysius shakes his head subtly, but doesn't comment.

"I'm sorry." I lower my volume. "But look, it's true... You know what I really hate? Everyone around here wants to pop up and tell me what I am, am not, should be, should not be. When they're getting me, where they're taking me. Well, I'm my own person, I've got my own shit to deal with, and I'm doing my best. Anytime something goes right, it's like one giant leap for Dane, and one massive kick in the ass to mankind. Up until just now you were one of the only people who *wasn't* being like that."

I fold my arms and lean against the door, bracing for her response, which I'm sure will be a gut-cutter. But she takes a deep breath and looks at me with glossy eyes. "I know. I'm sorry."

"No, *I'm* sorry." I move to the bed and sit next to her.

"I just feel really alone and left out lately," she says. "It's just us now, but I feel like it's just me a lot. And...I'm still dealing with...you know."

"I know."

Grant's energy hangs between us like a ghost, the missing piece of our puzzle. The third musketeer, before too much body spray and homophobia got him.

"I miss him." Hannah stands up and walks to the other side of the bed. "He was probably going to join the cult of the GOP someday, but I still miss him."

"I know. Listen, Saturday will be fun."

"Duh." Hannah unwraps a mini-Twizzler. "I've been collecting your blood in the dead of night for my satanic ritual."

"Funny." I side-eye her. "But I was *going* to say, no one's demanded my presence yet, so let's hang out that night. Just us two. Watch movies and eat junk and not let anyone else in the room."

"You don't have to go like, fly on a broom and lure children away from their parents so you can eat their souls or something?"

"No."

"If you're not going to tell me anything," Hannah says through a mouthful of fake licorice, "will you at least tell me why you smell like a cute guy?"

"It's just me."

"Gross. Cousin. No." Hannah looks at me. "You smell like another guy."

I pop a fun-sized Snickers into my mouth instead of responding.

"EJ?" Hannah's eyes light up. "Good for you."

She presses play on the remote and flicks the light off. The girl in the movie runs into a wolfman who wrestles her to the ground. He's about to sink his teeth into her neck when some hero dude shows up with a gun and scares the werewolf away.

"*Look behind you!*" Aloysius pleads.

The hero doesn't hear him. He also doesn't notice the vampire lurking in the shadows.

"Are you ever going to tell me what happened between you two?" Hannah asks. "You and Grant?"

My heart skips a beat and I reach for a Reese's Pumpkin.

"Dane?"

I take a bite. "Someday. Not right now."

"Any leads on who carved that thing in the tree?"

All I can do is shrug. We're twenty-four hours further along, and I haven't even tried. But if Hannah doesn't know who would've been close enough to Grant to know about our tree, then I definitely don't. I don't know what the final half year of his life was. I haven't known him since April.

Longer, when you think about it.

I'm starting to think the Grant I miss died years ago.

20

I NEVER LIKED JACK-IN-THE-BOXES

"**W**hat have you been up to?" Madelaine folds her arms.

She looks down at me from her place on the veranda of Collingwood Hall, Chloe and Elena flanking her like a scene out of *Mean Girls*. I swallow and adjust the lapel of my jacket.

"Huh?" I sweep my curls to the side of my forehead. "Whatever do you mean?"

"You have a glow," she says.

My fingers brush under my lip, hoping there isn't a mark. Five minutes ago, my lips were pushing against EJ's—just around the corner, in his car.

Aloysius scurries to my ankles. *"I told you! That's what you get when you parade about being a hormonal teenager."*

I tug the hem of my jacket down, hoping my bulge isn't so obvious underneath.

"I've just been walking," I say, ascending the steps and heading to the door. "You know, fresh air and exercise. Not all of us have a Pepto-mobile to zoom around in."

"You don't have to tell them anything." Aloysius scurries ahead of me. *"Gentlemen don't kiss and tell."*

He pushes himself onto his hind legs and tries to open the door for me, but he can't reach the knob. I open the door for the both of us.

"Let's go," I call back to the Reds. "We're late for charm school."

"Suddenly so studious," Elena notes.

We walk to the dining room and I take the liberty of tilting the mirror on the wall so that the trap door opens. A few nights ago, this seemed creepy and surprising. Now it's as casual as clocking in. Trekking down the stairs, we make our way into the basement where Jefferson Airplane's "Plastic Fantastic Lover" blasts.

Ada twirls in a lilac robe, Louisa slithering in time to the music around her sandaled feet.

I thrust my fingers at the record player, and it screeches off. Ada looks to it, then to me. "I don't remember teaching you that."

I shrug, unable to explain it. I didn't even think about doing it. It just happened. "I'm a man of many hidden talents. I'll prove it. Get me a bowl of cheese puffs and we'll play Chubby Bunny."

Ada claps. "Silence! Everyone sit. We aren't doing spells today. I have news."

My chest rises. Has she figured it out already? Do we know who's messing with us? We all plop onto the sofa, familiars in our laps. Ada paces and Louisa follows her, despite nearly being stepped on every so often.

"Sheriff Doyle called this morning to inform me that the bodies found in the woods have been identified."

My blood stops running through my body for a second. "And the lucky winners are?"

"Matthew Witt and Donovan Washington, both aged eighteen." Ada picks up a small notebook with a fuzzy orange cover, glancing at the notes inside. "Both were reported missing around the same time as Brett Baum...*and* Grant Allen."

My memories flash back to when I accidentally read in on the casket at the funeral. The body parts the morticians were working with. Brett. The body's name was Brett. I can still barely believe it.

"Both families saw them and confirmed," Ada continues. "This time there will be DNA testing to prove everything, but I highly doubt it will be wrong this time."

"So, what happens?" I ask, thinking of the fresh grave. "With the body?"

"He'll have to be reinterred," Ada says. "But that's only his family's business, and I'm sure your aunt will work with them on it."

"And I'm guessing that we don't know anything new about this rabbit guy," I say, and Aloysius nudges a comforting paw into my thigh. "Or who marked the tree?"

Ada stops pacing and gently shrugs one shoulder. "Nothing beyond legend. What we need is to figure out why this specific group of boys were the target."

"He's a perv," Madelaine says.

"Not so simple." Ada resumes her pacing. "A dead man doesn't crawl out of the ground and dismember three young men for kicks. I was hoping maybe our little psychometrist here noticed something when he grabbed that phone."

Everyone turns to me, and I sink into the sofa.

"Any sort of clue?" Ada asks. "Could you see what they were even doing out there that day?"

Oh, just trying on a dress.

"Anything that might give us some sort of direction?"

Because I dared him to, and if I hadn't, he'd probably be home and safe.

"No," I say.

"They weren't so much as playing hacky sack?"

"I don't know why he was out there," I say.

You damned dirty liar.

Ada sighs. "I was worried about that. We have zero direction, plain and simple."

"Could we not call up Mr. Hawthorne?" I ask. "Be like, 'Yo H., your demented ghost is in my yard, you might wanna get it'?"

"I *did* try to convene with Mr. Hawthorne," Ada says. "I've burned out five candles trying. He can't be bothered."

"I wonder why," Elena deadpans.

"I don't want to name any names." Ada smooths her robe, casting her eyes on me.

The Reds follow suit.

"Point taken." I cross my arms.

"But!" Ada turns and pushes through the curtains to the other side of the basement. "Just before you arrived, I received a delivery from the other side. It may be a sign that he'll help us after all."

She returns, carrying a black gift box. A black ribbon is tied around it like a Christmas bow in mourning. "It's addressed to you, Craven Kid."

My stomach knots. "I'm not supposed to take things from strangers."

Ada sets it in the center of the room. "He's not a stranger, he is your patron."

Aloysius climbs off my lap. *"Maybe it's another jacket?"*

I stand and walk to the dark gift, wondering what could be inside. Another crown? A pile of ashes? My cousin's ear? Beneath the bow, a note scrawled in silver ink on gray paper reads, *Mr. Dane Yuletide Craven*. Why would Mr. Hawthorne send *me* a gift, if it isn't something horrible, or some roundabout tactic to get me to devote myself to him?

The Reds push themselves from their seats and lean over to get a better look as I stoop and pull the ribbon.

The box shakes, and I jump back. "I'd rather have cash!"

"Go on," Ada says. "He's not going to send anything *lethal*. Well, not in *my* experience."

Slowly, I stoop back down and tug the ribbon away as the box continues to shake more and more violently. I lift the lid, just a centimeter, and am forced backward by an intense wind. I tumble to the floor, propped up on my elbows, as I watch a silvery silhouette rise from the box. It wails a piercing cry.

I gasp at the ghost of a young woman, standing in a long nightgown, wringing her hands. She scans the room blindly, with foggy gray eyes that are bugged out in fright.

"Put me back!" she shrieks. "Put me where I was! I don't want to be here!"

"Holy shit." Madelaine gapes.

The ghost thrusts her arms out to me in a plea, and I scamper across the floor toward Ada. "A gift card would've sufficed."

"Find out what she wants."

I turn around, staying on all fours, looking up at the ghost as she swivels to me. "Wh-who are you?"

The ghost girl's eyes aren't even really on me. Her hollow gaze wanders the walls. "Don't tell them," she whispers. "Don't talk to no one. Get back in, get back in. Don't stay."

"Hey." I push myself to my feet, my knees shaking so hard they could give at any second. "I won't hurt you."

The girl stops fretting, and her eyes fall on me. She lets out a long, freezing sigh. "Oh. You."

"Who are you?" I ask her again.

"I s'pose he'll be wantin' you next." She giggles. "You gotta nice face. S'why he took mine."

The giggles burst out of her as she raises a hand to her face, fingers splayed and trembling. She gasps and lets out a breathless, "Oh! Oh! Oh!" as her mouth gapes downward into an open frown that grows longer and longer. The tips of her fingers dig into the right side of her forehead and she pulls down.

The skin of her face peels off.

"Don't look at me!" she wails. "Don't look at what he done!"

"Ada," Elena starts, "what the hell is—"

"Who are you?!" Ada demands. "What do you want?"

I think back to the articles from the archives and my heart skips a beat. "She's Emily Black."

"S'not what I want, s'what *he* wants," the girl wails. "S'why he brought him back."

She erupts into more giggles and begins to dance an old-time jig, clapping her hands as she circles about, singing loud and fast and furiously. "Rabbit Skins. Rabbit Skins. Here to cleanse you of your sins. Drags you down and eats your bones. Keeps you for his very own."

She cackles and coughs, spitting out a bloody tooth.

"He'll take your face!" She points at me. "And suck your bones dry of their marrow, and you'll belong to him then!"

"To Rabbit Skins," Ada says.

"No!" Emily wails. "To *him*!"

The face of Mr. Hawthorne peering down at me in the clearing that night blazes in my memory.

"Boy, do you join me at last?"

Emily cackles and shrieks. My heart pounds, threatening to explode. My teeth chatter against my tongue, accidentally biting it, as a nuclear surge of energy pushes through my body. My arms burn like fire as it floods into my fingers, up into my ears. The ghost girl keeps jigging and laughing and reaching out toward me.

"STOP!"

The energy pulses from me, like a thousand invisible arrows shooting from my fingers, my forehead, my chest, and into the ghost.

Her silvery form turns black. Only her eyes, gray and cloudy, look out. A mere shadow with eyeballs. The shadow rips itself as Emily shrieks, the eyes rolling back and forth, up and down, until it all shreds away, falling into the box like discarded tissue paper.

I gape at the sight. *I did that, didn't I?*

Chloe cringes. "What the—"

My stomach retches. I double over and vomit on the box.

"Hell," Elena finishes.

"I never liked jack-in-the-boxes," I say, bent over with my head between my legs. "Did it come with a gift receipt?"

Ada snorts and drops a cold wet rag on the back of my neck.

I'm sitting on the toilet lid of the first-floor bathroom—the only room allowed to be updated and modernized in the museum portion of the Hall. It smells like lemons, and usually I'm all right with that, but right now it just makes me feel even more nauseous.

Aloysius pushes onto his hind legs and pats my knee with his paws. *"Take it easy."*

"That was a fascinating demonstration," says Ada. "I've never seen a witch your age take out a ghost by themself. Hell, I can't even do that."

"Well, she scared the shit out of me," I say. "I just wanted her to stop shrieking. I didn't mean to vanquish her."

"You need to seriously consider accepting Mr. Hawthorne's offer," Ada presses the rag harder against my neck. "It's for all of our best interest, and clearly he could use you."

"I don't trust him."

"You sound like your mother."

I think of Emily Black, pointing and shrieking at me, telling me that Rabbit Skins will want my face, like the others. A flash of Grant, out in the woods, floods my mind in an instant.

Could it all just be a huge coincidence? That whoever drew that star on the Tell No Tales Tree had no idea what they were doing, and that it *was* me wanting Grant to hurt that brought it back?

Did I accidentally cast a real spell when we made that pact? Our blood dripped onto the soil—our thumbprints still stain the headstone. I led Rabbit Skins to us both. Grant was the one still in town.

Or did Mr. Hawthorne have a hand in it?

"Is he trying to kill me?" I look up at Ada.

"What?"

"An evil ghost shows up and goes on a murdering spree. Was I the target and Grant was just in the way? Why else would he send one of Rabbit Skins' victims to mess with me?"

"I don't know—"

I push myself to my feet, leaning my arms against the wall as I fight a head rush. "Both of our blood has been on his headstone. We gave him a trail to follow."

"You should sit back down."

"He wants me to unleash his monsters," I spit out.

"What?"

I slide my eyes to her, then look down at her feet. "The night of my awakening, down in that other realm. He said something about me unleashing his monsters, and I don't think it's for a company picnic."

"He doesn't need help to do that if he wants to."

"Are we so sure? Think about it: why does he need us working for him if he has so much power? I mean, why would he want me and why would my mom skip town with me. Why would my aunt lie about me if something horrible wasn't going to happen?"

Ada takes a deep breath. "Beast-moon birth. You'll have a way with monsters."

I purse my lips, tears prickling the back of my eyes. "You said that my reading objects is incredibly rare. You said that you'd only heard of it once. Who was the witch who could do that?"

My worst suspicion is confirmed when she says, "Elgin Hawthorne. Back when he was alive."

I look down at my arms, at the red sleeves. I think of the flames burning through me. That dark snake deep down that wants to slither out to maim and destroy. It all makes sense now. How I do all of these things, the way it takes over me and *becomes* me. Why Mr. Hawthorne would pull me into his realm over any of the others and personally ask me to join him.

My father ran in the other direction when my mom ran with me. He wouldn't even let her have me in a hospital. The ghost audio of my mother rings through my ears, when I asked if she knew I'd be a witch. *"I knew while conceiving you."*

And it's why Aunt Bella lied and told Ada that I was a girl. They knew all along. They *knew* I'm a bad witch, they *knew* Hawthorne would want to use me. They were giving me the chance to be good. The chance to avoid whatever happens to an evil witch child.

"Did *you* know I could do this?"

With a sigh, Ada sits down on the toilet. I turn and push my back against the wall to look at her. "I could see the dark streak in you when you showed up. But I didn't think it was anything beyond teen angst."

I snort contemptuously. "So, you just blindly followed some dude in owl feathers and didn't stop and say, 'Hey, wait a minute'?"

"This is hardly my fault."

"It's mine, right? All of this. It's my fault. I'm a *wicked* witch."

"I wouldn't say that."

I reach over and pull the bathroom door open. "Well, here, we'll stop it. I'm done."

"Dane!"

I push out of the bathroom and run to the front door, pulling the red jacket off as I go. Ada is quick behind me.

"I'm finished! I'm not in this coven anymore! I'm not a good witch or a bad witch because I'm not a witch!"

The jacket drops to the floor. I fling the front door open, running out into the cold autumn wind and down the veranda steps. Halfway across the yard, a handful of dead leaves slice the air, hitting my face and shoulders, slowing me down.

"You already have the power!" Ada shouts at me. "Mr. Hawthorne gave you—"

"Then he can take it away!" I whirl around and stare her down.

She stands on the veranda, her robes billowing as the wind picks up, growing stronger, colder. The Reds rush out of the door behind Ada.

"And you!" I point at them. "I'm not your accessory! I don't say *hunty*! I don't want to talk about boys, and if you try to kidnap me again, I'll flip that goddamn car!"

"Dane," Madelaine says and takes one step toward me.

"No!"

My fists ball tighter, and the veranda light explodes behind them. They turn and gape at it. I stare as sparks fall from the dead socket.

Madelaine looks back at me. "That's *my* skill."

I laugh. "Didn't you hear? *I'm* the most powerful one, now."

Before they can respond, I turn and run the rest of the way down the drive. I thrust my hand out as I near the gate. It gives a shrill groan as it opens on its own, and I bolt through it, closing it behind me without touching it. Aloysius knocks into it and reaches between the bars.

"Dane!" he calls. *"Wait for me!"*

"Go home!" I yell back.

"You can tell me anything—"

"Go. Home!" I yell louder as I round the corner.

I feel bad immediately. I'll apologize later. I can't think right now, I need air and space.

Down the block, EJ has the car parked behind a tree like a cop on a stakeout. The passenger door opens as I near it, and I slide in.

"Whoa," EJ looks at me. "You okay?"

"Fine."

Someone beats on the window, and I jump, looking over to see Madelaine glaring at me through the glass.

EJ rolls the window down. "Can I help you?"

"So, this is what you've been up to," she says. I notice she's holding my jacket under one arm, wadded up like a dirty towel. "Hm. This will never do."

"Do you maybe want to take about five steps back?" EJ leans over and his shoulder bumps mine as he glares up at Madelaine. "Before you say something you're going to regret?"

"How about *you* take five steps back," says Madelaine, "from Dane."

"You don't own me!" I try to roll the window up, but it struggles, an inch up, one down, in a tug-of-war between me and her.

"You aren't dating *this* guy," Madelaine orders.

"You're just mad because he doesn't want you anymore," I say, my voice struggling as I use all of my strength to get the window up another inch.

Madelaine laughs. "You think I'm *jealous*?" Her laughter gets louder and her mental grip on the window breaks. But I stop rolling it up as her laughter cuts off and she stares directly into my pupils, her gaping smile locked tight. "You're such a disaster."

"Fuck you."

"Dane," says EJ, "let's just go."

Madelaine looks down at the jacket. "Guess I'll keep this, then."

"Fine!" I nearly scream. "*Thank you* for ridding me of it!"

I roll the window up as fast as I can. "Drive."

The gas pedal slams down and the car speeds forward on its own. EJ grips the wheel and shouts, "Let me!"

I mentally let go of the gas pedal and EJ steadies the car.

"I'm sorry," I say. "I didn't mean to actually do that."

"It's okay," he says, his voice tight. He stares straight ahead. "Just breathe."

I look into the side-view mirror at Madelaine. She watches us go, wringing my jacket in her hands.

21

EAT FRENCH FRIES. BE CUTE. REPEAT.

re you a good witch, or a bad witch?

I didn't expect the question to be answered—definitely didn't expect the answer to be bad. Was anyone ever going to tell me? Exactly how twisted can I get with these powers? How limitless is the destruction I could cause, and do I want to cause it?

"What're you thinking?" asks EJ.

I shrug and force the thoughts away. I can't deal with all this right now, and if I think any more on it then I might explode.

"Wish it wasn't so cloudy," I say instead. The grass is soft under my head as I look up at the black-and-purple sky. "Then we could see stars and it would be the absolute most cliché thing we've ever done."

EJ laughs, his head inches from mine. "We literally kissed for the first time yesterday."

"I'm really sorry about earlier," I say.

"Stop apologizing." EJ turns his head to look at me, but I keep my eyes on the sky. "You were upset. I think it would be okay if you took your hands out."

My hands are tucked into the sleeves of my sweater so that it looks like I don't have any. I want to reach over and graze my fingers against his, to touch him without being afraid I'm going to light him on fire. But I haven't lost my edge since speeding away from my own coven.

"I'm taking them out only to eat fries and that's how it's going to be for the rest of my life," I decree. "We'll have to learn to hug with our legs."

After a pause, I sense EJ's mouth pulling into a grin. "I think we can figure that out."

"I walked into that."

But my smile doesn't stay long. I keep waiting for something bad to happen. We're lying in a field in the park, after sundown. At any second, Rabbit Skins could show up and kill us before I even have the chance to do to him what I did to Emily Black. Or Mr. Hawthorne could appear and snuff me out like a candle. But I don't care enough to get up. If he wants me so bad, where's he been?

I slide my gaze from the sky to the hill ahead. The old hospital stands in the blackness. Hell, the monster could come gobble us up and they'd never find our bones. Then again, Madelaine said she's got it tracked. A monster that the coven takes care of.

To my other side, past EJ, I make out the dim outline of a Ferris wheel. A carnival's come into town, standing empty and alone before Hollowians flock in for cotton candy and rickety spins on the scrambler. This whole place is serial killer central.

I roll over onto my stomach and reach toward EJ's coat, which is now a makeshift picnic blanket for a takeout bag from a diner. I reach in, pull out a small handful of fries and shove them all in my mouth. I groan.

"You okay?" EJ asks.

I chew and swallow, letting out a sigh. "This is all I've wanted all week long. Have normal time. Eat french fries. Be cute. Repeat."

EJ laughs. "If I'd known this was all it took to make you happy, I'd have had a pocketful of fries this whole time."

"But then you'd be a creep, so good thing you didn't." I push myself up to sit on my knees. "I like you."

My cheeks burn as soon as I say it.

"I like you, too," he says.

"Can I ask a question?"

"Go for it."

My eyes go back to the sky. "What made you like me? I mean, at first."

EJ lets out a chuckle. "Well, to be honest, I thought you were really cute. And then when you freaked out, I just felt so bad. I understood because I feel awkward and in my head a lot, too. Also, I really liked your hair."

My fingers instinctively go to the locks around my ears, now silky and perfectly placed. "That frizzy ball of cat hair?"

"I liked it," he says. "On you. I don't know, it was just easy to see *you*, I guess."

"How long did you know I was a witch?"

"The second I saw the Reds talking to you across the funeral parlor."

"And you still wanted to talk to me?"

For a second, EJ is quiet. I should stop grilling him about it. But I want to know. I want to hear it from his own mouth so that I can believe it—that this isn't just me being lonely and imagining it. Like it's not going to turn out that this is all a colossal joke and I'm about to end up locked in a bathroom stall again.

Just when I'm about to tell him never mind, he says, "Part of me said to leave immediately and forget I ever saw you. But I don't know. I was really attracted to you."

"You know a *lot* more about this witch stuff than I do."

"I've tangled with them a time or two," he says.

I reach for another fry. "Yeah. About that. Why are you and Madelaine still acting like an angry divorced couple? I thought you were freshmen then."

"We were," EJ says. "We had a great relationship. As great as fifteen-year-olds can have, anyways. But then I had to come out to her once I'd figured that out. I felt like I needed to explore it, and I broke her heart."

"Okay," I say, "well, you were fifteen."

"There's more to it. She also came out to me in a way. The witch stuff. I mean, we got together not long after her brother went missing. Then she learned she's a witch, and her parents freaked out, and yeah."

"Whoa," I say, "repeat that, and this time, include the story."

EJ sighs. "Well, okay. So, for starters, the Wednesdays and the Kowalskis have never gotten along. Every town has their feuding families. Well, mine and hers are the Hollow's. It's ridiculous, really, going back to when my family first moved here. They didn't really like Polish people then."

"Okay," I nod. "We have chapter 1, and it's loaded with nationalism. Chapter 2?"

"So," EJ continues, "we already had shit from that. Her parents and my aunt. It was around that time that she ran for mayor the first time, too. Sorry, this is disjointed. No one's asked me before."

"I'm listening."

"Madelaine was already having issues because of her brother, and then her boyfriend tells her he likes guys. *Then* her boyfriend's only living relative runs for office, effectively becoming the last stop in coven-land. We've been smashed together ever since. And I guess it bothers her that I always know her coven's business, and there's still that wedge of family hate. And I know she still has problems with her parents about her brother and her powers. It's a whole thing, but I didn't tell you that. Meanwhile, I was still getting over *my* parents, and...it was just all a really bad time for everyone."

"And that's it?"

"That's it."

I nod. "Okay, so what about the brother?"

"What?"

"Weren't you two dating when he went missing?" I glance at the hospital and scan the windows for werewolves. "Do you know anything about it?"

"I feel like if I talk about it, she'll know," EJ says. "And I'd rather not have her fingers snapping to make me do god knows what. Not again."

"Again?"

"Oh yeah," EJ's voice rises a bit, anger trickling into the gravel. "She used to control me all the time. Another reason it wouldn't work."

I'm quiet for a moment. I pick up another fry but as I put it to my mouth to bite, I just end up tracing it around my lips. Finally, I sigh. "I promise never to do that."

His hand brushes against my leg. "I trust you."

"Is Jason Wednesday a werewolf?"

"What?"

"The one in the hospital. I know you know about it, if you know everything else."

EJ looks at the sky. "Ah, the ole monster of Jasper Hollow. Beast of urban legend. Stalker of the night."

"Is he?"

"Let's change the subject?"

I drop the french fry and think of Madelaine worrying about a Code Silver. Making sure I went in there and met him. Referring to him like a pet. Cutting off Chloe when she mentioned Jason. She's been protecting him this entire time. I can't help but feel sorry for her.

"Got it."

"Can we go back to being cute?" EJ's hand pushes a little harder against my leg. "Eat french fries? Repeat?"

I lower my face to his and kiss his forehead. "Best topic we've had all night."

He laughs and wraps his arms around my back, pulling me closer to him.

"Let's just stay here," I murmur, my face pushed against the side of his neck. "Forever."

"I have a better idea," EJ says and points toward the abandoned carnival. "Fall Fest is this weekend. Town tradition. Would you want to go? Like, an actual date?"

My lips tighten. Holy shit, a guy just asked me out, officially, on an actual date, for the first time. I thought I was going to have to lurk on Hinge all through college before that happened, and now...

"People won't care?" I ask before I can stop myself.

"I've never had problems in this town. But if they screw with us, aren't you capable of turning them into mushrooms or something?"

My tongue breaks through my smile and I bite down on it. "Fair."

"So?"

I nod and sit up. "Okay. Yes. A date. At a small-town festival. They'll make a Hallmark movie about us."

"Hey, yeah! What's wrong?"

"Nothing, I just gotta fix something," I say, running my fingers through my hair, purposefully messing it up. I think of the hairs, each one falling out of place, sticking up in that unruly way that it had prior to Elena's magical haircut. I look at EJ, feeling the frizz take over.

Even in the dark, I can see he's grinning. "There you are. Nice to see you again."

I lie back down, settling my face deeper into the crook of his neck and wrapping my leg across his waist.

THE HOLLOW: ESCAPE

Grant curls his nose as he rips the rotting flesh from a dismembered finger. He'd plucked it from a string dangling from the ceiling of the common room. With each tear, his stomach retches, as muscle and skin fall in curled flakes like grated cheese.

Not today. Grant will not die. He won't.

He speeds up his work, knowing that Rabbit Skins could reappear at any moment. The bone of the finger slips free of its fleshy wrapping. It's not a true weapon but it'll have to do. He'll stab it into Rabbit Skins' eye when he gets close enough. Stab, run. Even with his twisted ankle.

He hobbles to the stove for the skillet. It's caked in grease from day after day of sizzling that god-awful meat he's been force-fed. There was a time he could've stacked ten of these and lifted them. Now he has to steady himself as his arms quiver under the weight of one. He slides it from its place and nearly drops it on his one good foot.

Dragging it to the window, he swings the skillet back as far as he can. It whooshes down and back up. When he lets it go, it sails through the window, causing a thunderous crash as the glass waterfalls to the floor. Grant hobbles forward, careful not to step on the shards, and pulls himself onto the sill. He swings one leg over, then the other, and drops to the ground.

With a shout, he crashes facedown into the grass. He lifts his head and investigates the surrounding forest, almost invisible in the night. Pushing himself up, bone at the ready, he takes a few hesitant steps through the wet grass before something rustles behind him. He spins around, but nothing is there. Just the side of the cabin, the warm light inside dim and hazy. He lets out a breath and turns back.

Rabbit Skins stands inches away, as though he arrived from nowhere. "*S-st-stay.*"

Grant aims the finger bone, stabbing it against Rabbit Skins' face. It hits directly against his forehead, ricochets, and plunges into his eye.

The monster moans and reaches for the bone. Grant makes it around the corner of the cabin. He wants to break for the trees, but Rabbit Skins will catch up fast. He has to hide and throw him off the trail. He can't use the chicken coop again. Too obvious.

A wooden slope juts from the cabin and Grant hobbles toward it. Rabbit Skins' moans grow louder. *He's following! He's going to round the cabin any moment and—*

Grant feels along the slope until he hits a metal handle. What little light comes from the cabin cuts across the weathered green door as he flings it open. Stone steps lead into darkness. The smell that radiates from below is rotten and salty.

Limping inside, Grant pulls the door over him and holds it shut with what little strength he has left. Everything is quiet—not even Rabbit Skins' moans can be heard. Grant inhales the rotten air into his quivering lungs and thinks about his next move. How he'll get from the cellar to the forest. He won't die tonight.

In the dark of the cellar, someone begins to cry.

His heart picks up speed as the flame of an oil lamp flickers to life, illuminating the room, and Grant squints at the figure of a boy shivering at the foot of the stairs. This can't be right. Can't be real.

Dane waits for him below, his hair soaked, the word *fag* smeared in blood across his forehead. Grant squeezes his eyes shut. This is *not* real. It has to be a trick to scare him. It's not going to work. His knees knock together.

"Go away," he whispers. "Go-away-go-away-go-away—"

Dane doesn't respond. He only stands, shivering, as his body grows thinner, and weaker. Frail.

"I said I'm sorry! Please! Stop!"

Dane blinks, scanning his eyes down Grant. A laugh bursts from his mouth. Then another, until he lets out a full, barking belly laugh.

With shaking limbs, Grant looks down to see that he's wearing the white sundress. It's crisp, and fresh. And now, unlike before, it fits perfectly.

This is what you really are.

A cry escapes Grant's throat and he snaps his attention back to Dane, who is laughing even louder and pointing. "Stop it!" Grant cries. "Please! I don't want to be here. I'll never be an asshole again, just *stop!*"

Dane lifts a middle finger.

Something wet trickles down Grant's head, and he presses a hand to his forehead. The air whooshes from his lungs as he pulls his palm away to see that it's blood. He looks back to Dane, but sees only himself, frail and starved, barely able to hold himself up.

A word drips down his forehead. *Weak.*

The door of the cellar jolts and Grant's knees buckle. He grips the handles tighter with both hands and pulls as the door is yanked from the other side.

His fingers threaten to slip. He can't let go! Just hold on a little tighter, for a little bit longer, and—

His fingers fall from the handles and the door swings back, banging against the ground. Rabbit Skins looms at the entrance of the cellar. And now he's holding his knife.

Grant's knees want to give out, but he has no choice. He limps down the stairs, his bad foot thudding against each step, looking ahead for anything he can use to fight. Dirt. Stone. Lamp. Yes, that's it! If he can just reach the oil lamp and smash it, he can burn the whole place down and escape. He can do it. He just has to reach the—

The flame extinguishes, plunging the cellar into darkness. Grant steps forward. He can still get the lamp; he just has to reach for it.

But his arms won't lift. He wills his muscles again, tries to thrust his arms up, but they won't budge. An unseen force holds him in place as he pleads with every inch of his body for the strength to move.

A single voice sings from all corners of the room, in a rich, full baritone.

"Rabbit Skins, Rabbit Skins... Here to cleanse you of your sins."

The knob on the oil lamp turns, and the flame reignites and slowly brightens.

"Drags you down and eats your bones... Keeps you for his very own."

Rabbit Skins emerges from the shadows, knife in hand. He slides his fingers against his mask and pulls, removing it at last. Grant stares into the face of his soon-to-be killer. He can't be much older than Grant, with healthy, glowing skin on one side of his face. But the other half is void of flesh, a mess of singed muscle and broken teeth.

A scream rips across Grant's vocal cords but is unable to make it past his frozen lips.

"Mustn't," Rabbit Skins whispers, the missing half of his mouth barely able to form the word. "Not ready."

The killer takes another step forward, sweeping the dull side of his knife across Grant's cheek, a pained expression in his eyes. "But looks so tasty," Rabbit Skins mutters, then pulls back sharply. "No! He wouldn't like it."

Rabbit Skins heaves, a strangled sigh hissing from his chest, and doubles over. "I mustn't... But I want it!"

The youthful side of his face winces as he grips the mangled side and twists around. "Don't want to choose. Don't like it."

This can't be happening, repeats in Grant's thoughts over and over again. All he can do is watch while this monster debates whether or not he's going to kill him—while he has his nervous breakdown. As though Grant should be understanding of that.

Tears push through Grant's eyes as his bladder lets go. This is real. This is happening and there's nothing he can do. Because he did this. Didn't he? He broke his pact with Dane, and he locked him in that stall. And here he is. About to die at the hands of this monster. And so. Fucking. Weak.

Rabbit Skins' wailing dies down and he slowly straightens up, his grip on the knife loosening. Grant's heart lifts. Rabbit Skins hobbles three steps away, shaking his head.

"Not yet," he whispers. "Need the other."

He takes another step, and Grant's arms go slack. His knees bend and almost give way. He can move! Rabbit Skins is walking away, and he can move. He can run. He can get the oil lamp and smash it, he can get away.

Get the lamp and run. Just go.

His chest puffs out. He feels strong again, invincible.

Go!

But he can't help himself. He rises to stand taller and spits, "Ugly, weak-ass freak!"

Rabbit Skins whirls, his hand wrapping around Grant's throat, hoisting him into the air.

"I don't want to!" Rabbit Skins wails, to no one in particular. "Don't want to choose."

Grant's scream is cut off beneath his killer's grip.

"But..." Rabbit Skins runs a hungry tongue across his mangled lips. "I do like it fresh!"

Rabbit Skins plunges his knife into Grant's chest and drops him.

The room spins as Grant shivers. He must be against the wall, now. Yes, he's back against the wall and he's standing. He can't be lying half-dead on the ground. Not Grant Allen.

"Why did you make me?" Rabbit Skins mutters somewhere in the room. "Supposed to wait. You made me choose!"

A hand slides into Grant's and his head falls to the side where Dane is lying next to him, his face still smeared with blood.

"Do you want to know a secret?" Dane asks, smelling of Easter lilies. "We're all just memories."

Grant blinks, unable to form words or thoughts.

"It doesn't matter who you think you are, in your head. The only real you is the one people see. The version in their minds."

Grant remembers himself as a child, throwing birthday cake at his sister in a food fight. Wallowing with Dane on beanbags and sucking green juice from plastic popsicle tubes. Picking up Dane's broken plane. Holding Hannah's hand at their dad's funeral. He sees himself pricking his thumb, and Dane's, and pressing it against the headstone.

He sees himself, a little boy, putting on a mask of his own face.

"You're what everyone remembers. Your choices."

Grant shudders as Dane's eyes become white and he leans close, grinning.

"And you, Grant Allen, are a monster."

22

ONE NORMAL NIGHT

"*You'll be wearing your jacket, of course,*" Aloysius clicks firmly, pushing the red jacket across the floor.

Yesterday morning I went to get the mail for Aunt Bella and found it stuffed in the mailbox, between a home decor magazine and an ad promising the best Internet service in town.

I haven't heard from the Reds since Thursday and I can't lie, I've enjoyed it. I was finally able to catch up on my schoolwork yesterday.

"Why would I?" I keep my eyes on my reflection and continue to judge the button-down I put on.

"*Oh, I haven't the foggiest.*" Aloysius rubs a paw against one of the sleeves. "*Because it's who you are?*"

"I'm starting to think that the entire idea of a coven is just another form of oppression, like pigeonholing, perpetuated by psychotic people with a need to control others."

"*Witchcraft is the antithesis of oppression!*" clicks Aloysius. "*But even a witch cannot stand strong when they stand alone.*"

"Hilarious." I turn around to stare at him, folding my arms. "I don't seem to recall needing them to explode a ghost. Besides, did you even see what Madelaine did to it?" I stoop and lift the jacket, shaking it out from its crumpled state. "She ripped my buttons off and put these ugly ones on!"

I point to the bulbous buttons, a hideous dull silver. A black thread snakes its way around one, marking where the jacket was once perfect.

"She ruined it on purpose. Why would I—"

Aloysius puts his paws on his hips. *"I wouldn't be concerned with getting along at this point. Focus on yourself and work as a team. Like coworkers."*

"And our job is being petty?" I turn back to the mirror and spitefully rough my hair up until the curls are standing on end. "Shit! No! I look like a chrysanthemum!"

"That's what you get." Aloysius scurries under the bed and sticks his nose out.

I run my fingers back through my hair, thinking of the individual strands and imagining it perfect again. Slowly, the frizz dies away, and my hair lies down. "At least magic has *some* practical use."

"Hmmpf."

I cringe at my shirt and unbutton it, casting it behind me. It lands over Aloysius's snoot, and he sneezes. I reach across the pile of discarded clothes that I've already tried on and pull out the gray sweater I picked first.

Outside, the October breeze picks up and knocks against the window, making me shiver without even feeling it. If I wear the jean jacket, then I'll have to change again. Huffing, I bend down, grab the red jacket, and pull it on. I turn to my reflection.

"I guess it's not that bad," I say, folding back the lapel to detract from the ugly buttons. "You know, Aloysius, sooner or later you'll learn to just agree with me and save yourself a lot of trouble."

"No, young master." Aloysius pulls his snoot beneath the bed skirt, vanishing completely. *"Sooner or later, you'll learn to agree with* me.*"*

"Young master?" I step to the bed and kneel. "Since when are you formal again?"

"Since you abandoned your goals in favor of funnel cake."

"Aloysius!" I pull up the bed skirt. "Are you mad at me?"

I peer under the bed and spot him in the farthest corner, his body curled and face pointed at the wall.

"No. I am disappointed."

"Why?"

Aloysius slowly turns his head, his eyes catching the light and bouncing it back at me with a yellow glaze. *"Because you don't need me."*

"That's not true."

"All you've done for nearly two days now is hover around mooning over a boy. Have you forgotten why you're here? That a very powerful entity wants to use you? That your cousin—"

"No, I haven't!" My grip on the bed skirt tightens. "But god forbid I have *one* normal night! Aloysius, you need to understand. For me, it's *not* a given that

I can go out and have fun with someone that I happen to really like. I don't know how people will be around here. I don't know if—"

The pads of my fingers burn just at the thought of that bathroom stall. The green door keeping me trapped. I force a gulp of air.

"This is important to me. I want to experience what everyone else does. I want to be normal."

Aloysius shuffles forward. Just a few steps. *"But you're not."*

"You little—"

"My spirit has wafted about, searching for my master and friend since the first drop of human blood fell on this country's earth. Sixteen years ago, I was born into this body in the rafters of that Laundromat, and I peered down through a gnawed hole in the ceiling, down at you in your mother's arms.

"Neither of us are normal. Whether you want to be a witch or not, you've got a witch's familiar. And it hurts that you treat me like some stray who wandered in."

"Aloysius—"

"Go on!" He turns back around. *"I don't wish to speak anymore. If you truly want me, you know how to call me."*

"I'm sorry." I bite my lip. Aloysius doesn't respond. "I said I'm sorry!"

His tail sweeps back and forth, but no words acknowledge me. I yank the bed skirt down. "Fine! Be that way!"

I go to the door but pause. Crossing to the dresser, I pull open the top drawer and grab the box of Banana Moon Pies I bought for him this morning. I pull two from their wrappers and lay them at the bed skirt.

Outside, a car pulls into the driveway.

"He's here. I have to go," I say.

Aloysius doesn't respond. I leave the room, shutting the door behind me.

Hannah bounces up the stairs, her arms full of chip bags and Halloween candies. She wears costume devil horns, the red striking against her black clothes.

"I got the goods!" she announces.

"The what?"

She passes me and disappears into her room. I follow. With a grand gesture, she drops the bags onto her bed and kicks her Converse off. "I have the perfect lineup. We begin with *Pet Sematary*, the original, of course—not that blasphemy of a remake. Then! It's back in time, to *House on the Hill*, followed by *I Was a Teenage Werewolf*. I thought you'd relate to the main guy having an attitude problem and finding out he's a freak."

My jaw drops and I let out a vocal fry. It's Saturday. How could I have forgotten that I promised her we'd hang out? "Shit."

Hannah tenses and cocks her head. "What?"

"Hannah, I am so sorry. I didn't even think about it. I...I'm going to the festival. With EJ."

Her eyebrow raises. "Fall Fest? You mean the carnival with all the weird shit? Like the pumpkin patch and the fun house, and all that *fun. Nice. Shit?*"

"Yes?"

Hannah shrugs, overly casually, and sits on the bed. "Mom was talking about going tomorrow night. As like a fun distraction thing. Bring EJ then."

"I hear you," I look at the ceiling, "but it's kind of...my first. You know, like, my first actual date? Where I get to be in a normal couple? For the first time? Ever? In my life? I should act on that."

Hannah's eyes are almost gone, they're squinting so hard. "I see."

"You should come with us!" I offer. "It'll be fun, we can all just hang out."

"And be the third wheel on your mushy, gushy, *normal* date? If you're going to hang out with me, at least let it be because you *want* to."

"Could we do this tomorrow?" I ask. "Just us?"

"You said that last time."

"I'm really sorry, Hannah."

"I get it! You have a life now. You have things to do. Whatever, it's fine."

"I think you're being a little bit dramatic—"

Hannah cackles. "*Me?* You, Dane *Yuletide*, are calling *me* dramatic?! Okay, Tinker Bell."

I squeeze a fist and half of her chip bags explode.

"Enjoy your movie night." I bolt from her room, slamming her door behind me.

Bounding down the stairs, I nearly face-slam into the front door. In the living room, my worst fear is realized.

Mom sits on the couch, across from EJ, who's sitting very stiffly with his hands on his knees in the armchair.

"Ah, there he is," Mom says with a painted smile.

"What are you doing?" I ask.

Mom shrugs. "I'm just getting to know Elton here."

I cringe. "EJ."

"I don't mind," EJ is quick to interject. "It's nice to officially meet you, Ms. Craven—"

"Oh, please!" My mother holds a hand up. "Ms. Craven was my mother. You can call me...'Ms. Dane's Mom, Ma'am.'"

I'll explode if I don't get out of this house. "I can think of a few things to call you."

Mom gestures to me. "Dane, sit down. You look like a nervous chicken."

Realizing I've been bobbing my elbows up and down frantically, I force my arms to my sides. I go to EJ and sit on the arm of his chair, shooting a scowl at my mother.

"So, you're going to the Fall Fest?" she asks.

"Yes," I say.

"And there's a serial killer out there prowling?"

EJ coughs. "We plan to be very careful. It's pretty well-lit I think, and I'm sure it'll be crowded."

Mom gives a glazed smile. "Good! So, Elton. What are your intentions with my son?"

"*Mom*!" I bolt to my feet.

"What?" My mother looks at me innocently. "I've always wanted to say that!"

"Okay." I grab EJ's hand and pull him from the chair. He goes along with it, looking stunned and confused as I yank him to the door. "We have to leave now."

"It was nice to meet you, uh"—EJ gulps—"Ms. Dane's Mom, Ma'am."

My mom laughs. "You can call me Robyn."

"I don't think I can," he says as I push him outside.

"You stay!" Mom calls out. "I need to talk to you a sec."

I give a loud, exaggerated grunt, but the look Mom responds with tells me not to push it, so I nod to EJ and close the door. "Yes?"

"I heard shouting upstairs," she half whispers. "Everything okay?"

"Yeah," I spit the words out more than I mean to. "Fine."

"I know this is a big deal for you. But please keep in mind that we're here because of a tragedy. This isn't a family vacation."

My grip on the doorknob tightens. "I'm aware of that."

"Hey. Tone."

"What?" My jaw clenches. "I've already heard it from Aloysius *and* Hannah. I know that I'm terrible. I know why we're here. But I can't help the timing."

Mom pushes her palms together and inhales sharply. When she speaks again, her voice is very low, and unnaturally even. "I understand, honey. I'm trying to tell you, from experience, that it's important to have a balance when you meet someone new."

"Balance? I've spent the week learning that I'm not only a witch, but that I'm the fated GBF of an entire coven. And to top it all off? I have to find a murdering ghost. But look at me! I'm doing good. I'm dressed in nice clothes. I'm friends with a group. I'm dating."

"You seem to forget that we have a life in Lexington we'll be going back to."

"Yeah, you, me, and an apartment where you've faked my entire shitty life."

Her eyes lock onto mine. She takes three breaths before saying, almost inaudibly, "Well, I'm sorry I gave you such a shitty life. Maybe that boy will save you and the two of you can ride off into a perfect future."

"Well, he definitely won't abandon me after making me have our kid in a Laundromat."

The words fall between us, landing in silence.

Aunt Bella comes into the living room, taking quiet, slow steps. "Everything all right?"

"Yeah," Mom says, her eyes still on me. "We're finished."

23

HERE COMES PETER COTTONTAIL

"**M**y side hurts," I massage my right hip through my jacket. "That was like driving with Hannah."

EJ snorts, but my heart dips a little. I think about texting her again to ask her to come, but she hasn't responded to my last three apologies, or my gif of a man begging. Aloysius also hasn't responded to my inner calls, telling him that there's a ton of greasy fair food lying around and that he should scurry on over, either.

And then there's Mom.

Maybe, it was a little harsh. But Jesus H., she can't keep shoving away things she doesn't want to talk about. She can't keep putting duct tape on our problems. It's peeling. Fast. But still. Maybe I shouldn't have said it *that way*.

I shake my head and swallow, as though these feelings are merely saliva. This is my normal night, and it's been going well. No one has given us shit, things have felt easy, and there haven't been any mean girls in red jackets showing up to ruin it, or any temptation to light the place on fire.

"Are you having fun?" EJ asks as we step in line for the Ferris wheel. His face is cast in purple light. He's the cutest blueberry I've ever seen.

"It's a good change." I nod.

EJ mocks offense. "I thought you always had fun when I was around."

I consider. "Not always true, but in your defense, we haven't done a lot of fun things yet."

My face breaks out in a blush the instant I say this, and I move my eyes away from him, resisting the urge to slap my own hand. I focus on a guy dressed as a zombie a few yards away instead. Just the way I like my monsters—from Halloween Express. This whole place is like the Jasper Hollow version of Disney World, with creatures walking around waiting for someone to get a picture with them. Frankenstein's monster is trying too hard and failing to scare a group of middle schoolers in line for the Ring of Fire. I nearly bump into a werewolf wearing a torn red flannel. He wiggles his arms at me, clanking the broken chains around his wrists.

I turn back, look at the Ferris wheel. Through the slats I see the old hospital up the hill, overlording the entire fair. Jason Wednesday is probably in there. I wonder if Madelaine is keeping him company.

"What are you thinking about?" EJ asks.

"Hm?"

"You're making a sad face." He imitates what my face must look like, with pouty lips and knitted eyebrows. "You aren't afraid of Ferris wheels, are you?"

I blink away my thoughts of werewolves and witchy sisters. "Only if you rock it."

"Oh." EJ stands up straighter and bobbles his head like he's trying to be cool but failing miserably. "I *always* rock it."

I crinkle my nose. "Boo."

He laughs, his eyes falling to my lips as he thrusts his hands deeper in his coat pockets. He wants to kiss me, doesn't he? I glance at the crowd around us, then I push onto my tiptoes and lean toward his ear.

"I can't wait to get stopped at the top," I whisper.

He squints at me mischievously. "Why do you think I've been trying to ride it since we got here?"

I wiggle my eyebrows as I settle back onto my heels. EJ glances at the sky, and I glance over the crowd.

Not far off there's the facade of a Victorian-style house, painted lavender with a blue roof and made to look dilapidated with boarded-up windows and neon graffiti telling people to keep out. The windows above the front door look like evil eyes that glow red beneath a banner. It says, in red paint splattered to look like blood, *HOUSE OF TERROR*.

In the "front yard" of the house, a pitiful stream of fog rolls past foam headstones and a cardboard tree.

My eyes catch one of the costumed actors wandering toward the house.

Two tall rabbit ears, a mask of fur. A faded yellow plaid suit. He carries a knife. He passes a few people, but they don't notice him as he stalks closer toward the house.

My hand shoots out next to me, knocking EJ in the stomach. "E-EJ—"

"Ow!"

"Holy shit"—I can hardly breathe—"Holy *shit*."

Rabbit Skins crosses through the foam tombstones. On the steel ramp that leads to the door, an attendant dressed as Dracula lets out a forced vampiric laugh and gestures to the next person in line, a guy around my age. He pulls open the door and disappears into the blackness of the house.

"What? What?" EJ follows my pointing finger. "Holy shit."

Rabbit Skins passes through the house's entryway, following the guy in.

"Wait. Dane, don't!"

But I'm gone, running from the Ferris wheel line to the house, my heart thundering. I knock into a woman carrying a large stuffed cat.

"Watch it!" she screams.

"Sorry!" I run faster.

A symphony of strings, horns, and drums screeches from speakers placed around the house's yard, the music like something out of a Hammer Horror movie.

"*Velcome*! Mua-heh-heh!" the Dracula attendant announces to the line, in a hokey Transylvanian accent. "*No* flash photography. *No* stakes or garlic! Bleh! Bleh!"

"Excuse me. Sorry." I push through the line, elbowing my way past moms, a gaggle of preteens, and one guy wearing a camo hat. "Sorry! Coming through!"

"Hey buddy!" the Dracula drops his accent and shouts at me as I come up the ramp. "No cuttin'!"

"You don't understand," I say as I reach the front. "I need inside that house right now."

"*No* cuttin'! Now get to the back and wait your turn."

The people in line boo and shout. I flash a frustrated smile at the attendant. "I don't like to throw my name around. But I am John *Fest*. Founder of Fall *Fest*."

"Back. Of. The. Line."

"Dane!" EJ is catching up, shoving his way through. He has a harder time than I did, and one of the moms smacks his shoulder with her purse.

The horror music warps on the speakers, cutting off with a death-drop *boom*. The speakers crackle as a new song screams to life—"Here Comes Peter Cottontail."

Grant's least favorite song.

"Christ." The attendant scratches his chest and paws a walkie-talkie clipped to the collar of his cape. "We got tech trouble at the house. We need to shut it down a minute."

The lineup erupts into a symphony of groans and boos. I take a step toward the door, and the attendant grabs my arm. "Did you not hear me?"

My eyeballs heat up. "Don't touch me."

"You gotta go, kid."

"Let. Me. Go!"

Heat blasts through my arm and he falls backward, tumbling off the ramp. The door opens on its own, and I run inside.

The entryway of the house is nearly pitch black. Letters glow in red before me, reading TURN BACK and BEWARE, along with a neon-green arrow pointing to the left. I follow it, passing through a slitted rubber curtain into a staged dining room.

A cobweb-covered chandelier hangs above a dirty table piled with fake rotting food and a giant rubber snake positioned like it's slithering between the plates. Skeletons of blue and orange sit holding goblets, glowing in the dark. I make my way around the table and stop.

"Dane!" EJ runs into the room behind me, whispering loudly. "What the hell are you doing?"

But then he's quiet, too. In front of a Styrofoam fireplace, the guy Rabbit Skins followed in stands with his back to us. There's something familiar about him, but I can't place it. He holds one hand out, fidgeting his black-polished fingers. I watch them bobbing and weaving around one another as recognition clicks in my mind. It's the guy I ran into with Hannah outside of Hallow Bean.

"Why does he want her?" he's muttering. "You better leave her the hell alone. The one you want was getting on the Ferris—"

"Hey!" I take a few steps. "Hey, dude! You need to get out of here."

The guy turns around suddenly, and blinks. "You're the—"

"You need to come with us." I move forward and try to take charge of him, but I feel ridiculous because he's about EJ's height and twice my width. "It's not safe in here."

"Not for *you*," the guy says.

I gape. But I don't have time for this shit, so I grab him by the arm and pull him along.

"Get offa me!" he shouts.

"Dane!" EJ scolds, following me. "You can't just drag people!"

"It's for his own good!" I shout back.

"Let me go!"

I push him through the black curtain leading to the entrance and follow, searching for the door.

But this isn't the room we came from. I thought... Must be a maze. Great.

The music warps until the words are slow and deep—like the groan of a monster. Blue-and-green lights flicker, and I stare at twenty of my own reflections. We're in a hall of mirrors.

"Shit." I say. "Shit. Shit. Shit."

"You made him mad," the guy says.

I tilt my head toward the guy, trying to read in on him. How does he know I made Rabbit Skins mad?

Tap-tap-tap. A finger rapping on glass pulls me out of the reading before I can get in. I whirl around, confronted by a bunch of Danes, mouths hanging open, eyes wide.

EJ ducks around a mirror and I jump. He reaches for me. "Back this way."

I tighten my grip on the guy's arm and we make to leave.

"*Hello.*" A deep voice half whispers behind us and we slowly turn back.

A hundred men in rabbit masks stare back. The lights flicker and fail, plunging us into darkness. A surge of electricity sounds over us and the lights flash on, revealing one singular Rabbit Skins making his way down the hall.

I try to remember what I did before, how I destroyed Emily Black. I need to get really upset. Really angry.

"What did you do with Grant?!" I scream.

"F-f-fresh Grant." He giggles and flashes his knife, which is dripping with blood.

"*Run!*" EJ screams.

We trip through the curtain, scrambling back into the dining room, just the two of us. "Where'd that guy go?"

"He's still in there!" EJ makes for the curtain, but I break back through before he can.

"Dane, no!" EJ comes after me.

I'm met only by shaking mirror-Danes about to piss themselves. I run to the side and down a different stretch of hall, knocking against a mirror. A tired, terrified Dane stares back two inches away. A blue light flickers on behind the reflection, revealing the Hallow Bean guy behind the mirror. He's at the end of the maze, in some sort of plant-filled chamber. I push against the glass.

Somewhere in the hall, Rabbit Skins giggles, drowning out the sounds of EJ calling for me.

"Leave him alone!" I kick the glass.

The light goes out and the guy disappears, leaving just my reflection—and the reflection of Rabbit Skins behind me.

I whirl, my back pressing to the mirror, as he hobbles toward me.

Kill him! My brain screams at me. *Destroy him! Get mad!*

He waves his knife back and forth. I'm going to piss myself.

"What did you do with Grant, you sick bastard?" I spit at him.

Not mad enough!

He raises his knife.

"Hey, asshole!" EJ screams from down the hall.

Rabbit Skins jumps out of the way as EJ barrels forward. I step aside just as he's about to slam into me, and he goes falling through the mirror. Shattered glass rains down on us as I stumble to him over the mirror frame.

"You almost got killed!" I pull EJ to his feet by his collar.

"So did you," says EJ. He pulls a shard of mirror glass from the sleeve of my jacket and pushes me farther along, into the plant room the Hallow Bean guy was standing in.

This one is staged to look like a conservatory, with potted plants spray-painted black and a scorpion the size of a sofa. Above us, a plexiglass dome in the ceiling reveals the cloudy sky. The guy leans casually against the wall in the corner behind a cobweb-wrapped telescope.

"We need to keep going!" I tell him. "There has to be another door!"

"It's behind you." The guy rolls his eyes.

I spin and stumble back. Rabbit Skins stands waiting, his head tilted, beneath a black-curtained arch. He saunters in, right toward me, his knife raised.

"Yeeew. You." He hobbles closer. "Come...play."

EJ lunges at him, knocking him to the ground. I've never seen anyone able to fight a ghost before.

The clouds part above the dome, revealing the full, red-ringed moon. Its light hits the plants and scorpion, the half-built coffin in the corner, and trickles down, illuminating us in pale gray. EJ rolls out from beneath Rabbit Skins, pummeling the ghost's face again and again.

I stand, stunned, looking at him. And at the fur growing across his fists.

A guttural snarl rips from EJ's throat, which is growing longer by the second. His entire form is swelling, twisting, and elongating as he growls. Rabbit Skins kicks him off and he lands in a darkened corner.

Frozen, I watch as growls and the gnashing of teeth float out of the darkness.

Don't be true. Don't be true.

A large, clawed paw steps into the moonlight. The beast of my hospital nightmares emerges, flashing its fangs at Rabbit Skins, who vanishes.

Rabbit Skins is afraid of my boyfriend.

EJ throws his head back and unleashes a deafening howl. My hands clap over my ears.

Because my boyfriend is a monster.

"EJ?" I ask, barely able to make a sound.

The werewolf swings its head to me, his sunken eyes glowing red against his gaunt, wolfish face.

I recall the first time I ever saw him at the Hallow Bean. What I thought of him then. *A dog waiting for a frisbee.*

He runs from the conservatory, knocking down mirrors and plastic skeletons.

I look at the Hallow Bean guy, who's still standing behind the telescope.

"I'm not done with you."

I run from the room, following the path of broken mirrors and ripped-down curtains. I need to talk to my EJ. The monster of Jasper Hollow.

24

ALEXA, PLAY "BAD MOON ON THE RISE"

I climb over the wrecked door of the House of Terror and stop at the top of the ramp. The crowd runs, frenzied, cowering around game stands and overturned popcorn carts.

EJ leaps atop the roof of the milk-bottle game, and its attendant rushes out from under him, covering his head with his arms. The wood of the roof cracks as EJ climbs, a massive claw scraping into the paint as he gnashes his teeth and growls at the crowd.

"Hey, kid!" the Dracula attendant appears beside me, fists on his hips. "I gotta kick you out. Please leave the fairgrounds immediately."

I shoot my hand toward the werewolf. "Are you kidding me?"

He grabs my arm and before I even think about it, I wheel my free fist into his jaw. He falls backward, landing on the wrecked door. Sometimes, I guess I don't *need* magic.

I rush down the ramp and push my way through screaming mothers and whooping teenagers who must think this is some kind of show.

EJ leaps from the roof and lands in the dirt, lowering himself onto his front paws, like a cat preying on a mouse.

"Hey!" I call out. "Stop!"

EJ turns his attention my way, and his eyes glow right into me.

I halt, holding my hands up, fingers splayed. Deep in his throat, EJ emits a low, heavy growl.

"Easy," I say. "Easy now. I *will* bitch-slap your nose again."

Is he really in there, conscious of me? Or has he gone feral and I'm just a raw steak ready for him to swallow in a single gulp?

Click.

EJ snaps his gaze to the side. Four policemen surround us, guns cocked and ready, pointed directly at EJ's giant wolf body.

"Back away slowly, kid," an officer behind me says evenly. "Don't turn your back to it."

"I can't do that," I say.

"Back it up, now. Quickly, please."

"I'm not moving." My fingers twitch.

"Come on, kid!" another officer whispers loudly. "Get outta there!"

"If I do"—I take a slow step closer to EJ—"you'll shoot him."

"What the—"

"It's me," I whisper, never breaking contact with those glowing eyes. "It's *me.*"

The fingers of my right-hand bend, and my wrist follows, slowly descending onto EJ's nose or...his snout, I guess. When he doesn't gnash at me, I bring my other hand behind his fuzzy, pointed ear, and scratch. He whimpers, shutting his eyes. When they reopen, his irises have turned blue.

The crowd is silent, everyone trying to make sense of what they're seeing.

He's as big as a van and looks like the undead corpse of a wolf, but he's definitely in there. I smell the faintest trace of his soapy, fresh scent that I've grown familiar with.

He's in there.

"What do you say you and me get out of here and have a talk?"

His big eyes blink and EJ whimpers again, lowering his head to the ground. I swing my leg over the back of his shoulders and pull myself on. The crowd screams.

"What the hell are you doing?!" an officer shouts.

"Back away!" I say. "Back it up!"

The officers don't lower their guns. I need them to, before EJ takes a bullet and maybe me too.

I think of holding Grant's face under the water. Of controlling Aloysius. I hate it. I don't want to do it. But I'm glad I can.

I look at the first officer, thinking about that night in the bathroom stall, and imagine him lowering his gun, pointing it to the ground. The officer frowns at me, as though he can feel what I'm doing. But slowly, his gun descends.

"What are you doing, Greg?" another officer asks. Then *his* gun descends.

A third officer keeps his pointed straight at EJ's head. "Enough of this."

His finger presses against the trigger before I can focus on him.

"DON'T SHOOT!" a voice booms. "Don't shoot!"

I heave a sigh as Sheriff Doyle runs forward.

"Todd, it's—"

"You heard me, guns down!" Doyle's face is flushed, his eyes locked on EJ's. I really wish I had my hoodie on so I could pull the hood over my head. "You'll hit the kid!"

They lower their guns.

EJ takes off, and I struggle to stay on, barely managing to wrap my arms around his neck as he bolts through the screaming crowd.

"Wait!" Doyle shouts, but we're gone.

EJ heads toward the Ferris wheel. With a leap, he latches onto it and climbs the spindles. The riders scream as their seats swing back and forth, and he pulls us upward, to the very top. He balances on the steel beams. I look out over the Fall Fest, a sea of colorful lights beneath us.

Well, he got us to the top, finally.

He jumps, and my stomach shoots up into my throat as we land on a semitruck with the carnival company's logo painted across it. EJ's impact dents the sheet metal.

He leaps off the semi and bolts across the fairgrounds, into the blackened park, and straight to the old hospital.

When we reach the crumbling entrance, he stops and lowers his head. I slide from him, my knees shaking so hard I almost drop to the ground.

He runs against the doors, knocking them down, and disappears inside.

I stumble toward the doorway, leaning myself against the frame as I enter. My hand hits a hinge.

"I'm sorry, sir, but Mr. West is not allowed to receive visitors."

"There's nothing wrong with him. If he knew I needed to see him—"

"I'm sorry, sir. Please leave."

I stuff my hands into my pockets and make my way across the floor of the foyer, my throat wanting to close from the smell with every step. Taking the stairs two at a time, I squint through the dark.

"EJ! Where the hell are you?"

As I hit the final step, I stagger back and grip the rail. EJ stands before me. He's slung an open flannel on his bare torso and is buttoning a pair of jeans. His hair is messed up in unruly spikes.

"What was that?!" I shout. "Were you saving this for the third date, or were you just hoping I wouldn't notice?"

"Dane." He holds his hand up, and even in the dark I can tell his eyes are pleading. "I wanted to tell you. I wanted you to know from the beginning, but I couldn't—I didn't... I didn't know if you'd believe—"

"Somewhere between 'a ghost serial killer took your cousin' and 'you have wicked gifts from a dark lord,' you thought this was beyond believability?"

"Believe that I'm not bad," EJ says. "Because I'm, I'm—"

"A coward?"

"A monster," his voice rises. "I'm a monster. The very thing you're supposed to keep in line. The reason Madelaine's telling me to keep my nose out of everything, and why they're so shitty to me, and—and—I'm way below you in the paranormal food chain."

I turn my back to him and rush a few steps down. "So that's it. That's why she doesn't like you, because *you* are the werewolf."

"It's more than that." He closes the distance again, and now he's shouting. "This is her family's fault!"

"What?"

"You think I just have an aversion to red jackets?" His voice climbs octaves, and his fists shake. "The Wednesdays are the reason I'm like this. *Look* at me!"

He points to his face, and as my eyes adjust I can tell that he's not entirely human again. The skin on the right side of his face is still all fur. Specks of red glow in his eyes. His ears have tiny points.

"Her family cursed mine," he says, and I remember him mentioning feuds.

I look to the ceiling and thrust my arms out. "Universe! Oh, universe!" I shout. "You got the wrong person! This is supposed to happen to straight girls in teen novels! Not me!"

"Please don't joke," EJ says.

"I'm not joking!" I shout. "That's the shittiest thing about it!"

"Aren't you wondering why I kept putting my hands in my pockets and didn't kiss you when I wanted?" EJ asks.

Slowly, he puts his hand to my jacket, his fingers brushing against the silver buttons. He winces and pulls his hand back, points his fingers up for me to see. I barely make out the promise of a tiny burn.

"I couldn't," he says. "Even if I wanted to."

"Silver. Werewolves. I get it." My voice breaks. Madelaine wasn't trying to be petty. She was trying to protect me. "So that night they made me come in here—"

"I didn't want to hurt you. I didn't know it was you until I'd come down the stairs and there you were."

"That's why Ambrose screeched." I chuckle with anger. "So you'd think the Reds were here and come down. And why you kept looking at the sky."

I think about the other night, when we lay out in the park with our makeshift picnic. I'd even mentioned it. Everything was so perfect. Except for the clouds that were blocking the moon. God, I'm such a dumbass!

"I thought it was Jason." I laugh hysterically. "And you just let me go on thinking that!"

"I'm sorry."

I take a few more steps down, but this time, I won't turn my back on him. "So, if you're a monster, what do you do? When you're a wolf, what do you do?"

"I hunt," he says, sounding a bit ashamed.

"That's why you were in the woods." Another angry laugh escapes me. "When you found the bodies and said you were 'hiking.'"

Tears push from my eyes before I can stop them. I hate that I'm crying. I hate that I care this much.

"I would never hurt you, Dane."

"Why are you saying that?"

"Because it's true."

"No." I plant my feet, the breath in my chest threatening to leave me. "Why at this minute? I'm talking about when you found the crime scene. Did you actually find those bodies, EJ?" My voice raises. "Or did you—"

"Come on. You know I didn't kill them."

"Did you rip them into pieces?" I push.

His sigh makes me slide my back against the wall as my knees give out from under me.

"I didn't eat the other half of them, if that's what you mean," he finally says. "But..."

My hand pulls up into a fist that plants into my forehead. "If you don't just tell me everything, I swear to god—"

"I tried a binding ritual." He comes down a step, and I slide down to the next one. "I found it years ago. But it requires, you know, bodies... So when I stumbled across them...I had to try, Dane..."

"So, *you* arranged them that way."

EJ nods. "Yeah."

"You found it years ago." I picture a fourteen- or fifteen-year-old EJ, dating Madelaine and having access to Collingwood Hall. Must have had a lot of time to rip pages from Ada's books, I imagine. "Have you just been using me, thinking I'll help you?"

"No!" EJ takes another step down.

"I have to go."

"Wait for me." EJ comes toward me. "I'll change back, just give it a minute, and I'll help—"

"I have to find that guy Rabbit Skins was following. He obviously knows things and he's probably the one who started all this shit. I have to find him so I can find Grant. I can't deal with *this* right now."

EJ's voice cracks. "Let me help you."

"I don't know you!" I stumble toward the door. "For all I know, you're part of it too."

He grabs my shoulder. "Dane—"

"Get off!"

Against his will, EJ stumbles back and sits on the bottom stair. When I let go of my mental hold, he looks at me, trembling.

"You promised you'd never control me," he says, his voice shattered. "You *promised*."

"Well, sorry. I broke that promise."

THE HOLLOW:
THE NEXT VICTIM

annah Allen shoves a potato chip in her mouth and stares at the television. Someone knocks on the bedroom door.

"Mm," she mumbles in response.

The door creaks open, revealing her mother's face in the dim hallway.

"Aunt Robyn and I have decided to go out for dinner," she says. "Where would you like to go?"

"I'm good," Hannah says and doesn't look away from the screen.

A quiet sigh. "I know you're mad that Dane went out, but you shouldn't let that stop you from having a good time."

"I *am* having a good time," Hannah says as the last victim of the movie gets slashed with a kitchen knife and the credits roll. Hannah laughs, pointing at the screen. "See?"

Her mother steps into the room. "I don't like you watching this stuff."

Hannah sits up. "Funny, you didn't notice until it was just us."

"What do you mean?"

"You never gave a flying shit what I did or didn't do."

You liked Grant more.

Her mother shuts the door behind her. "That's not true, and you know better."

Even Dad knew it.

Hannah ignores her. "Besides, last thing I want to be is a third wheel to my mother."

A moment of quiet passes between them, the only sound coming from the TV as Hannah points the remote and searches for the next movie.

"I get how you feel," her mother says finally.

Hannah rolls her eyes. "What a parenty thing to say. You have no idea—"

"To feel like your sibling's the better one?" Her mother raises an eyebrow. "Right. No idea. Or to find out that the person you're closest to is actually a witch, and then you watch them do everything you can't and hope for a scrap of their time? You are right, daughter. I have zero idea what that must be like."

"I don't want to play last brownie."

"Or to lose someone you can't imagine losing!" Her mother nearly chokes on the words. "Not once! But twice! Who the hell am I, right?"

"Jesus," Hannah grunts. "I'm the ungrateful bad seed, I get it."

Her mother holds her palms up. "I'm trying. Okay? I shut down a lot. And I don't always have it in me to be present, since your father...and now Gr— I'm trying, Hannah."

Hugging herself, Hannah drops her voice. "I get it."

"As I said, Aunt Robyn and I are going out. Will you come?"

"As I said, no."

Her mother shrugs. "Then don't say no one ever includes you." Hannah clicks play on the next movie. "We'll be home in an hour or two. Keep the doors locked."

Hannah snorts as her mother leaves the room. She mutes the TV, waiting for the sound of her mom and aunt leaving the house. There's a muffled conversation, the jingling of metal keys, then finally the door clicking shut, and the garage opening.

She pushes herself from the bed and hitches up the waist of her black sweatpants. Leaving her room, she makes her way down the hall, stopping for a moment outside the upper guest room. She turns the knob and peeks in. Dane's raccoon is asleep on a pile of clothes, the remnants of Moon Pies at his side.

Leaving the door open a crack in case he needs to roam, she heads down into the basement.

She pauses as she passes through the den. It's been her mom's escape room for years, a plainly decorated box of nothing. A low sofa, a Zen Garden on a coffee table with a miniature, battery-operated waterfall next to it.

There's a new picture hung on the wall. Hannah snorts as she stares at her brother, kneeling on a football field in his uniform.

There is no picture of Hannah in the room.

At the far end of the den is a door. The one that leads to the unfinished part of the basement. A bunch of junk stored to be ditched at some vague time in the future. But it's more than a basement to Hannah.

"Hey, Daddy," she says, shutting the door behind her and surveying the large concrete room. "Can we talk?"

She heads for one of the shelves and trips on the cord of an old boom box radio, nearly knocking it from its place on a dusty barstool. She catches it, pushing it back into place. With a sigh of relief, she wraps the cord around it and lays the plug on top.

Resuming her path to the shelves, she makes for the box that holds all her old stuff. Dog-eared copies of R. L. Stine books, sentimental ornaments her mother claims she'll want someday, old notebooks from middle school scrawled with barely started stories about backwoods hill witches and sexy vampire lovers. But what she wants is wedged to the side between four white candles and a box of matches.

The Ouija board.

She hasn't used it for years, not since she discovered tarot cards.

Thrusting the board under her arm along with the candles and matches, she steps to the taped red X on the floor. Hannah sets the board here, the very place where she found her father, dead of an aneurysm, when she was twelve, and sets up the candles, lighting each one.

"How long did I stand there before anyone found us, Daddy? One hour? Three? Or did it just feel that long?"

She places the planchette on the Ouija board and closes her eyes, focusing solely on the image of her father in her mind's eye. The blond hair that belongs to her and belonged to Grant. The blue eyes, too. The man who understood her and let her watch scary movies, and watched Ozzy Osbourne concerts with her, and wasn't worried that she'd turn out to be a psycho.

"Are you here?" she asks the empty room.

Beneath her fingers, the planchette begins to move. She gasps and looks down as it slides beneath her fingertips in a careful, methodical pathway, until it reaches its reply.

YES.

A tiny smile breaks over Hannah's lips. She can't ruin this chance. Finally, a real connection.

"Are you all right?"

YES.

Hannah lets up on the planchette a bit, worries that she's just doing it herself. "Do you know what Dane isn't telling me about Grant? About why he was in the woods and what happened between them?"

The planchette jerks away from her fingertips and she jumps. *YES.*

Upstairs, the front door opens. Hannah looks to the sound, up at the ceiling. Her mom must have forgotten something. She doesn't have a lot of time.

"Do you know where Grant is?" Hannah asks. She wants to ask if he's alive at all but isn't ready for the answer as the planchette zigzags across the board, spelling out an answer in dizzying speed.

I. KNOW. EVERYTHING.

"Holy shit," Hannah whispers. "Where is he?"

The planchette slides faster.

I'LL TAKE YOU THERE.

The blood in Hannah's heart pumps cold. "Daddy? Is this you?"

NO.

Hannah stands, nearly kicking the board over. Behind her, the boom box powers up with static. She turns to it, wide-eyed, and its yellow lights glow as the radio tunes itself. The unplugged cord slides to the ground.

An organ groans out a melody that sounds familiar to her. Some sort of nursery rhyme. A children's choir sings.

"Rabbit Skins, Rabbit Skins... Here to cleanse you of your sins."

"What do you want?!" Hannah screams over the choir.

The planchette zooms back over the Ouija.

Y

"Be gone!"

O

"Leave me alone!"

U

Hannah falls backward, knocking into a coatrack she hadn't even realized was there. She reaches out and catches the sleeve of an old coat. A faded yellow plaid coat. Her eyes freeze. She blinks.

There's a dirty, deteriorated hand sticking from the sleeve.

Slowly, Hannah lifts her eyes to see that it is not a coatrack. White eyes peer down at her through holes in the mask of a rabbit's head.

She screams, and the man screams. He stumbles to the side and something furry swipes at her ankle. She looks down to see Dane's raccoon biting the man's leg, fighting him away from Hannah.

"Aloysius?"

The raccoon clicks fiercely between bites, as though telling her something important. Hannah wastes no time in acting on what she thinks he might be telling her.

She runs.

25

TO LEND A HELPING FIST

I tighten my jacket as the pink car pulls toward me outside of the ticker-taped fairgrounds. It was probably stupid to wait here, since there's still a slew of mothers wailing to a cop about how a monster almost ate their baby. Doyle's been strutting around and of course he knows who I am. Yet, no sign of the Hallow Bean guy.

Maybe I want to be found. Maybe I want to be thrown in a jail cell where no one can get me.

Madelaine stops the car, and I stare blindly into her headlights like a deer about to get pulverized. I run to the passenger side, yank the door open, and slide in.

"What did you do?" Madelaine asks, eyeing the police tape.

"Why didn't you tell me?" I ask. "If you knew about EJ, why didn't you tell me?!"

Madelaine looks at me, surprised. "So, you... I thought you'd figure it out."

I huff and stare out the windshield, the blocked-off carnival a way too perfect metaphor for my one "normal" night. A moment of silence passes between us.

"So," Madelaine begins cautiously, "you *did* figure it out?"

"Fall Fest was ruined when a rabid, mutated wolf burst into the crowd," I say curtly. "*And then* proceeded to climb the Ferris wheel with me on its back."

"You rode away on him? You didn't!" Madelaine cackles. "My god, you're so extra!"

I wince, heat flaring in my cheeks. "Is that why you took me to the hospital? To figure it out?"

"I just wanted to warn you."

"I know your family did it to him," I accuse her. "Just undo it and cut the mean-girl bullshit."

"Yeah, because I'm so astute at undoing a century-old curse. EJ thinks I can just wiggle my nose and *poof*. No more beast boy. He thinks I'm letting it go on because he broke up with me when he came out. Like I'm some tragic thing who didn't know her man liked other men, too. But that's not how it works. And news flash: I knew he wasn't straight the minute he *begged* me to see *Wicked* on tour with him. So."

I rub my temples. "I thought your *brother* was the werewolf."

"Not at all." Madelaine's voice quivers. She takes a deep breath. "Jason is just...gone. Probably dead."

"Like Grant." I shudder. "No way he's not. I didn't care enough to find him in time."

To my surprise, Madelaine grabs my hand. "Hey, don't do that."

"I have to!" I laugh dryly and tears well up in my eyes. "I chose a date over him. I'm a terrible person."

"We are going to find him."

"Well"—I breathe in to force the tears back—"we do have one clue. Rabbit Skins showed up. That's why EJ transformed, to protect me. But there was a guy in the House of Terror. He seemed to know the ghost. Like, he could talk to it."

"Who's the guy?"

"I've briefly met him before, but beyond that I have no idea. But I would recognize him. He's in there somewhere." I nod toward Fall Fest. "They're not letting anyone leave until they've been 'looked at.' I think they're searching for me."

Madelaine unbuckles her seat belt and pulls at one of her sleeves. "Then we'd better take these off before we're instantly caught while we look for him."

A few minutes later we're sneaking past the backside of a balloon-darts game, arms folded across our chests to brace against the cold. Red and blue lights flash up the sides of the game stands, overpowering the purples and greens of Fall Fest.

We peek around the corner and freeze. Sheriff Doyle stands with his back to us, a cell phone to his ear. Madelaine pulls me inside the game stand, and we crouch behind the counter to listen.

"That's not gonna work, Bridget!" he says. "I've got half a town in hysterics because a werewolf's running around with a witch ridin' it like a bronco... Of course we aren't followin'! And now I got a team of officers questioning me because we aren't. Can't very well tell them it's just the mayor's nephew havin' a testosterone surge."

Madelaine snorts.

"Sheriff Doyle!" a voice calls out, and gravel crunches under feet. I peek around the side of the counter. "He was in my house!"

"It's Hannah," I say. "What's she doing here?"

"Shh," Madelaine whispers.

Hannah pushes her way to Doyle, past officers trying to hold her back.

"Let her through!" Doyle calls.

The officers look at him with confusion but lower their arms. Hannah runs to him, scowling ever deeper.

"I gotta go." He clicks his cell phone off and turns to Hannah. "Who was in your house?"

"Who the fuck do you think?"

"Language!"

"Rabbit Skins. He was in my fuc—my house, and he tried to frickin' kill me."

My head droops and I feel like I'm going to be sick. Could he have been there looking for me? Is that why he came to the fest in the first place? Hannah was nearly killed, and I wasn't there.

"Okay," Doyle sighs. "You need to be calling Ada—not me. I don't do ghosts."

"I went to Collingwood Hall." Hannah shakes her head. "No one's there. I can't find Mom, or my aunt, and Dane isn't answering his phone."

You didn't answer the phone.

"I don't have time for this!" Doyle snaps. "EJ went and turned wolf, and—"

"What?"

"So just keep callin', bang on Ada's door, figure it out!" He stomps away. "Jesus fucking Christ."

As Doyle storms off, Hannah gapes at him looking like she wants nothing more than to jump and maim him. I stand and wave her over.

"Hannah!" I whisper. "Over here!"

She swivels her head to me, and her eyes grow twice their size as she bolts over. "There you are! Where have you been? I've been—"

"Calling, I know. I haven't exactly been checking my phone. A *lot* has happened."

"You're telling me!"

Madelaine sticks her head up from behind the counter like an angry whack-a-mole. "Will you two get back here and be quiet before we have mug shots for senior pictures?"

I take Hannah's hand and pull her behind the counter with me. I crouch, gesturing for her to follow.

"What is going on?" she whispers, spit spraying on my knee. "And don't you dare say you can't tell me."

Looking at Madelaine, I raise my eyebrows. She rolls her eyes. "Fine. Igor can know."

For the second time tonight, I give the abridged version of everything. Hannah squints at me the entire time, waiting for a plot twist that never comes. When I've finished, she says, "Well, I hope you've learned your lesson about canceling movie night."

"The hard way," I agree.

"So, basically..." Hannah squeezes her eyes closed. "This guy brought Rabbit Skins back to murder my brother. We need to find this guy and make him talk."

"Yes," I say, "but we're stuck back here."

"I think I can help you," a voice says above us, and we all jump.

From the other side of the counter, a face stares down at us, looking scared. An accessory to murder.

The guy from the House of Terror. We stand in unison.

"You," I say.

"You?!" Hannah shrieks.

"Let me explai—"

Hannah knocks him out with a single punch as Madelaine and I both gape in surprise. Righteous fury paints her expression.

"That was for Grant." Then, she cradles her fist. "Goddamn it, that hurt!"

Much like getting arrested, dragging a body isn't so bad once you've been attacked by a serial killer. But here we are, dragging him from the trunk of Madelaine's car to Aunt Bella's porch. Chloe looks between him and us like it's all a big punch line she isn't getting, but Elena doesn't seem fazed at all, her eyes trained on him, controlling him. Ensuring he doesn't wake up.

"Watch his head," Madelaine says as we pull him up the porch steps. "He needs it to tell us everything."

"I could just lobotomize him with the Dum-Dum stick in my pocket," says Hannah, shuffling to get a better grip under the guy's arms. "It would make me feel better."

"You can feel better once we've vanquished the ghost of a serial killer," I say, heaving his legs higher. I glance at Elena. "Don't let him wake up until we're ready."

"Duh." Elena keeps her gaze on the guy. "And don't any of you deny that I'm the best at control again."

Madelaine pushes the door open, and we carry the guy inside.

"Honey, I'm home!" I call out.

There's no answer in the darkened house. Madelaine waves her fingers, and the lights of the living room flip on. I drop the guy's legs, and Hannah almost loses her own grip.

The living room is a mess, the couch and armchair overturned and slashed, stuffing and October leaves scattered over the floor. A gaunt brown rabbit scurries from the room and out onto the porch.

"Nope"—Chloe makes her arms an X—"I don't like this!"

"What the hell?" Hannah whispers.

"Here, let him down easy," I say, and we lower the guy to the floor. "Mom?! Aloysius?"

"Mom!" Hannah shouts.

No one answers either of us. Madelaine goes into the kitchen and flicks the lights on. She cries out. We run after her.

"Nope!" Chloe shouts.

"Hell no," Elena mutters.

I push my way past them.

Flecks of blood cover the linoleum, droplets falling from the ceiling, where, in large, smeared script, it reads, *COME PLAY.*

26

PLAYTIME

"He must have waited until they came home," Hannah's voice breaks.

"Holy hell," Madelaine whispers.

My head swims. I can barely think, barely breathe. I can only picture Mom, staring at me during our last conversation. I hurt her. I'm sure of it. I hurt her and now she's gone. And Aloysius...

"It's all my fault."

"Everyone breathe," Madelaine says, holding her hands out like a conductor cutting off an orchestra. "This doesn't mean anyone's dead. Think about it. If he *is* after Dane or Hannah, then he could be using them as bait."

I need her to be right. "Yes. Bait. Okay, we need to talk to that guy."

"Logan," Hannah says, and our eyes meet. "His name is Logan Hockstetter. Remember, we ran into him at Hallow Bean?"

"And he was acting really strange," I recall.

"He's in our class. Grant was never nice to him. Like, *especially* him."

"A motive," Madelaine says. "All right Elena, we can wake him up."

"Not so fast," Chloe says. "Not that I'm threatened by that guy, but shouldn't we ensure that he can't run off?"

I nod. "Yes."

"Let me find something." Hannah stoops, opening the cabinet under the sink and tossing me a large roll of gray duct tape.

With quaking knees, I go back to the living room and try to keep my hands steady as I tape Logan's wrists together. This is the guy. The person who had Grant killed and got us all into this mess in the first place. My hands grow hotter the more I look at him, threatening to melt the tape. I could light him on fire right now. Just turn him into ashes and move on.

"This is such bullshit," I whisper, more to myself than anything else.

"What?" Hannah asks.

"This is bullshit!" I say louder. "This guy is why everything's shit, Hannah. What are we going to do? Solve this and go back to our lives like that answers anything? Rabbit Skins took Grant. Now he's taken my mom. And your mom. We're next. And we're alone."

Madelaine is who responds—so quietly I barely hear her. "You're not. Your friends are here."

I whirl on her. "Are you kidding me?! All you can think of right now is the freaking coven being complete?"

"Did I say coven? I said friends."

A hysterical laugh breaks out of me. "All you have done is GBF me! The clothes, the hair, ordering me around—"

"We aren't doing that," Elena says.

"Well, I was," Chloe admits, folding her arms. "Just a little bit—you know what? Not now, Chloe."

"Dane," Madelaine speaks up. "We don't want to GBF you. I realize *now* how that all came off, but to be honest, we were excited to have a new kid. We wanted you to feel welcome."

"You have *not* made me feel welcome."

"I know. I'm sorry. I'm not great at making friends and I need to work on that," she says. "But. Come on. Why do you think we even run in a coven? And stick together? We"—she gestures to all of us, even Hannah—"can only count on each other."

"We're outcasts, too," says Elena. "Both sides of my family are from Puebla. Why do you think I had to magically wire a boy's jaw shut? He wasn't paying me a compliment, let's just say that."

"And people think I'm stupid," Chloe interjects. "I'm not. I just don't like being serious considering my life is nothing but scary stuff."

Elena nods in solidarity. "We all have targets on our backs. We're *witches.* On our own, we're just lonely weirdos. But together, we're unstoppable."

"Yeah," Chloe adds. "We rule our lives, and we get what we want, because we deserve it. *You* deserve it."

"Love me, hate me, I don't give a shit." Madelaine steps closer. "We're a family, whether you want it or not. Why else did I come to the fairground when you called me crying?"

I have to fight back fresh tears, because I realize now that I *did* call her first. I didn't even try Hannah. Like the magnets in my bones were pulling me to who I needed. My coven.

"When Jason disappeared," Madelaine continues, and now I can see that *she* is fighting tears, "I was lost. I didn't just lose my brother; I lost my best friend."

Elena puts her hand on Madelaine's shoulder. I shift my weight and sense Hannah doing the same. The room is filled with the threat of spilled secrets, and we all wait for the words to tumble.

"Jason is a trans man," Madelaine says. She glances at Chloe and Elena. "I don't know if they told you already."

"Oh." I nod.

"My parents... They weren't okay with that. My family's so careful about appearances that it's toxic. My father is one of the only Black CEOs in this area. My mother is the whitest woman I know. *And* she didn't take his name. Here. The dirty looks they get in this state never ends, and it tore them down by the time my brother and me were growing up. Imagine, a trans kid *and* a witch for children?" Contempt bakes into her voice. "What would the neighbors think?"

I dig my fingernails into my palms. Shame sweeps the back of my neck and I bow my head. I'd assumed for so long that the Reds wanted to use me. Never once did I think that maybe they were just allies. "I'm sorry, Madelaine."

"He was running away," she continues, "and I wanted to go with him. So we ran. No real plan, we just packed a bag and bolted. But out in the woods...something got him. I couldn't see anything, and I couldn't help. All I could do was listen to whatever it was attacking him. The last thing he said to me was 'run.' We all tried to find him, but there was no trace. He was just *gone*. Eventually, everyone stopped looking, but I won't."

Chloe holds her hand out. "Madelaine—"

"Anyways!" She waves us all off. "So. Yeah. No, no one was trying to make you a project or anything. And I think we all agree that we're sorry it came off so gross."

"Hey, it's okay." I shrug, still upset with myself for being so obtuse. "We're all learning, I guess." We all stand in silence, for once. No one's being petty or trying to work each other's nerves. It's a nice feeling. "I'm glad you're here."

"And look how we've worked together," says Elena. "Madelaine's got the electricity covered. I've got this asshat trapped, you've got the explosions, and Hannah you"—she looks at Hannah, who returns her gaze with a glare—"you've still got a Dum-Dum stick in your pocket."

"And I've got my skill!" Chloe rushes forward, hand outstretched. "Take my hand. It's time." With a sigh, I take her hand and she gestures to Logan.

"Look."

I look down and—he's in his underwear! I pull my hand away. "What the hell!"

With a squeal, Chloe claps her hands and bounces on the balls of her feet. "I've got X-ray vision!" Everyone groans. "What? I thought we could use a laugh. Day-umn."

Instinctively, I pull the hem of my sweater over my crotch. Has she tried this on *me*? She must know what I'm thinking without having to read in on me, because she shakes her head but mouths, "A little bit," at the same time.

With a shiver, I position myself in front of Logan. I'm glad we're all getting along, and the air is clear. But now it's time to finish this.

"Ready?" I ask once everyone has picked up on it and flanks me. "Wake him."

Elena raises her right hand and snaps her fingers. She looks relieved to be done, and a bit tired.

Logan's eyes snap open and he struggles against the tape. I stare at him, a worm on the floor. Everyone gathers behind me, and I wonder how we must look to him, like a cult in our red jackets.

"Let me explain," Logan says.

"That's the only reason you're not in jail," I respond.

"You—you don't understand," he stammers. "I never wanted anyone to die. I didn't even mean to bring Rabbit Skins back. I just, just—"

"Just *what*?"

"I wanted to scare him!" Logan sobs, and he stops struggling. "Grant. You weren't here. You didn't see him. He'd scared me for so long. Terrorized me all summer. He'd catch me walking alone and throw insults—the way I walk, or my nail polish, whatever he could think up. He'd threaten to hurt me. He'd cruise around until he could. I wanted to fight back."

Saliva pools on my tongue and I swallow as I do the mental math. I wasn't around. This guy was the closest he could get. The surrogate to take all the anger out on. The room suddenly feels very cold.

"I thought if I could curse him, or hex him, or—"

"But you didn't," Hannah shouts. "You didn't curse him. You killed him. By fucking with things you know nothing about."

"I *thought* I did. I've been practicing witchcraft for years. Obviously, nothing like"—his eyes scan our jackets—"like what you all are capable of."

"Yeah, same," Hannah spits. "Ever hear of the rule of three?"

"I didn't care," Logan says. "I found a hex on TikTok and that night, when I went to the old church graveyard and performed it, nothing happened.

The next day, he was missing."

"It was my birthday," I say, more to myself than anyone.

"And then he showed up outside my window. Rabbit Skins. I thought he was coming to kill me next, but he promised not to if—"

"If?" Madelaine asks.

Logan takes a big swallow. "If I led him to the other boy who left blood on his grave."

The room falls silent, but my thoughts are screaming. By making that pact with Grant, I cursed us both, cast a spell that I didn't know I was capable of. I left it there, waiting, for someone to light the fuse. At the end of the day, this is my fault.

"He said he'd go away when he had both of you. When I saw you at the coffee shop, it all clicked." Logan shakes his head. "I can't explain how, but I could feel it was you."

"Maybe your respective spells connected you," Elena deduces.

"Maybe." Logan shrugs. "But I wish I could take it back. I returned to the graveyard, and I tried to send Rabbit Skins away, but I couldn't. My only hope at that point was to help him find you."

"The star in the tree." I nod, my tongue stabbing at the inside of my cheek. "And that's how Rabbit Skins knew I'd be at Hallow Bean. *And* the courthouse. *And* Fall Fest. You've been *following* me."

"Yeah." He winces.

Fire zips through me and a flame bursts to life in my palm. "I'll kill him!"

Hannah yanks my free arm but instantly pulls back, as though she's touched a hot burner. "Dane, stop!"

"Do you know where Rabbit Skins' lair is, then?" I shout. "Did you know where Grant was this entire time?!"

"Yes."

"An ear!" I lunge, and the Reds have to hold me back. "I swear to god, just let me singe off one ear! Or a finger! I don't care what—"

Somewhere upstairs, something shuffles across the floorboards, and we all look to the ceiling. Something scampers around in circles.

"Aloysius," I say, the flame dissipating in my hand. Then, to no one in particular, "Keep an eye on this guy."

"Careful," Madelaine says. "It's dangerous!"

Hannah steps toward me. "We'll both go."

"No!" Chloe whimpers. "We need to stick together."

"This isn't a slasher movie, Chloe," Elena grunts. "We aren't going to get killed just because someone leaves the—"

"Stop," Madelaine says. She shoots me a worried glance. "Hurry."

Treading lightly, Hannah and I climb the stairs. The lights are out, the hallway in almost complete blackness. I flip the light switch at the landing and make my way toward the scurrying sound in my bedroom.

"Aloysius!" I call out. "It's just me."

The light of the hallway slices across the floor as I push the door open. "Aloysius."

Empty Moon Pie wrappers crinkle beneath my shoes as I cross to the bed and kneel.

"Aloysius?" my voice cracks as I slowly lift the bed skirt and peer through the dark beneath.

Nothing there.

"He's gone, too." My heart plummets. "Everyone's gone and it's all my fault."

My lip trembles. I hate that I'm losing it again, but really? My familiar too? I close my eyes tight to prevent tears, but when Hannah rests her hand on my shoulder, it's almost too much. I reach up to take her hand in mine and squeeze.

Her hand feels strange. Dirty. Like candle wax and dried mud. My eyes open wide and I glance over at Hannah, who is standing in the doorway, frozen except for her panicking eyes, which dart between me and the killer behind me.

I scream. Rabbit Skins screams too, mimicking me, mocking me. His fist knocks against my temple, my vision floods with white—

27

RABBIT SKINS, RABBIT SKINS, HERE TO CLEANSE YOU OF YOUR SINS

"What're you thinking?" EJ asks.

I blink at the cloudy night sky, void of the moon and starlight. My thoughts are hazy. The salt of french fries sticks to my lips and if I don't lick them, the little granules are going to burn them off.

"I can't move my tongue."

Next to me on the makeshift picnic blanket, EJ laughs. "Then how are you speaking?"

My eyes wander down to the trees on the opposite end of the park. Their dusty tops billow in the breeze that I can't feel. In my state, I laugh. "I don't know."

EJ sits up and leans over me. His blue eyes twinkle, even in the dark. "You can take your hands out of your pocket, you know."

My right index finger twitches, and I realize it's locked inside the fingers of my other hand, nestled inside the front pocket of my hoodie. EJ dips his head toward it. "Why do you always wear that?"

"There's a purpose," I say, not directly to EJ Just in general. "I wanted to... I wanted to feel secure. Like I could hide away inside if anything bad ever happened. If anyone could see."

"See what you are?" EJ tilts his head. "Or just see you?"

"Both." I try to take a breath to refill my lungs, but I don't need air.

"That reminds me of a story. May I tell it to you?" When I don't respond, EJ smiles, flashing eyeteeth that I hadn't noticed were so sharp before. "There was once a pretty man. He lived in a pretty little house. Every Sunday he led a flock inside a pretty little church. He was a pastor, you see, and a good one. Only, not quite. He had these gifts, you see, these—these strange little abilities. If anyone found out—"

"He'd lose his job."

The smile closes. "No. He'd be condemned as a witch." Staring into those eyes, I realize that EJ has yet to blink. "So, the man wished to hide away as well. In the woods. Where he met the crooked man who wore the feathers."

EJ smiles again, lifting my hand to his cheek. My fingers graze his flesh, but all I feel is muscle and teeth. "And that man burned him."

"That was a very sad story," I say. There is no emotion in my voice. "What does it mean?"

With a laugh, EJ lets go of my hand. "That hiding is pointless." His fingers twist the strings of my hood, pulling the collar tighter. "That no matter what you do, or how powerful you think you are, the crooked man is still able to bend"—tighter—"and break you until you do as he says." Tighter still. "That someday you will explode with flames that rain down through the veil, and there will never be an underbelly again. There will only be monsters and mortals, feeding upon each other in the sunlight."

The clouds behind EJ part, and the full moon appears, a scarlet-red ring around it. The moon hits EJ's face and I freeze.

He has vanished, leaving a young man in his place.

His face is angelic. Round and smooth, with fair skin that glows iridescent against the warm, buttery yellow of his fresh plaid suit. A fat brown rabbit perches atop his shoulder, its left ear tickling a soft wave of the man's caramel-colored hair. He seems about my age.

This is Charles Frederick, long before he became legend. Before he went bad and killed all of those kids. My insides squirm. It's like I'm gaping into my past and my future at the same time. Because in this moment, the two of us aren't so different. Not now.

The difference, I need to remind myself, is that he chose his path. I haven't chosen yet.

He smiles. "I just wanted you to see me as I was before I kill you."

With a suck of air I sit up, my hands pushing along the rough, dirty floor, sending clouds of dust swirling through the air. I grab both sides of my head, thunder rolling through my cranium from the impact, and squint. Orange-yellow light paints the room around me, but I can't see its source. The place is threadbare. Just four wooden walls, a dirty wooden floor, and a wooden table.

"Dane," a voice whispers, and I look over to see Mom, kneeling next to me. She curls an arm around my face and pulls me to her chest. "Oh, baby. Thank god."

"Mom." I throw my arms around her. "What's going on?"

"We're in his lair." Hannah stands in the middle of the room with her arms folded, looking down at the long table. "Rabbit Skins."

Aunt Bella leans in a corner, eyeing the ceiling. "This is it. This is where he killed my"—her voice breaks into a sob—"he's dead."

I stand, but my knees are weak and threaten to give out. Hannah isn't staring at a bare table. She's staring at a corpse. Grant's corpse, hacked up with his arms and legs in a pile. Flies swarm over it, buzzing around the sockets of his eyes. There are no eyeballs. The right side of his face has been removed, leaving only skull and muscle.

A sob escapes my throat. "Oh my god."

"I wanted to see him," Hannah says, more to herself than anyone else. "Remember at the funeral? I wanted to see him. To be sure. Well, I'm sure."

I slip my arms around her and pull her close. "I'm sorry, Hannah."

"My baby is dead," Aunt Bella cries.

"But not gone," Mom says.

Aunt Bella's eyes slide to Mom, glaring. "That *thing* up there is not my son."

"What are you talking about?" I ask.

The ceiling quakes again, and someone, or something, within the house groans.

"It looks like Grant," Hannah explains. "But it's not. It's Rabbit Skins fucking with us. He's like if the bad side of Grant broke off and became a thousand times worse."

Ada's words about dark necromancy zip through my memories, and I look at Mom. "We have to bind him."

"That's way too much for the two of us," she says. "We need the entire coven for something that large, and I don't know the words."

The smell of blood wafts through the room and I cover my mouth, looking around as other scents invade my nostrils. My eyes fall on a dirty white heap in the corner next to a bucket of shit and piss. Grant's final text flashes in my mind:

Okay, I did it. Happy birthday. Forgive me?

I pull from Hannah's embrace and crawl toward the corner, to the heap.

This has to be it—the sundress I'd dared him to wear. He made my worst nightmare come true in that bathroom stall. I wanted to make *his* come true. To humiliate him and totally break that toxic masculine mask he'd been hiding behind.

All of us are hiding, aren't we? Mom from the past and Aunt Bella playing strong through it all. Hannah, hiding her grief and emotions. And me, trying to hide away into a hoodie, hiding myself. The fire. The darkness.

Hiding got us all trapped here. I have to tell them why Grant was in the woods. It's not going to be easy and they'll probably hate me, but I have to.

Reaching for the sundress with shaking hands, I say, "I need to tell you all something."

"Don't touch anything," Mom says.

But I'm already grabbing the white cloth, holding it up in front of me and watching it unfurl, covered in dirt and blood. Images of Grant, barely alive, trapped in this room, flood my mind. My heart thunders in my chest. I try to drop the dress, but it clings to my fingers, shooting a hundred ghost reels through my mind, until the room fades away completely, and I land somewhere else entirely.

28

DRAGS YOU DOWN AND EATS YOUR BONES

"I'm all right, you know," Grant says. He has no irises. Just foggy whites, swirling like milk in a cup of tea. His face is expressionless, tired, as he comes forward. Behind him, white fruit falls from the tree boughs and pink cherry blossoms sprinkle through the air. "I want you to know that I'm all right and that thing, it isn't me."

"Where are we?" I ask, realizing that I'm sitting cross-legged on the ground. I can feel the early morning dew soaking the backs of my legs. I can smell the April breeze, all lilies and grass.

"In a simpler time," says Grant, coming to sit next to me on the soft, springy earth. "Where it's good."

"Is this the real you?" I ask. "Are you actually here? Or am I dreaming again?"

"Both," he says.

Air catches in my lungs and I fight back tears. "I'm sorry. I'm so sorry how it all turned out."

But he's barely listening to me, looking out at the trees, where the spring blossoms are quickly fading to autumn leaves.

"I never realized we could choose," he says. "Like, we spend our entire lives obsessing over good and bad. Our side and theirs. We never... We never stop to think that we can be both. We just play whatever part people cast us in and think we're doing it on our own. I didn't live long enough to figure that out—

that I could've stopped." He looks at me, revealing that his face is a little paler, a little more translucent. "I'm sorry for what I did. That doesn't change it. But I am sorry. Tell Mom and Hannah I'm sorry, too."

"Seriously?!" Inside me, the fire rages. Grant doesn't react, just stares at me with a complacent lip and level brow. "So that's it, then? You're just *dead* and that's that? I've been looking...everyone has been looking for you. You're not supposed to be dead! You're supposed to be alive!"

He lifts a fading hand and gestures to the autumn leaves withering and drying up before us. "I don't have a lot of time."

"I should have answered the phone." The words sting my throat as I say them. Words I never thought I would say to his face. "I really wanted to hurt you."

He lets out a singular chuckle. "I get that. But don't choose stuff like that anymore, okay? Being here isn't so bad. I feel chill." The dead leaves fall from their twigs, landing on scorched earth. "But you can choose."

I blink in time with my heart, which is speeding faster than Hannah down Main Street. "What do you—"

"I've seen the other side. Don't give in," Grant says, his voice urgent. Pleading. "Don't say yes to him. Keep on fighting. Don't be bad. Don't be good. Just be. Be Dane. And don't let anyone tell you who that is." His voice shakes. "And don't say yes. If you do—if you choose only the dark—well, then it *is* your fault." He nods to the landscape, and I follow his gaze to the trees, as the last leaf falls. He's so faded now that I can make out the landscape behind him. "I have to go now."

"No, wait!"

I reach for my cousin just as he shatters into a thousand owl feathers. They swirl in the breeze as a winter chill creeps over my shoulders. All I can do is stare at them and whisper one syllable in the silence.

"Grant?"

A rotten hand pushes through the soil and latches onto my ankle, dragging me into the earth.

My temples sting and thud as heavy footsteps awaken me.

If a Dane falls in the forest and someone makes paper—no, that's not it.

I blink, roll my eyes across the rotting ceiling of the cabin. I try to sit up, but I can't. I'm tied to the table.

Grant's body parts have been tossed carelessly into a pile on the floor.

"H-Hannah?" I slur. "Mom? Aunt Bella?"

I look to my right. They're on the floor, eyes closed, silent and still, but I can't scream, my throat is too tight. Their chests rise and fall slightly. Breathing. They're out cold. But not dead.

"Guys!" I half scream, my voice still not obeying me. "Wake up!"

The footsteps grow closer, and I look over as eight long, dirty fingers and two bony thumbs creep around the doorframe. A patch of fur appears, the mask of a rabbit.

"Rabbit Skins. Rabbit Skins… Here to cleanse you of your sins."

Rabbit Skins hums his melody and saunters toward the table.

"Get away!" I scream, finding my full voice.

"Drags you down and eats your bones."

"You sick fuck!" I fight against my ties.

"Keeps you for his very own."

Rabbit Skins brandishes a long knife at me in warning. He raises a corroded hand to his mask and grips the fur. He pulls upward slowly, and the mask pulls from his head. I can hardly breathe; Grant's face is staring back at me, all green and gray and covered in maggots. I fight against my ties.

"Well, well," he says in Grant's voice. "Look at what we've become."

It's not him. It's not him. I think it over and over like a mantra. But that is his face and his voice, and he's rotting away before me because Grant is *dead*.

"I should have answered the phone," I sob.

"Why should *you* get life, huh?" A maggot wiggles down from Not-Grant's hair. "Why should you be able to go and be this crazy awesome living person, when *I'm dead*?!"

My eyes water with hot tears that burn my skin as they fall.

Not-Grant laughs, pointing at me. "I have an idea! I'm going to stab your back just like you stabbed mine. And we'll see if you like it, you little queer."

"Don't talk to my son like that, you piece of shit."

We snap our attention to Mom, who has woken up and is pushing herself to her feet. Her hair is wild, and she's covered in dirt.

"Mom!" I scream.

"Why, Auntie"—Not-Grant shoots her a grin—"it's ever so charming to see you."

"Get real." Mom puts her hands on her hips. "Here's how it's going to work. You are going to untie my son, and then you are going to apologize. You're going to march your ass to the coffin you crawled out of. And *then*, I'll put you in the ground, asshole."

"Oh my god, I love my mother." I look at the ceiling.

Not-Grant stands tall. "You and what army?"

"Graveyard Reds, fourth generation." Ada sweeps into the room, her robe tattered, autumn leaves stuck to her. Louisa slithers around her shoulders, hissing. Behind her, Madelaine, Elena, and Chloe push their way in. Beyond them, a half-wolf EJ holds Logan by the arms. Even in this state, my heart leaps a little. And even though I broke my promise, he came to help.

After a second of silence, Not-Grant cackles. Then he stops laughing and stares directly at Madelaine. "Don't you want to know where Jason is?"

Madelaine trembles as Rabbit Skins' face twists and changes, transforming into the freckled, light brown face of a boy not much older than Madelaine. His eyes glow violet.

"Don't listen to him, dear," says Ada. "That isn't Jason."

"I know where he is," Not-Jason says. "I've seen him. I'll show him to you."

"Jason?" Madelaine whispers.

Ada takes a step forward. "Mr. Frederick, do not bait my girls with false hope. You're only pissing me off."

"Like you could do anything, you dried-up hippie," Not-Jason says, his voice deep and demonic as his face twists back into Not-Grant.

He lunges for Ada with a growl. She pulls Louisa off her shoulders and swings the copperhead around. Louisa hisses and her fangs plunge into Not-Grant's face, knocking him over. When he sits back up, he's turned back into Rabbit Skins.

"Get him, girls!" Ada shouts.

The Reds scream a battle cry and pounce. Chloe scratches at him while Elena kicks his shins. Madelaine punches him repeatedly.

Shouldn't we be humming like they did at the coffee shop?

"As for you!" Ada turns her attention to Logan. She snaps her fingers, which knocks him out again. "I'm great at control, too."

Mom darts around the chaos and comes to the table, pulling at my ties.

"I love you!" I shout. "I love you I love you I love you."

"I'm so sorry about everything," she says, pulling the ropes off. "I should have told you everything. I should still tell you everything."

"I'm sorry, too. I don't have a shitty life." I roll my eyes and sit up. "But if we don't finish this, I'm not going to have a life at all."

"Fair enough."

Ambrose, Efron, and Caesar run into the room. They leap at Rabbit Skins, stabbing their claws into his legs.

I slide off the table and stoop over Hannah, shaking her hard.

"Wake up!" I shout. "Come on!"

"Wh-what's happening?" Hannah sits up, grabbing the back of her head. "Did you bind him? Did it work?"

"Does it *look* like it worked?" I gesture to the mosh pit of fighting witches. EJ kneels next to me and helps me get Hannah to her feet. "What are you doing here?"

"The Reds came to the hospital," he says, "after you were taken. I couldn't just sit by. I gave everyone a ride."

"Thank you," I say. "I'm sorry that I—"

"No need," he says. "I get it. *I'm* sorry I kept secrets from you."

"Hey, Prince Eric," Hannah says to him, "kiss Ariel later. We need to bind this demon now."

Rabbit Skins is gaining strength against the Reds, despite Mom joining their effort.

"The ritual," I say. "How do we do it?"

"Can you read in on my sleeve?" He sticks his arm out. "I was wearing this coat when I tried it."

My stomach flips. "But I promised I wouldn't—"

"This is different," he says. "I trust you. If you—if you trust me."

"Oh my *god*!" Hannah screeches as she nudges Aunt Bella awake. "Just touch his damn arm, Dane!"

Nodding, I grab EJ's sleeve and shut my eyes, dipping into the fibers of the fabric with my mind. My inner eye fills with the sight of EJ in the woods, standing above the star of body parts, chanting.

"I cast you into the ground. I bind you to the star. You are dead, demon. You are dead. You will nevermore rise. You will never return. I cast you into the ground."

"Not exactly bibbidi bobbidi boo." I pull my hand away.

"I'll arrange the star." EJ glances at the pile of Grant parts. "You say the words."

Aunt Bella rubs her head. "Did we slay the bastard yet?"

Rabbit Skins heaves Madelaine off him and her back slams against the wall as she lands. In an instant he's on his feet, rushing at me, his face Grant again. EJ moves to pull me back, but the ghost is too fast, and he shoves me against the wall, knocking the wind out of my chest. He grabs my throat, lifting me by my neck. I yank at his arms, but they don't give.

"We could've been fine!" he screams in my face. "We could've worked it out!"

"You aren't...Grant." I choke the words out, punching my fists against his wrists.

But he's too strong.

Behind him, the Reds have joined hands and started humming, but it doesn't do anything to weaken him. He only digs his fingers deeper into my windpipe.

My vision is going dark, the air squeezing out.

With a scream, Rabbit Skins drops me and falls backward, grabbing his ankle.

"You taste terrible." Below me, Aloysius wipes his mouth with the back of his paw.

"Aloysius!" I scoop him up in my arms. "I've never been so glad to see you!"

"Remember that the next time we argue." Aloysius raps my knuckles with his paw. *"Now unhand me, I've got my dander up!"*

Just as Rabbit Skins lunges at me again, I fling Aloysius and he flies from my arms.

"Excelsior!" shouts Aloysius, latching onto the ghost's face.

The ghost flails, knocking the raccoon off him. He bounds for his knife as Aloysius hits the wall.

"You bastard!" I push myself forward.

"Dane, no!" EJ shouts.

Rabbit Skins raises his knife. I stretch my palm out and a thousand tiny invisible flames shoot from it. He swings his knife, deflecting the flames, and ducks just in time to miss them. I run at him, grabbing him by the skull and what's left of his face. Heat flares inside and burns all through me—it blisters my skin and turns my vision red.

The floor leaves us. We're levitating as I continue to shake him by the head, pulling at the skull and muscle. He raises the knife again as I will him into a thousand pieces. Just like Emily Black.

His knife plunges into my left side.

29

KEEPS YOU FOR HIS VERY OWN

I let go. Rabbit Skins slips through my fingers, falling to the ground.

"Dane!" My mother screams somewhere below me.

My pupils are changing shape. Dilating. I feel ice and heat at war in my side. The world moves in slow motion around me as I descend to the ground. The knife sticks from my side.

I clatter to the floor, my cheek slamming against the dirty, cold wood.

"No!" EJ comes into view, his hands digging into my shoulder blades. I stare directly ahead. His voice is just an echo, a faint sound against the blood pounding in my ears. "You aren't allowed to die! Dane! Dane!"

"Stand back!" I hear Ada shout as everyone rushes around me. "Everyone, stand back!"

"Let me go!" Mom screams.

Their shouts fade until they speak without sound, and they slowly stop moving, freezing in a big, unfinished circle, unable to reach me—as though someone has pressed Pause on the world.

Only the dust moves around the room, falling from the ceiling like snow.

Snow. Cold. That's what surrounds me now. And the fire inside me doesn't make it any better.

"Well, well."

I slide my eyes upward. Mr. Hawthorne smirks down at me, his arms splayed against the ceiling, the ends of the owl feathers on his coat sleeves unfurled like wings. The air around him is distorted, warping his edges. A being from beyond. He's an angel of death, here to take me to his underground world.

"It appears this is going to end poorly for you."

He pushes his fingers against the ceiling and floats down, landing over me, his face less than a foot above mine.

"Knife wounds are nasty business." He casts a sad, sidelong glance at my mother. "I don't think Mommy can kiss this one and make it better. But you do have a choice, now that you're this close to forever."

Air whooshes through my still lips and I can't speak as the answer slides into place. He wanted this, didn't he? He knew Rabbit Skins was brought back. He wants me this close to dying so he can make his deal.

The blood in my ears pounds harder.

"Do you want to go or stay? You could slip away and join me below. It would be such an honor to have you. Down in the underbelly, you'd be free to let the fire rage at last. It would feel so good. Or you can stay here, and well, things would be harder, an unbearable onslaught of pain and suffering. I promise."

He leans down and whispers in my ear. "For sixteen long years I've waited for you. Dreamt of you. Ever since you were born with this fire—this...this wickedness." His fingers slide against my cheek, tilting my head sideways. "Fear not your wickedness. Embrace it for it makes you strong."

My heart makes one beat, just one, as his hand pushes against my cheek.

"Charles wouldn't embrace his fire and so"—his hand grows hot against my face—"I burned him."

His hand grows hotter. And hotter. But I can't push him off. Can't do anything but feel the blistering heat against my skin. He burned Rabbit Skins' face off. And I'm next. A strangled cry escapes my throat.

"Don't try to fight it," he tsks. "This world is full of wicked little things. And you're my favorite one."

Inside me, the fire crackles. Maybe he's right and going to the underbelly would be the best thing. Maybe it wouldn't be so bad, letting my fire out, burning so hot it rips a hole in the screen door that separates the living from the dead.

I think of all the times I've given in and let it out. How good it felt deep down.

But I also think of how awful it felt later. The guilt. I picture Grant fading before my eyes, telling me to say no. That if I say yes, then it's all my fault.

Another heartbeat.

Are you a good witch? Or a bad witch?

Another.

Beneath Mr. Hawthorne's hand, my skin blazes, but my flesh doesn't broil. He can't do much but hope I die, can he? I can choose to keep going. I can be me and not let him or any person dictate what Dane Craven is. Good. Wicked. Cousin. Boyfriend. Witch. Fag. It's up to me, and he can't tell me that any more than he can burn me from the other side.

You have no power here.

"No," I mutter. One syllable.

Mr. Hawthorne sighs. "I thought you'd be wiser. Dear, dear. I'll just have to get a little more creative, then. Won't I?" He slides his hand from my face, the sharp nail of his index finger scratching my skin.

"Go on then." He almost spits the words. "Keep fighting, suffering. I'm a patient man."

He stands and glides between a still-frozen EJ and Hannah. He blurs as he begins to disappear. His final words echo as a single owl feather wafts to the floor. "Until then."

I blink. My heart beats again, and again, pounding in my ears in full force as everyone begins to move. I reach for the knife in my side.

"I cast you into the ground," I whisper.

"What did you just say?" clicks Aloysius.

I lift my head. Rabbit Skins stalks toward me. My lip quivers.

"Do it!" Hannah shouts. "Now!"

I grip the knife tighter and yank it out of my side. Everyone gasps. The blade is red, dripping with my blood, a lot darker than I thought it would be. I clutch the wound with my free hand.

"I cast you into the ground!" I scream through tears.

The Reds, Mom, and Ada gather around us, joining hands. They begin to hum, one long singular note. EJ runs forward, grabbing arms and legs, arranging them into a star on the floor between me and the ghost.

"Don't," Rabbit Skins whispers, his eyes getting larger. Sadder.

"I bind you to the star!"

His face twists. I'm looking at Grant again.

"Dane," he whimpers, "please! I want to come home."

Aunt Bella covers her ears. "You aren't him. You aren't him."

"You are dead, demon!" I sob and raise the knife. "You are dead! You will nevermore rise!"

I push myself to my feet, raising the knife higher. The witches raise their humming voice, nearly drowning Rabbit Skins out as an unfelt breeze billows our hair.

Grant's lip trembles. "I'm sorry, Dane!"

"You will never return." Tears stream down my face. The lights flicker.

Then, Grant's eyes turn angry, and Rabbit Skins' head appears on his body, his face whole again. Aunt Bella creeps behind him as he says, "Say yes."

"I cast you into the ground!"

I stab the knife downward, down, down, toward Rabbit Skins' chest. He backs away and I almost miss.

"Die, monster!" Aunt Bella screams. She raises her leg and kicks his back, sending him toward me again.

The blade plunges into the breast of his plaid suit.

He falls backward, convulsing and kicking. His head spins around and around. Beams of green light break through the tiny holes in the fabric of his suit. His hands crumble to dust, turning to ash before us all, as the lights grow brighter and brighter.

Everyone moves back as he writhes and screams unintelligibly.

The room fills with the green light. My blood boils, the power stinging and shooting all through me as the light blinds us all. I cover my eyes with the back of my hand.

After one long scream, the light fades and is gone.

A brown fur mask lies atop the pile of Grant's limbs, lifeless and still. Rabbit Skins, Charles Frederick, is gone.

My cousin is gone, too.

"Shit." Hannah breathes.

I look to the corner, where Logan remains unconscious.

"Don't"—I point weakly at him—"don't let...him...leave."

I collapse to the floor. The Reds crowd around me, Ada pulling at my jacket. "We have to heal him fast. He's losing blood."

Smoke plumes from my fingertips. I feel so hot—like I could burst into a giant fireball at any moment. My heart pounds in my ears. Hotter. Hotter still.

Mom pulls my head onto her lap and wipes her hand over my forehead. "You're gonna be okay, baby. It's gonna be okay."

"Is he going to die?" Chloe asks, grabbing my hand.

"It's not allowed." EJ wraps his hands around my ankles.

Aloysius runs up by my leg and pats my chest. *It's going to be all right. I am here.*

My eyes droop shut and Hannah lightly slaps my face. "Nope! Stay here!" Her voice is breaking.

"No more death," says Aunt Bella. "No more."

Ada's pulled her phone out. "Siri? Play 'Make Your Own Kind of Music.' Mama Cass. Dane, you just focus on this."

"What're you doin..." I slur as I try to sit up, but Mom holds me down.

"Robyn," says Ada as her music starts up, "we have to cauterize this wound. Now."

"Mom?" I feel woozy. And so hot. "Mommy?"

"Breathe, baby." She wraps her hand around the sleeve of my wrist and gently pushes my hand toward my side. "Breathe."

I scream, drowning out Mama Cass, as my hand sends fire against my own flesh, caramelizing it where the knife went deep.

THE HOLLOW:
MORNING IN JASPER HOLLOW

"I've been filled in on everything, Logan," Dr. Richert says pleasantly.

Logan Hockstetter doesn't respond. He just colors with crayons, listens to the radio they let him have. Some woman sings about making your own kind of music. He scribbles. He has to do *something*.

Dr. Richert is too nice. He wants answers.

"So," Dr. Richert continues, adjusting his blue tie, "I'm just going to ask you some questions—things I ask a lot of patients. Some of them you might not want to answer just now, and that's all right. But if you could answer to the best of your ability, we'll be on a good track. Does that sound good?"

He adjusts his tie again. Logan keeps scribbling.

"You look like John Krasinski," says Logan.

Dr. Richert smiles. "Oh! I'll take that as a compliment. Thank you."

"You're eyes though. And hair. Reminds me of this one guy."

The red crayon's just a nub now. Logan finishes coloring in the jacket and drops the nub to the floor. He picks up the brown crayon and fills in Dane's hair, squiggles, and circles, moppy curls all around. Then, the black crayon. He draws two Xs where the eyes ought to be and shows it off to Dr. Richert.

"This Dane kid. You know him?"

"Now, how did you—"

"I know a lot of things now. Way more than I'd like to, Dr. Luke Richert."

Logan looks at his own work. He admires the vampires and werewolves.

The ghosts and monsters crawling out of the earth. The stick figures with Xs for eyes piled high. A corpse burning in red and yellow flames, a pile of severed heads in the corner. He admires the dead Dane Craven, combusting into flames.

Dr. Richert narrows his eyes. "Tell me, Logan. Have you been speaking with a man wearing owl feathers?"

Outside the jail cell window, a blue jay flies past.

Sweeping above the rooftops of Jasper Hollow, it glides around the dome of the courthouse and swoops down to the street, nearly hitting Sheriff Doyle's car. It lands on the hood and cocks its head.

"I don't care what the situation is," the Sheriff says to Mayor Bridget Kowalski. "Your nephew steps so much as one toe out of line, and I'm gonna have to do what I gotta do to keep this town safe!"

"I'll remember that during the next election cycle." Mayor Kowalski folds her arms. "But you might want to be careful, considering the mother of— what was it you called him? 'The curly headed punk bitch'?"

Sheriff Doyle hops into his car and starts the engine. The radio flips on. The lyrics insist on making your own music—that doing your thing is the hardest.

"Oh, don't worry about that none." He flashes a smile at the mayor. "If anyone knows how to handle Robyn, it's good ole Todd Doyle."

Mayor Kowalski rolls her eyes. "You could be a bit nicer. They *did* find our killer."

Sheriff Doyle snorts. "Logan ain't the killer. Just the mastermind. But we'll nail him either way. We got his therapist over there analyzing him right now."

The blue jay resumes its flight, gliding above the courthouse and out toward Jasper Hollow Memorial Hospital, just as Robyn Craven lights a cigarette and leans against the door of her car. She lets a few tears fall as she takes a drag and presses the phone closer to her ear.

"No, we'll be here awhile," Robyn says. "But I'm still a call or an email away... Yeah, he'll be okay. Just one of those freak accidents, you know."

The blue jay flies down, landing on the car's side-view mirror. Robyn stares at it, unblinking.

"Sandra, I gotta go. There's a hurt animal in the driveway... I know... Okay, bye!" She hangs up and goes to the blue jay, smiling, tears welling up in her eyes. "Hello, Delilah."

30

I PROMISE I CAN'T MAKE ANY PROMISES

barely sit up in the hospital bed, wincing at the sharp pain in my side. But it's okay because I'm not dying. Not today. Today, I'll just get fed a lot of green Jell-O. Aloysius, who had to piggyback into the hospital beneath one of Ada's flowing robes, snuggles closer to my hip, nuzzling his snoot against my lap. I pet his head and he purrs.

"Perchance, could you ask someone to find a vending machine? I could go for some salty pretzels."

"In a minute."

Ada looks us all over from her place by the window. The sun makes her hair seem an even more vivid orange.

"To say that I'm proud," she begins, "would be a disgusting understatement."

The Reds smile, pleased with themselves, but Mom rolls her eyes and looks up from feeding seeds to Delilah. "Ada, now is not the time for one of your speeches."

"Just let her," Aunt Bella says. "She's going to give it anyways."

"Actually," Ada continues, as though no one had interrupted her, "I'm overwhelmed with pride. Not only did we stop the ghost of a serial killer. We all came together and completed our circle at last. Oh, our world is changed forever, girls and boy...witches. And now, we won't answer to anyone."

With raised eyebrows, I look to her. I told everyone about what Mr.

Hawthorne said to me. About letting the wickedness out, about letting fire rain down and destroy the veil that keeps the underbelly separate from the world. It became clear and unspoken, for everyone, that I would not be accepting Mr. Hawthorne's offer. Whether he gave me this power or not.

"Here I was," Ada continues, "so upset at having a male in my coven that I didn't stop to think we've been blindly following an old straight white man, and who knows what would have happened had we made Dane say yes to what he wants. No, I won't be following anymore. Let him try. Let him see what we can hurl at him."

Elena snaps her fingers poetry slam style in agreement.

"Make no mistake." Ada raises her hands. "This is only the beginning. Who knows what he'll try to do next."

"Well," Madelaine beelines next to Ada and stares out the window, up into the sunlight, "I know what I'm going to do. I'm finding Jason." She looks to Ada, with an expression that only dares Ada to try and stop her. "When Rabbit Skins turned into him, his eyes were violet. Jason's eyes weren't violet."

Ada sighs sympathetically. "That was a ghost's vision, Madelaine. His goal was to distract you. Not to bring a message."

"But it could mean something."

"I don't want to get your hopes up."

"But"—Madelaine throws back her shoulders—"it *could* mean something."

She heads for the door. On her way she shoots me a half smile. "Feel better." Then she's gone, leaving the rest of us exchanging silent glances.

"Well, that was a bit heavy," says Hannah.

Elena narrows her eyes. "Nobody asked you, Igor."

"It's Elvira!" Hannah gives the old Sicilian curse again. "And so what? I'm the mascot now. I nominated myself, and I was so flattered that I humbly accepted."

"All right, all right," Ada says. "Everyone has been through a lot in the past twenty-four hours. I vote we let Dane rest and treat ourselves to cafeteria cookies."

She winks and pats my leg on the way out.

Everyone stands to follow, but I shift in my spot. "Wait. Can I talk to you, Aunt Bella? Hannah?"

Aunt Bella's face falls, but she nods. Hannah sits in an empty seat.

Mom leans over and takes my hand as Delilah alights on her shoulder.

My stomach is in knots, but I have to do this now or I'll lose my courage.

"I need to tell you something," I start. "But first, I need you to remember that we're family. And that we love each other. And also, that I know it's going to take a while to deal with...with everything."

Aunt Bella is rigid, as though she knows what I'm about to say. "Okay."

My chin quivers. "I need to tell you why Grant was in the woods."

When I come to the top of the hill, I spot EJ sitting on the picnic table, looking out over the Hollow. I take a deep breath.

This isn't the hardest thing you've done, Dane Craven.

I move toward him, lifting the collar of my jacket to brace against the early November air. He turns at my movement. His eyes double in size when they land on me, and he tenses.

"How'd you find me?" he asks.

"You weren't at work, and Scout said you brooded on the clock, so they cut you early. I figured there's only one place where you like to mope. You wanna talk or not?"

He shrugs. "Yeah. I guess."

"You guess?" I try not to raise my voice. "I've barely heard from you since the night at the cabin. I'm only just now able to walk around without care."

"I'm sorry." He pushes himself from the table and paces. "I didn't know if you wanted to see me."

"I texted you. I called."

"I know," EJ sighs. "I'm having a hard time forgetting that night."

I shiver. "That makes two of us."

"How've you been?"

Shaking my head, I bite my tongue. "I can't sleep through the night. Nightmares. Rabbit Skins at the foot of my bed. Mr. Hawthorne hiding in my closet, waiting to kill me if I fall asleep. That feeling that something is around every corner. And meanwhile, it's awkward around my family. I told them all. Everything. About, you know, me and Grant."

"How'd that go?"

"They're coming around." I shrug. "It'll take time."

"I'm sorry. That's terrible." He furrows his brow. "Did Hannah drive you here?"

"I walked." I smirk. "I didn't know how long this would take or if, I don't know, if you wanted to do something. Get french fries. Be cute."

EJ blushes. "I'm sorry I've made it awkward. To be honest, I can't stop thinking about Fall Fest and the hospital. The look on your face when you found out about me. How much I scared you. I'd never hurt you."

"I know."

"But if I do? What if I accidentally scare the shit out of you again? Or you see what happens when I cross a deer? And boom, I've hurt you again."

I can't help but smile. "You're seriously playing brooding hero for me right now?"

He laughs. "Dane, I'm being serious! I'm a monster, remember? Certified. And it led to you controlling me—"

"I was scared! I promise I won't do it again."

"And you almost died."

"But I didn't. I promise not to die."

"That's two promises you can't guarantee you'll keep."

I smile. "Then I promise I can't make any promises."

EJ laughs and my shoulders relax. "This is all so messed up."

"You're telling me." I look out at Jasper Hollow. "And what's more, I'm thinking about going to your school next semester. Whatever shall we do?"

EJ steps next to me. "Are you serious?"

"I'd have told you sooner, but you didn't answer the phone." I look at him. I try to stop myself, but I add, "You know that kills people, right?"

"Don't." EJ shakes his head. "Don't do that to yourself."

I smile even bigger. "If you can't laugh at your own trauma, then whose can you laugh at?"

"No one's!" EJ's mouth breaks into a smile. He laughs. "You are so not right!"

"I've stopped trying to be," I chuckle. "Look. All I know is that I'm here for a while. And there's a lot of weird stuff happening, and I don't know what's next. But, if you're willing to try, I am too."

EJ's smile gets bigger, then drops. He wrings his hands together, letting out a long sigh. "You're a witch and I'm a monster. I'm afraid we'll do things that freak each other out, things we maybe can't deal with, and then we'll both get really hurt."

He has a point. I can't argue with that. I need to work through the idea of him mutilating those bodies in the woods. Also, the whole hunting thing. But he also has to work around me being a half-wicked witch who occasionally starts fires and might have a slew of demons and ghosts headed his way. That, and I pal around with his ex-girlfriend.

"Look," I say, "before I came here, I wanted to be hidden. I didn't want people to know a thing about me, or what I was. I genuinely disliked myself. I thought gym clothes were formal attire." EJ chuckles and I continue. "I thought

I was a bad person deep down. Well, you know what? There *is* a lot of dark, deep down. But I know that I'm not *bad*. I can choose. And I'm going to have to fight it down time after time."

I pull back the left flap of my jacket and lift the side of my sweater. "But it's still there."

EJ stares at the wound, which is forever marked on my skin by a black web of veins in place of a scar. Evidence of my wickedness oozing out.

"Just like your—um—issues?" I add, letting my sweater fall back over the mark. "But I'm trying. Really hard. And I'm going to get as strong as I can. And then! I will work very hard to lift your curse. I think I can get there. But I don't want to do it by myself. And I don't want to stay hidden, either. I'm not scared anymore."

EJ's eyes lock onto mine.

"I'm not scared," I repeat. "Can we just try? You be you, and I'll be me. It's all I'm asking for."

With a deep breath, EJ takes a step toward me. I don't step back. His hands run up my arms, which haven't tingled in a week. His lips tilt above mine, and as they descend toward me, he lifts his fingers to my chest.

"Ow!" He jumps back. A small plume of smoke rises from his right index finger. "See? I can't even touch you because of my shit. How can—how—"

I unbutton my jacket.

"Dane."

I smile. "I don't need this protection, EJ Because I trust you. Do you trust me?"

I shrug the jacket from my shoulders, and it slides to the ground. My fingers lace around EJ's trembling hand and I pull it to my chest. I look up at his blue eyes and wait. He gives a nod, and I lift my lips to his. His free hand slips around my left hip. He barely lifts my sweater and sweeps his palm over the black web. As though to show he's not afraid of it. When he pulls his lips from mine, we smile.

"Now," I say, "let's get queso and be wicked."

ABOUT THE AUTHOR

Justin Arnold is a storyteller, occasional comedian, and junk food connoisseur. He lives in the bluegrass region of Kentucky, where gnarled woods and abundant ghost stories fuel his inspiration.

When he isn't writing, he spends most of his time trekking the wilderness, planning getaways, and experimenting with ways to make the most amazing vegan cheeses and pizza crusts (he's dangerously close!).

ACKNOWLEDGMENTS

There are so many people who, over the years, have skipped with me on the twisted yellow brick road that is *Wicked Little Things*. Writing this book has been one of scariest, most deeply personal, and most eye-opening things I've ever done, and "Thank you" will always feel like an understatement.

The first person I can't praise enough is my editor, Joshua Perry. Dane Craven can read thoughts, but Josh can read them before you've finished thinking them and make them even better. I had no idea when this book started out that he and the Tiny Ghost team were building its perfect future home, and his sincere love for the protagonist and the story world is undeniable on every page. So thank you for taking such great care of Dane and Co., and for listening to me ramble about story threads that make zero sense to anyone who isn't me.

Speaking of Tiny Ghost, I want to thank Dana Keller and Julia Wortman, who work so hard to make each book in this house a success. It's hard to find one person to understand and believe in what you're doing with your book, so to have three people in one place is a unicorn of an occurrence, and I will always be amazed by what sheer awesomeness they do for their authors, present and future.

To Lio Pressland, who designed the book cover and allowed me to see Dane, Rabbit Skins, and Aloysius for the first time by way of ink and paint. There really are magical, Red witches among us, and they are one of them. Knowing the characters would appear on the cover was enough to make my nails bite themselves off. But they brought them to life. Because they are magic. Thank you.

As I said, writing this book was scary. One of the scariest moments was back in January of 2021 when I held my breath and sought feedback on the second draft. Too shy to sit in an in-person critique group, I joined Scribophile and went all in. It turned out to be the best thing I could have done, because it brought me my very own Scarecrow, Tin Man, and Lion. (And no, I will never stop referencing *Wizard of Oz* where this book is concerned!) Rocío, Artie, and Elizabeth have my whole heart. Without them, this book would not nearly resemble what it does today. All three kept me writing when I felt like procrastinating. They demanded my vulnerability and honesty when I wanted to goof off, and their own writing inspired and taught me how to be better.

Speaking of betas, I want to thank author S. Legend, who answered my notice for an additional beta reader and whose generosity with her time and sincerity with her feedback pulled me through the final stretch before submission. She is a rock star, both on the page and off. She takes the things that she wants to read and makes everyone else want to read them, too. An original through and through, her encouragement and advice for this work added ingredients that I never would have noticed were missing if not for her eye. Thank you!

They say that to write is to purge, and that was painfully true with this book. So many people and things have touched this story than I can ever thank here. But there are three very special ladies (why do magical ladies always come in threes?) that deserve much more credit than can ever be given.

The first is the incomparable, the wonderful, the mystical—Rachel Nipper. She not only gave me permission to include a snake-toting, fun-house-mirror version of her, but scooped up my broken pieces and gave them a red jacket so long ago. There was no way this wouldn't happen. And she has my endless gratitude for reading the drafts, for listening to me talk through rewrites, for sending me memes that remind her of the story, and for vocally daydreaming about a screen version of it. She's dealt with my zero-to-sixty self for years and isn't even getting paid for it. Thank you. Now stop sniveling and call me.

To the second special lady in question—Cayla Blankenship. Queen of darkness, mother of loyalty, she graciously lent her black dress, the "shiv" in her pocket, and a bond that I have been fortunate to know since I was twelve years old. She listened to me talk of my idea about a little gay boy who casts spells since 2015, and didn't stop checking in until it was done. I never would have started otherwise. The spine of *Wicked Little Things* was missing for so long. When certain someones kept calling, she taught me that it'd be all right if I didn't answer the phone. Because what's the worst that can happen? Now let's get queso and be wicked.

Now for the third special lady. Bekah Knight, Galinda to my Elphaba, what a journey we have had. From rooting for each other as ensemble members, to being Peter Pan and Wendy together, to our late-night car concerts, her obsession with *Heathers* and thoughtful conversations about cliques, stereotypes, and toxicity, she was such an unseen yet instrumental thread of this book. She had no idea how many times our talks flipped on light bulbs in my head, or how much our time apart and eventual reconciliation taught me about real friendship, fate, and how much stronger power is when it's not alone. I, and *Wicked Little Things*, have been changed for good.

www.ingramcontent.com/pod-product-compliance
Lightning Source LLC
Chambersburg PA
CBHW011150190726
48288CB00010B/3260